P9-DXL-267

Praise for *Family and Other Catastrophes*

"The perfect book for anyone with a calamity
of a family who wants to laugh along in knowing hilarity.
Alexandra Borowitz has written characters
who we hate to love but yet we do (love them)
because we know these people intimately,
they are our own family."
—Ann Garvin, *USA TODAY* bestselling author of
I Like You Just Fine When You're Not Around

"*Family and Other Catastrophes* is, hands down,
one of the funniest novels I've read this year.
The members of the Glass clan are as hilarious
as they are cringe-worthy, and Alexandra Borowitz's
rendering of family dysfunction is charming,
insightful, and wickedly smart. Honestly,
the only real catastrophe here is that
this wonderful book had to end."
—Grant Ginder, author of *The People We Hate at the Wedding*

CALGARY PUBLIC LIBRARY

NOV   2018

CALGARY PUBLIC LIBRARY

NOV 2018

Family & other CATASTROPHES

ALEXANDRA BOROWITZ

If you purchased this book without a cover you should be aware that this book is stolen property. It was reported as "unsold and destroyed" to the publisher, and neither the author nor the publisher has received any payment for this "stripped book."

mira

ISBN-13: 978-0-7783-1755-5

Family and Other Catastrophes

Copyright © 2018 by Alexandra Borowitz

All rights reserved. Except for use in any review, the reproduction or utilization of this work in whole or in part in any form by any electronic, mechanical or other means, now known or hereafter invented, including xerography, photocopying and recording, or in any information storage or retrieval system, is forbidden without the written permission of the publisher, MIRA Books, 22 Adelaide St. West, 40th Floor, Toronto, Ontario M5H 4E3, Canada.

This is a work of fiction. Names, characters, places and incidents are either the product of the author's imagination or are used fictitiously, and any resemblance to actual persons, living or dead, business establishments, events or locales is entirely coincidental.

This work was written in the author's personal capacity. The opinions expressed are the author's own and do not reflect the view of the author's employer.

® and TM are trademarks of Harlequin Enterprises Limited or its corporate affiliates. Trademarks indicated with ® are registered in the United States Patent and Trademark Office, the Canadian Intellectual Property Office and in other countries.

For questions and comments about the quality of this book, please contact us at CustomerService@Harlequin.com.

BookClubbish.com

Printed in U.S.A.

Recycling programs for this product may not exist in your area.

Family & other CATASTROPHES

NIGHT 0

David

"DOES THIS DRESS make my nose look big?"

Emily Glass stood at the mirror brushing her hair. Her pink sundress was tight around the torso and flared out at the hips.

"How could a dress make your nose look big?"

"You'd be surprised," she said. "With my nose, you have to be careful. I read on PopSugar that I shouldn't wear black, for example. It's harsh against my skin and it'll accentuate my nose."

Emily's nose wasn't small, but it wasn't enormous either—long, prominent, but nothing anyone would point out unless she pointed it out first. She had brought her nose up on one of their first dates, when she self-effacingly said that she was tired of her parents' friends telling her that she looked like a young Barbra Streisand. David hadn't thought to give the correct response: an incredulous look and a shocked "Why would anyone ever say that? You're far more beautiful!" Instead, he only nodded. She had never let him forget it.

As she turned around, her hair whipped over her shoulder and revealed the candy-pink straps of her sundress. David wasn't sure what this type of dress was called. He had recently heard the term *bodycon* but still didn't completely understand what it meant or if it applied to this dress. He playfully reached out to pinch her butt but wound up groping a handful of poufy fabric. She spun around and laughed.

"I love you so much, sweetie." She threw her arms around his neck and kissed him on the cheek.

"You know you don't need to wear a dress to the airport. This is going to be just like Las Vegas all over again. And this time, we're not shopping for leggings halfway through the trip because you only brought miniskirts."

"You're not still mad about that, are you?"

"I wasn't even mad then. I just want you to be comfortable and I don't want you to complain during the flight."

"I want to be comfortable too. But every outfit this week needs to count." She opened her eyes widely for emphasis.

"Don't go too sexy on the night of the bachelorette, okay? Trust me, I know guys, and guys don't care if you're on your bachelorette party, they'll just go for it."

"I wouldn't wear anything sexy anyway, with Lauren there. If I want to avoid her usual criticisms, I'm going to need a giant androgyny cloak." Emily's arms released from David's neck as she pantomimed a cloak over her head.

David laughed. "I don't understand why you think she's such a bitch. Lauren's always nice to me."

"Because you aren't her sister. And you should hear the stuff she says about you behind your back."

"What does she say?"

She paused. "She thinks you're boring and that you attempt to make up for it by projecting hegemonic masculinity. I disagree, obviously. But when she found out you played basketball in high school, she kept sending me all these articles about sexual assault and high school sports."

"What the hell does 'hegemonic masculinity' mean?"

"I forgot you didn't major in something useless at college like I did. Let's put it this way. She's been engaged to an unemployed lumberjack with a neck tattoo for ten years—if she doesn't like you, it's probably a good thing."

"But I want your family to like me."

"The rest of them do!"

"Yeah, okay." He reached over to close his suitcase where the zipper was gaping, and then realized Emily might see this as literally turning his back on her.

"Are you upset now? I shouldn't have said anything. I knew something bad would happen this week. Why do I always do this? Now we're going to be mad at each other all week."

"Look, I'm not even… I'm just going to feel so weird seeing her now."

"You should always feel weird seeing her. I can't remember the last time I didn't feel weird seeing her. She's a huge jerk."

"Well, huge anyway."

"Mean!" She laughed. "Get that out of your system now. If Lauren didn't like you before, any comments about her weight will put you into the same category as the guy who accidentally called her 'sir' at Panera four years ago."

"Who did that?"

"None of us knows. But she's written six blog posts about him."

Emily

By the time they got to the airport, she was already starting to regret wearing her sundress. So many women managed to look chic at airports, and she didn't understand why she couldn't be one of them. She saw a six-foot-tall Latina woman in leather leggings and a simple black blazer, her highlighted hair barrel-curled and cascading down her back.

She was standing at the ticket kiosk with a sleek black rolling suitcase, unburdened by a heavy laptop bag, huge overpriced bottle of water or any of the other unwieldy items Emily always lugged around at airports. A few feet away, she spotted a college-aged girl in a casual, loose crop top, a pair of high-waisted jeans shorts and clunky white sneakers, taking selfies near the end of the security line. She also looked flawless. Why was it so hard for Emily? She could spend four hours getting ready and still somehow feel inferior to every other woman in the room. Already she was shivering, her knobby legs were covered in goose bumps and she realized that she should have worn a bra when she looked down and saw her nipples poking through the thin cotton bodice of her dress.

"They won't let you take the NaturBuzz bottle through security," David said.

"Right. I guess we should just drink it now. Is it bad to drink it if you haven't actually worked out?"

"I don't think so. Better to drink it than throw it out anyway."

"Sir." A TSA agent approached. She was short and heavyset with blond hair in a tight, oiled bun as if she were on duty in Iraq and not just working the security line at the San Francisco International Airport. "You need to remove that bottle from the vicinity immediately."

"Can't I just drink it? We're not even in the line yet."

"If I can see you, you're in the line."

"Um...okay." He handed the bottle to Emily. She looked at the label: white pomegranate and kaffir lime. She would have preferred to savor it a little rather than guzzle it near the TSA line. There went nine dollars' worth of NaturBuzz, none of it contributing to muscle growth, just winding up as urine in an airplane toilet.

"I don't have all day, ma'am," the agent said.

"Oh gosh, please don't call me that," Emily said, half jokingly. "It makes me feel middle-aged. I'll just drink this now, okay?" She thought she might get a little "I hear ya, sister!" from the TSA lady, but all she got was a steely stare and a defiant arm cross. Emily untwisted the lid and chugged half the bottle. She handed it to David, who finished it off.

"Okay, thank you, finally," the TSA agent said.

As she went through security, Emily couldn't help feeling anxious again. She looked at the other people in the line. She felt a familiar whirring in her chest and flipping in her stomach. A redheaded man in a suit took off his wing tip shoes for security. She turned to David.

"He could kill all of us right now and it would be too late for anyone to stop him. Ugh, this is why I hate airports. Everyone is a suspect." Maybe that was why the gorgeous women were there—to divert attention from all the terrorists in the security line. Genius.

"Everyone is a suspect in your world," he said. "This is the woman who called the cops on the building's handyman for 'sitting around outside.'"

"First of all, I'm still not convinced Chan wasn't up to something. And second of all, that guy in the line could kill us and nobody would be able to stop him before the first few casualties. And that's assuming he's carrying a gun and not a bomb. I can't do this."

"This guy isn't carrying anything."

"Oh, really? You've inspected his clothing and you know he doesn't have a gun? You can't just blindly trust everyone at an airport."

"Emily, he isn't even…"

"If you were going to say that he isn't even Middle Eastern, that's the point. They're dropping in people we least suspect. And you know I call the cops on white people all the time, I make sure to do that. Remember the guy at the St.

Patrick's Day parade? I suspect everyone equally. This guy looks exactly like someone who doesn't want people to think he's a terrorist. Look, he isn't even bringing a carry-on, just a backpack. Ready for jihad."

"He's probably going to New York for business."

"Do you just think that nobody ever has a gun? That there aren't at least a few terrorists on dry runs in this line? Did you think 9/11 was Photoshopped too? Please tell me you haven't become one of those people in the YouTube comments section."

"Actually, you're one of those people. You honestly believe there are terrorists in this specific security line?"

She could tell he found this somewhat amusing. Her therapist called this "flaunting her pathology." Sometimes her anxious rants were intentionally comedic, if only to break the tension. If she acted believably insane, it was a problem, but if she hammed it up so much that she could later claim to just be joking, that gave her an out. She knew David found her anxieties annoying, but in the moment she was too worried to care. She would deal with the embarrassing aftermath of being wrong after they landed. Better to be wrong about a terrorist attack and feel like an idiot, than to be right about it and dead. Life had to win every single day. Death only had to win once.

"All I'm saying is that there could be terrorists in this line," she said. "It would be so easy to pull off. Just look at that guy." She pointed to a young white hipster with a scruffy brown beard and a bowler hat, carrying a black violin case.

"Okay," he said, lowering his voice. "I'll play this game with you. If you were going to do it, how would you do it?"

"I don't know, I'd have to call some terrorists to learn some options. But it's easy. For one, last time I packed a full-size conditioner and they didn't stop me."

He squeezed her shoulders as they moved toward the body scan. "You really are nervous about this week, aren't you?"

he whispered in her ear. His one-day scruff tickled her neck and she smiled. The shoulder massage felt good. She wished she could stay in this moment forever, his face against hers, his hands on her shoulders. She would always feel safe then. Except in the event of an aneurism.

"Well, yeah, my mom is going to be a nightmare, but that's not why I'm worried about the plane blowing up. Two different things, babe."

"She'll be fine. And don't say 'plane blowing up' at an airport. Watch, you'll be freaking out about terrorists and then you'll be the one they arrest. It would be more typical of you to be detained for terror threats before your wedding day than to be killed by a terrorist before your wedding day."

"Judging by how lax they are about checking that guy over there, they're not going to pull me aside for saying that. They should, though. How do they know I'm not a terrorist? How would they notice a real terrorist if they don't even notice a run-of-the-mill crazy person like me?" She forced herself to smile. Sometimes smiling made her feel better. Her fourth-grade teacher had told her that if she pretended to be happy, there was some chemical reaction in the brain that would trick her into being happy. She had believed it, and smiled like a lunatic whenever she was even mildly worried. Her teacher had probably said it to help her do better socially, but as a result she just looked like a grinning freak. She toned down the smiles in middle school when someone put a note in her locker with a picture of the Joker, but she still kept the habit into adulthood—just a watered-down version. David seemed to appreciate her periodic attempts to seem normal, and she often wanted to remind him that he should count himself lucky that his bride's wedding anxieties weren't about second thoughts and cold feet, but about bombs and Ebola. Fuck—Ebola bombs. Surely someone was planning that.

"You'll be less crazy on the honeymoon, right?" he asked, wavering slightly as he said *crazy* since he meant it in an endearing way but was aware it sounded mean.

"I mean, I've always been crazy. I've known that since I was four. Thank you, Mom."

"Your mom definitely didn't call you crazy."

"Well, of course not. She says I'm mentally ill and reminds everyone whenever she gets a chance because it makes her look like such a saint for putting up with me. And I can't even argue with her, because then I look even crazier. This would all be so much easier if I could do my crafting. It always calms me down."

She was one of the first Pinterest users and an avid crafter in her spare time. Her crafts ranged from no-sew pillowcases to embroidered handkerchiefs to the ominous and pointless "glitter balls" that she insisted she would use if she ever threw a snow-themed holiday party. She spent hours studying the Pinterest pages of her favorite crafting bloggers. The women always looked so pristine and perfect with their strawberry lipstick and winged eyeliner, their pure white kitchens bathed in natural summer light, their unused copper pots hanging from the ceilings. When they baked, they never got flour on the counter. When they crafted, they never got glue on their manicured hands. Who were these women? Emily's crafts always got messy, and even when they were successful they were useless, like the glitter balls. David was nice enough not to bring it up, but she could sense his amusement every time he ran his fingers across the abandoned glitter balls still sitting on the kitchen counter.

Sometimes she worried that she was unbearable—disorganized, distracted and high-strung, leaving a trail of glitter behind her that nobody could clean up. But she knew so many women who were worse. Kathleen, her former friend from college, had cheated on her fiancé during her bachelorette party with a spray-tanned club promoter named TJ and hadn't even felt bad about it because she said it was part of "finding herself." One of her cousins repeatedly referred to her husband as "the Idiot" in her irritating Long Island accent, acting as if the nickname was witty and sassy instead of abusive. Emily could have been lazy, materialistic, demanding, emasculating, frumpy, unavailable or cold. She was none of those things. For all her shortcomings, she was outgoing, loving and never once turned David down for sex—even that one time she had a stomach bug—a badge of honor she wished were appropriate to share with other people.

She would never dream of ridiculing him over bottomless mimosas with "the girls," calling him "the Idiot" or joking about how she pretended to be asleep to get out of sex. Unlike the way some women she knew regarded their men, she loved David because of his flaws, not in spite of them. Her favorite thing about his face was his slightly large ears. If he suddenly became rich (which seemed more and more likely every month he continued working at Zoogli), her favorite things about him would still be the little things, the goofy things. Other women would try to seduce him if he had money, that was for sure, but they would never love him for his weird ears, or feel a wave of warmth in their hearts whenever they heard his off-key rendition of "Smells Like Teen Spirit" in the shower. She hoped he knew this. Men always claimed to want women who loved them for them, not for their money, but rich men always seemed to wind up with women who only wanted their money. She wanted to believe she could trust David, but why was he any more trustworthy than the thousands of other future Silicon Valley billionaires who would leave their loyal wives for Russian models?

Even if David never became rich, there was still something else for her to worry about: aging. She was twenty-eight, zooming toward her thirties, a decade she had long believed marked the beginning of a woman's journey into her new identity as a sexless, living Roomba. Meanwhile, David at twenty-eight was more handsome than ever. Just shy of six feet, with a full head of chestnut hair, and a face like a grown-up all-American lacrosse frat boy but without the arrogance. He was the man she dreamed about marrying when she was a little girl—except back then she had pictured him sporting a shaggy '90s haircut parted in the middle and a puka-shell necklace. She thought David was better-looking than everyone else did, which was obvious from the incredulous looks her friends gave her every time she referred to him as "out of her league." Regardless of what her friends said to reassure her that she and David were equally attractive, she didn't buy it. David was tall and fit—that could carry a man his whole life. It could only carry a woman for a few years before the estrogen dipped and she became another crazy-armed Madonna look-alike, veins popping out and skin sagging over preserved mummy muscles, boobs like two half-empty water balloons bagged in wrinkled beige napkins. She could gain weight and avoid the gaunt face of middle age—perhaps wind up looking like a jolly, pie-baking Mrs. Claus—then use push-up bras and shapewear. That wouldn't be very sexy, but at least then she wouldn't have the desperate, roast-chicken look of all the Real Housewives. Her therapist told her these concerns stemmed from her body dysmorphic disorder, but she knew he was just saying that to be nice.

She knew that one day—perhaps not today, perhaps not even in ten years—David would look at her, look at himself and realize just how much better he could do. He was far too sweet and devoted to realize it now, but it was bound to happen by the time he hit middle age. As a result, she had to be vigilant. Plastic surgery was out of the question because of her fear of ineffective but paralyzing anesthesia—it had happened to some woman in Kentucky and the story had trended on social media—but there were other things she could do. Her fitness routine was intense. In college, she only did the occasional dance workout video, but she had come a long way since then. Darius, her fitness instructor at LifeSpin, assessed her as a Level Four during her StrengthFlex test. Her new LifeSpin routine involved light weights, yoga, Pilates and NaturBuzz hydration. She did squats in the shower while the conditioner was in her hair in the hopes of attaining a Photoshop butt.

Aboard the plane, she rolled on two tight black knee compression socks. They looked stupid with her dress, but this was one of the few health-over-beauty sacrifices she made. If there was anything she worried about more than her declining looks, it was her health. She had recently read a Dr. Oz article about deep vein thrombosis, the silent killer. There seemed to be way too many silent killers out there for one thing to be given the title, but as far as silent killers went, deep vein thrombosis—and its aggressive cousin, the pulmonary embolism—played the part quite well. They could strike any person, at any time, and one of the symptoms was "no symptoms." She shuddered just thinking about it.

"You should listen to some music," David said, handing her a pair of white earphones, the speaker area lightly dusted with his orangey earwax. They would be so gross if they came from anyone but him. Maybe that was something she could incorporate into her wedding vows.

"I actually popped a Benadryl right before we got on the plane. I'm going to sleep."

"I wish I could sleep on planes. My neck always hurts and then I wake up as soon as there's any turbulence. I don't know how you can be so anxious and still have such an easy time sleeping in public places."

She laughed. "That was a compliment, right? You should

try to sleep too. We won't get much sleep when we arrive. Everyone is going to ask us how work is going and a gazillion other questions we don't want to answer."

"Ugh, I hate talking about work."

"Me too. I want to talk about fun things."

"Like parasites?"

She gave him an indignant look. "Like fun things."

"You're cute."

"Want to have sex in the bathroom?" she asked perkily. Sometimes she liked to throw out offers like that. David was too vanilla to ever take her up on them, but they made her appear kinky, so she could fulfill the roles of both seductive "other woman" and loyal, nurturing wife. If she were giving him so much sex, he wouldn't have any energy left for all the other women she imagined were sneaking around him, waiting to strike as soon as she turned thirty. Sometimes she swore she could hear the popping of their bubblegum and the sizzling of their hair underneath curling irons when she walked down the street.

"Sex in the bathroom sounds illegal, but you can give me a hand job underneath my blanket." She assumed he was kidding, but he really did have one of those fleece blankets given out by the flight attendant, so maybe he was serious.

"Just you? Like, I don't get any...you know...under my blanket?" Having sex with a guy in the airplane bathroom was sexy, *Pan Am*, *Mad Men* stuff. Giving a hand job under a fleece blanket while everyone on the plane watched reruns of *How I Met Your Mother* was just sad. But if David really wanted it, she'd look so cold and withholding if she said no.

"Finger banging is harder to maneuver," he said. "You don't have to give me the hand job, though. I just thought..." He gave her a flirty smile.

"I'm just joking. I'll give you the hand job."

"Wait, seriously? I was joking too."

"I don't know why you would joke about that. People do this stuff all the time."

"Have you?"

"No. Just people do." He never wanted to hear about, or even think about, her previous sexual experiences, even though on their first date she was twenty-five and had obviously had relationships before him. No one-night stands, though—she was too afraid of antibiotic-resistant chlamydia. He had never even divulged his own number, which led her to believe it was either embarrassingly high or low.

"Okay, you can give me a handie, but only after the safety demonstration."

"I *can* give you a hand job? I'm not begging to do it, I was just offering."

"I mean, *can* you give me a hand job after the safety demonstration?"

A peppy blonde flight attendant popped her head into the row and reached her arm around David's lap to make sure his seat belt was fastened. She pursed her mauve lips.

"Sir, in the future please do not have a blanket on your lap when we are checking seat belts," she said, in a way that managed to be both unnecessarily friendly and unnecessarily rude.

"Uh, sorry."

"And, ma'am?" the flight attendant asked. Emily realized her blanket was covering her seat belt, as well, and lifted the blanket to reveal that it was, in fact, fastened. Not that it would mean anything, if there were a terrorist on the plane. Why did anyone even check this? They should have been going around making eye contact with all the passengers to check for secret signs of nervousness, the way she once heard people did in Israel. Why didn't *she* live in Israel? Her cousin Rebecca did Birthright in 2007 and kept going on about how the police presence "ruined the experience." Of course, Rebecca was being stupid, because police were the only thing making the experience possible in the first place. Maybe if Emily lived in Israel, she'd feel safer. Except there would be a lot more threats in general—she wasn't sure if the police presence outweighed the increase in threats.

"Thank you," the flight attendant said.

"Oh, I have a question," Emily said.

"Sure, ma'am."

"Did you call me *ma'am* because you thought I was old, or because you say that to all women over the age of eighteen?"

She cocked her head. "I'm confused. Would you prefer something else?"

"I mean, I don't prefer anything because it's not like I'm going to be hanging out with you loads of times, but I just want to know what calculation went through your mind when you looked at me and thought, *She's a ma'am.*" Emily could see David wincing out of the corner of her eye.

"Well, you're an adult woman, so we say *ma'am* to be polite."

"It's not that polite, though. I mean, you obviously weren't trying to be rude, but when I hear *ma'am* I don't think the person is being respectful. I think my crow's feet are showing and that I look forty."

"Well, how old are you?"

"How old did you *think* I was?"

"I don't know, thirty-two?"

"I assume you were rounding down not to offend me. You probably meant thirty-five or older. I'm twenty-eight. Thanks."

The flight attendant looked like she was about to say something but thought better of it and walked off.

"What the hell is wrong with you?" David asked. "She thinks you're a weirdo now. Why do you always do that? For the last time, you don't look older than your age. Stop freaking out."

"Everyone thinks I look older than my age. You only say

that to flatter me, which, trust me, I appreciate. But this isn't just my anxiety. You can attribute a lot of stuff to my anxiety but not this. Everyone agrees with me except for you." Emily longed for the days when "I thought you were so much older" was a compliment. It was great when she was nine and trying to look grown-up, useful when she was eighteen and trying to buy alcohol, mildly annoying by the time she hit twenty-three and devastating now that she was twenty-eight. Worst of all, nobody else seemed to relate. Even people she thought looked terrible for their age loved to regale her with their arsenals of stories of how they were mistaken for fetuses when trying to see R-rated movies.

David shook his head. "It's really not you. People are just terrible at guessing ages. The other day at LifeSpin, one of the new trainers asked me if I was there with a parent because you need to be eighteen to have a membership."

"See? This is exactly what I mean. Everyone else gets guessed as younger. That never happens to me. I was actually offered a free Jazzercise class."

"If you're referring to JazzSweat, that's not for older people. It's actually super intense. They give you free cashew powder if you get through all six classes without passing out."

"Sure. Fine. But that flight attendant definitely thought I looked old."

"No, she didn't. Even if she thought you were thirty-two, that's, like, no different from twenty-eight. You're freaking out over something so tiny. Even for you."

"Okay. Full disclosure, I asked her that because I actually *was* offended by her use of the word *ma'am* but the good news is, she thinks I'm crazy, so now we don't need to worry about her bugging us while I give you a hand job."

"You're actually going to do that?"

"After the safety demonstration."

DAY 1

Emily

AT SOME POINT during her Benadryl-induced stupor, Emily had gotten chilly, stolen David's heather gray sweatpants from his carry-on, and put them on underneath her dress. By the time they landed at JFK around seven in the morning, she was too tired, and still too cold, to remove them.

"I thought you said you needed to look good every day this week or it would be embarrassing," David teased.

"Not now. I'm freezing. Why do they make planes that cold? And then they offer air-conditioning on top of that? When it's negative a hundred degrees outside, why not offer adjustable heat dials instead of AC? I know why—because they're sadists."

"Let's just get to your mom's house. We'll feel a lot better when we see Lauren, my biggest fan."

"Are you still upset about that? I shouldn't have said anything."

"It's actually not a bad thing. I can finally stop pretending to like her."

"So you didn't like her before?"

"I didn't really interact with her long enough to form an opinion. I saw her—what, once, that time in Brooklyn? We had lunch in that Americana dim sum place with the grilled cheese gyoza."

Emily turned to David. "Be honest. Is there anyone else in my family you don't like? I may even agree with you."

"Same question to you."

"I like your family."

"Okay, same answer."

"Except you don't actually like them. Your family is a million times nicer than mine."

"Yeah, my family seems great, but trust me when I say they can be annoying too. What about my brother?"

"Oh, well, I mostly meant your father."

"He's not perfect either, believe me."

"Emily!"

She turned and saw a young woman with long curly brown hair, a wide friendly smile and a Muppet-like bouncy walk. Emily couldn't place her at first but squinted and got a better look as she approached. Finally she recognized the ten-year-old frayed cross-body bag with the faux tribal stitching. It was Stephanie Morris, an old friend from high school—so old, in fact, that Emily hadn't seen her since her sophomore year in college when she was home for spring break. They had gotten coffee in Chelsea, but had very little to discuss other than Stephanie's love of silent movies and hatred of designer fashion. The two of them once had a lot in common—they were both artistic, extroverted and energetic—but since Vassar, Stephanie had changed dramatically. Of course, Emily hadn't spent enough time with her to know this firsthand, but she assumed as much from Stephanie's social media posts. If Stephanie wasn't posting about the dangers of vaccinations, she was posting about how meditation could cure cancer or how the only good decision a young person could make is to quit her job and live in Bolivia for a year without doing any research first. After Stephanie got her bachelor's degree in psychology, she went backpacking in Europe and presumably had sex with a flock of rich hippies named Travis or Jared in hostel beds for a year and a half. She had neglected to find another job since returning to the United States. It had been six years. Of course, such important life-changing experiences were a lot easier when your parents paid your rent and subsidized your shrooms habit.

"Emily, is that seriously you?" she squealed. "How are you? You didn't tell me you were back!"

Emily never told Stephanie when she was back home—because, naturally, they barely knew each other anymore—but every time Stephanie got any whiff of Emily's return to New York on social media, she eagerly asked her if she wanted to meet up for coffee in Brooklyn. She never stopped to consider that Emily's parents lived in Westchester.

"Oh, I've just been so busy with the wedding stuff."

"When's the big day?" she asked, her electric-green-lined eyes widening. She had gotten a nose piercing. That was new.

"Oh, just…in a week," Emily croaked.

"A week? Oh, so, like, it's a small ceremony with just you and your parents?"

"Um…not really. We have a few other people coming."

Emily watched it slowly dawn on Stephanie that she wasn't invited to the wedding. Eight years ago when they met up in Chelsea, Stephanie had promised Emily that she would give a kick-ass speech at her wedding. It seemed intrusive and weird even then, especially since Emily was single at the time. She racked her brain for all the consoling things she could say to Stephanie—for example, that her parents were limiting her to inviting five friends. Of course, the real reason she invited so few friends was that she didn't have many friends. Her mother had actually urged her to invite more and said that she feared that she was self-sabotaging by "pushing people away" because it was implausible for a woman her age to have only two close female friends. Surely, her mother assumed, Emily had other friends she was intentionally alienating.

"I didn't realize you wanted to come," she said to Stephanie. "Also, we don't have a raw vegan option for dinner. You're still raw vegan, right?"

"Yeah, but it could still work out! Especially since I'm currently fasting, except for alcohol, so you wouldn't even need to provide a dinner for me. I'd even bring my own craft whiskey. Can I still come anyway?"

Emily desperately wanted to turn to David and share incredulous looks, but she knew that doing that would plunge them both into fits of laughter. It would be just like the time they were riding the 47 bus downtown in San Francisco and a middle-aged man wearing nothing but a clown wig and leather harness got on, his soft, leathery penis flopping around like a very large skin tag. Everyone pretended not to notice, because that was the go-to San Francisco reaction to a lunatic. Emily, however, had made the mistake of mischievously glancing at David. He began to laugh, and so did she, and before long the naked clown was serenading both of them with a surprisingly competent rendition of "Every Breath You Take."

Emily smiled tensely. "Um… I mean… I can talk to my parents and see if they're okay with it, but they're being really strict about it. They're paying and they're on a tight budget, so it's kind of their rules."

"Well, I won't even eat anything, so I don't think anyone would even notice me. What day is it again?"

"Next Saturday."

"Oh," Stephanie looked down at her hands, as if discovering them for the first time. She shrugged. "Saturday is actually no good for me. I'm going to a reconstructed Druid bonfire that day. Poop! This totally sucks! There's no way we can do another day?"

"What, like, reschedule my wedding?"

"Oh, of course not! What was I thinking? You probably already paid all the fancy caterers and whatnot. Can we hang out a different day?"

"Let's totally do that next time I'm in town," she said with no intention of returning to New York for at least a year. Next holiday season, she would definitely try to go on vacation with David alone, to somewhere warm and peaceful where she could wear a bikini and a breezy cotton kimono. Slighting both sets of parents for the holidays seemed easier than slighting only one—at least they couldn't be accused of favoritism. The previous year, they had visited his parents, because they had seen her parents the year before that. With her parents in Westchester and his in Fairfield, Connecticut, they could easily visit both in one trip, but whichever family paid for the ticket seemed to feel horribly insulted if they spent even a few minutes seeing the other family. Emily learned that the hard way when she visited her own family for the holidays and made the mistake of seeing David's parents for lunch one day. For the rest of the week, her mother lamented that they were "stealing" her and deliberately trying to destroy what little Emily's parents had left of a family. This somehow devolved into the accusation that David's Catholic father was trying to steal her away and convert her to Catholicism because "for them it's not enough for Jews to be only two percent of the population, they want us at zero percent." The holidays had gone from something Emily enjoyed celebrating as a child—in a secular, Claymation-movie-based sort of way—to something she dreaded each year.

"What about Friday?" Stephanie asked. "Are you free to chill at my place?"

"Your place in Brooklyn?"

"Yeah, it'll be low-key. We can just chill for an hour or so."

"I mean, I'm staying with my parents in Westchester. Also, that's the day of the rehearsal, the rehearsal dinner, you know…it's kind of a busy day."

"I'm sure you have an hour free. Come see me! I never see you anymore!" She jutted out her lower lip like a kid begging for a rainbow slushy.

"Well, actually it would be like, three or four hours if you include the commute."

"Figure it out! Don't be a party pooper! We can smoke a little weed, drink the home brew that my neighbor made and watch *Nosferatu*. It'll be rad."

"Okay, I'll see what I can do." She squeezed David's hand, as if to send a distress signal, but he already knew she was distressed and seemed to have no intention of intervening.

"Sweet, let's totally do that!" She tried to high-five Emily. "Shit, my Uber is here. I have to go."

"No worries, I'll see you later."

Emily waited until she was gone and turned to David.

"Why does she even like me? What about me is even likable to a person like that?"

"Don't take this the wrong way, but her interest in you is just as confusing to me as it is to you."

"We're talking about someone who uses her emergency allowance money to go to Burning Man. What does she want with me? My organs?"

"Possibly," David said with a grin. "Since you went grain-free, your digestive system is probably top-notch."

★ ★ ★

Emily got chills when she saw her father, Steven, behind the wheel of his gray Volvo waiting to pick them up at the airport. This sight brought her back to the terrifying days when Steven attempted to teach her how to drive, shouting "Ah!" and "Ooh!" every time the car went above two miles per hour. Now, at twenty-eight, she was still afraid of actually taking her road test. Fortunately, in San Francisco everyone just took Uber.

Steven looked older to her, even though he and Emily's mother, Marla, had visited her in San Francisco the year before. He had gained some weight that had settled in his lower face. He had slightly less hair and a slightly longer beard with more gray in both. He was only sixty-three, which she knew wasn't really that old, but she often felt ripped off when she considered that her older siblings would wind up with more years of living parents than she would. Then again, he was only thirty-five when he had her. Having a child at thirty-five was no longer old by current standards. If anything it seemed recklessly young compared to what people attempted in San Francisco. Emily always dreamed of having her first child at thirty, but now that she was in her late twenties, such an act seemed outrageously premature. People who had children before thirty were part of the multitudes who occupied the land mass between New York and California, watching game shows, trampling each other in Walmart on Black Friday and remaining shockingly unaware of gluten. She knew it was classist to think that way, but she couldn't help it. She blamed Linda.

Emily's boss was an overachieving blonde Amazon who firmly believed that a person was incapable of committing to another person properly until they were both forty and had a net worth of over a million dollars (each). Linda proudly regaled her with stories about how she had the foresight to freeze her eggs at the age of thirty-seven, only to fertilize them at the age of forty-eight when she met her sixty-year-old husband. "In this technologically advanced day and age," Linda said, in her usual chipper but abrasive tone, "women no longer need to get married. My little Harper won't get married until I'm dead. That's the rule." Then she laughed and added, "Not literally, of course. But she better not be under forty, or I'm not paying for that wedding! Unless she's already at C-level. She's gifted, so it's not a totally crazy idea!"

Whenever Emily thought about how difficult her own mother was, she contemplated little three-year-old Harper, only allowed to watch PBS and forbidden from playing with dolls or anything that would discourage her from a career in science or engineering, the only acceptable fields for a woman in Linda's world, despite the fact that Linda worked in PR. Linda didn't want Harper wearing makeup or pink frilly dresses, but Linda got her roots touched up every few weeks, wore fitted, surprisingly sexy sheath dresses to work and never left the house without her fuchsia lipstick and heavy mascara. Eventually, Harper would start asking questions, especially if she was really so gifted, and the result wouldn't be pretty. Emily still recalled Linda's chilly, thin-lipped response when she had told her about the possibility of an American Girl Place opening up in Union Square and how much fun Harper would have there. Poor Harper was a science experiment from day one, as if Linda were playing *The Sims* and wanted to build the perfect Sim from the beginning— complete with the right genetics, the right skills, the right interests. But wait! Screw Harper! Harper only saw her mother for two hours a day, but Emily had to work with her and suffer her unsolicited pseudo-maternal advice for nine hours a day. Every time Linda opened her mouth to dispense some pointless aphorism, usually along the lines of "dump your fiancé and focus more on your career, but of course you can have it all, just not in your twenties," Emily cringed as she realized she was literally growing older with every second that she spent with her. Emily deserved far more sympathy than stupid Harper. Harper was naturally blonde anyway—life would come easily for her.

"Emily!" her dad called out. She ran toward the car. The sweatpants were too hot now that she was being hit with the humid air of New York in June, not to mention that her legs were double-insulated with both sweatpants and blood-clot-preventing socks. Sometimes she felt she should be compensated just for living with anxiety and all the inconveniences that came with being a hypochondriac. Could she possibly enroll herself in some kind of medical study? It would certainly beat scheduling Linda's meetings all day.

"Good to see you, Professor Glass," David said, climbing into the back.

"Haha, 'Steven,' please. So how's work? Is there going to be an IPO?"

"We're out for a second round of funding. Once that closes, we'll start the countdown to an IPO. So fingers crossed and say a prayer."

"I'm an atheist, so I don't pray," Steven said, peeling out and cutting off a taxi, then nervously slamming on the brakes so that the taxi almost rear-ended him. "But it is fascinating how, historically, people have resorted to prayer as a way to feel in control of a completely chaotic universe."

"Oh…well, I just meant—"

"Sorry. Didn't mean to bore. I recently wrote a book on early Jainism but you probably wouldn't find it very interesting. So who's your funding coming from? Google? It seems like they're buying up everything."

"No, actually—"

"Apple?"

"No, um…it's a VC firm called BluCapital."

"Like Blu-ray? I've heard of Blu-ray."

"No, it's…it's something else. I don't want to jinx it anyway." Emily could tell David wanted the topic to end. Whenever they traveled back East, people Steven's age were always ravenously interested in his work for a start-up. Half of David's stepmother's friends thought he worked for Amazon, and the only reason he didn't correct them was that he didn't feel like explaining what he actually did.

"So what happens when you do the IPO?"

David fiddled with the zipper on his backpack. "We'll hopefully make some money."

"I'm sorry, but what is your company called again?"

"Zoogli."

"Right, right. And what does Zoolie do again?"

"Zoogli, and we—well, we are the liaison between mobile tracking SDKs and the mobile app developers. We help to aggregate spend in a way that is more accessible for the developer. Our slogan is, *So easy, even a marketer can get it.*"

"Oh, so you make apps? I have this flashlight app on my phone, it's outstanding."

"Oh, no, we don't make apps."

"So you…how would you say it…promote the apps?"

"No, not exactly." David cleared his throat. "We are the *liaison* between the people who make the apps, and the people who track how many installs the apps get when the apps are being promoted."

"But you don't promote the apps?"

"No, we don't."

"Oh, so you're the guys who…track the installs the app gets when the app is being promoted?"

"No, we're the liaison between them and the app developers."

"Oh, okay. Well, hopefully, the IPO will happen soon." He looked back at Emily in the rearview mirror. "Em, what are you wearing?"

"Oh, they're just compression socks because of the flight. I don't want to get blood clots." She took off her sweatpants and compression hose. She had unflattering red marks around her knees. "Are Lauren and Jason at the house?"

"Yes. You know, sweetie, it would really be nice if your boss were a little more understanding about the time you need to plan a wedding out here. Your mother had to do most of it herself and she's driving herself crazy with it. How is it that Lauren and Jason had no trouble getting a week off for your wedding, and you practically had to beg for it?"

Emily took several deep breaths, as one therapist suggested she do when she felt filled with rage. "Well, Dad, Jason is the pretend CEO of a company that doesn't exist and Lauren is a writer for a magazine that barely exists. You'd be surprised at how lenient bosses are with vacation days when your job isn't real."

"Jason and Lauren are taking risks. You aren't happy where you are—why not do something of your own? Your mother keeps saying you're wasting your creativity over at TearDrop."

"ClearDrop. And I'm not *meant* to create my own company. Why does everyone in the world think they're equipped to start a company? I like my job security. The work's boring, but I get to do my own fun stuff on weekends. David and I just want to make enough money to live comfortably, and enjoy our life together." She looked at David, who nodded in solidarity. Every time she mentioned her future with David, she felt the urge to make sure he was on the same page. Even though they were getting married in a week, she still worried about the age-old problem of "What *are* we?" Sometimes she worried that if she referred to him as her fiancé, he would say, "Whoa, whoa, whoa, I didn't realize we were doing labels." There was no legitimate reason to worry about this, but there was no legitimate reason to worry about any of the things she worried about.

"Obviously, I'm thrilled that you have established such a stable life for yourself," Steven said, almost sideswiping a bread truck. "But what about your creativity? What if your crafting was your job, and you got to come home whenever you wanted? Whatever happened to that cute little craft blog you were making?"

"A bunch of teenagers started commenting on it and said I looked like a naked mole rat in my profile picture. So I had a mini nervous breakdown and deactivated it. And besides, it never got enough traffic to make me any money."

"Well, after David's company goes public—"

"It's actually not my company," David said. "It's my boss Robert's company."

"My mistake. But as I was saying, once Zookie goes public—wait, David, did I get the name right?"

"Yep."

"Then you can focus on something that actually utilizes the stronger areas of your mind. Then you can both come home more often, see your niece and nephew…"

"Did Mom ask you to say this?"

"I do not recall," Steven said, as if giving a deposition.

"Well, off *the record*, if Mom brings up the fact that I haven't visited home in a while, and how she's had to do everything for the wedding, let her know that's a byproduct of me having a real job. If she wants to pick on anyone for not coming home enough, tell her to yell at Lauren and Jason. They both live in the city. They don't even need to take a plane."

Steven nodded. The car's front tires squeaked as he absentmindedly drove into the curb.

Emily looked out the window at the house where she grew up. It was a pale blue colonial on a winding road lined with oak trees. The street would have been picturesque if people from other neighborhoods didn't use the vacant wooded lot on the corner to dump their old TVs and mattresses. When she was eleven, she had sworn she saw two deer humping on one of the discarded mattresses, but her mother had dismissed the story as a ploy for attention, and briefly diagnosed her as histrionic.

"Ah, your mother is home," Steven said, pulling into the driveway. In the carport she saw her mother's Subaru Impreza, maroon like her trademark shade of lipstick. Her brother Jason's used red Corvette—his first postdivorce purchase—was parked nearby as was a white Nissan Altima, which she assumed her sister, Lauren, had rented. It had to be a rental, since Lauren had sold her car to reduce her carbon footprint, and if she ever wound up buying another car, it was unlikely that it would be free of pro-choice or anti-meat bumper stickers. The last bumper sticker Emily recalled her sister having was a black one with white lettering, reading Got Privilege?

David and Steven lugged the bags inside, declining Emily's mostly empty offer to help. She carried her wedding dress, still in the white garment bag. In the car, she had checked it every few minutes to make sure it hadn't ripped, but every time she checked it, she worried that the zipper had ripped the lace, so she eventually stopped checking.

"Here comes the bride!" Her mother was at the front door. She was wearing her usual summer outfit, which Emily was convinced was the warm-weather uniform mandated to all sixty-year-old female Jewish psychologists: blue cotton shell top with a long beige linen kimono, matching palazzo pants, flat, thick-soled sandals with nondescript "ethnic" beading on them and a chunky amber necklace.

"Hi, Dr. Glass," David said.

"Oh, come on, it's 'Marla' now. We're all family!" She hugged Emily, keeping her hands on her daughter's shoulders after the hug ended. She looked her over.

"You look skinny. Are you eating enough? I hope this isn't wedding nerves." She rubbed the sides of Emily's arms, as if trying to warm her up.

"Hi, Mom."

"I'm a little worried that your wedding dress isn't going to fit you now."

"I went in for a fitting last week. It's fine."

"Why do you do this to yourself?" She threw her hands up in exasperation. This was a new record for her—normally she waited until Emily was actually inside the house to start criticizing. Emily supposed there was a first time for everything. "You had such a wonderful figure, and now you're some kind of heroin-chic toothpick runway model. I know weddings are stressful, but you need to remember to eat."

"I did eat. Actually, I think I gained weight."

Marla crossed her arms. "Well, I haven't seen you in a very long time. Maybe I just can't remember what you look like."

Emily refused to take the bait, even though that comment was difficult to ignore. She gave her a fake smile. "I didn't lose any weight, Mom."

"I'm not paying for any extra alterations that were caused by your unhealthy body image," Marla said. "I'll only pay for alterations done before you dropped below 130 pounds, because while I love you to death, sweetheart, I can't be an enabler for your anxiety."

"Mom, you're not helping," came a shout from inside the

house. "Don't blame women for their own oppression." Lauren was home.

Marla stayed focused on Emily. "We'll talk about it later. Let's not argue now."

"I actually didn't go under 130. I'm 132. I'll weigh myself in your bathroom if you want."

"You don't look it. You probably gained muscle and lost fat, that's why. You used to have such a nice lovely shape, and now you're looking a bit…hard. It's all that LifeSpin garbage."

"Mom, stop body-shaming," Lauren called out again, this time in a harsher tone.

Emily could hear Lauren's four-year-old son, Ariel, ask "Mommy, what's 'body-shaming'?"

Marla shook her head in a long-suffering way. "I promised myself we wouldn't fight this week. I must just be overwhelmed with all the planning that I've had to do all by myself. Let's just get you settled in."

Emily stepped inside. David followed her but stood frozen, still carrying the two bags, afraid of putting them in the wrong place. The living room hadn't changed much since Emily was a kid. Her father's antique Japanese bronze bowl sat in the middle of the low cherrywood coffee table, while a few family photographs hung over the mostly decorative marble fireplace that hadn't been lit since 1992. Light flooded through the windows. The only light fixture in the room was a dim, Japanese lantern-style floor lamp next to the black leather sofa. The television was the same bulky, old-fashioned one that Emily had watched throughout her childhood because Steven and Marla both believed television made people dumber and saw no need to upgrade. Emily had seen discarded ones in the vacant lot that were more up-to-date.

"Hi, Lauren," Emily said. Lauren got up from the sofa. She had gone from slightly soft to legitimately big, a label that Emily knew Lauren wouldn't mind. Matt, her beanpole-shaped, perpetually silent "partner and parental unit," stood next to her. He apparently had a strong preference for larger women. Emily knew this because Lauren told her about it every time anything tangentially related to weight came up. But Emily was happy that her sister had found someone she loved. For a woman who raged so much against body expectations, Lauren's taste in men had always been very conventional: thin, white, young and tall. Matt checked all those boxes, but his neck tattoo and long blond Viking beard were a good disguise for his conventional looks. Thanks to that beard and tattoo, Lauren didn't look like too much of a sellout.

The two sisters hugged, Lauren's black cat-eye glasses jabbing into Emily's forehead. Emily still couldn't get used to being taller than her older sister, after so many years of looking up at her. She hugged Matt, his bony sternum pressing against her chin.

"Don't listen to Mom," Lauren said. "She's been on a warpath all morning. Ariel ate the last of her nectarines and it's been downhill ever since."

"I heard that," Marla said. Beyond the living room was an open kitchen, where Marla was opening the fridge to get a mixed berry Greek yogurt. For as long as she could remember, Emily had never seen her mom eat a full meal. Marla ate constantly, but all her meals looked like unsatisfying snacks you would grab quickly before running to the airport.

"I like your hair," Emily said. Lauren had cut her dyed black hair to her chin with baby-short bangs across her forehead that made her look a bit like a creepy 1920s doll. Emily didn't really like it, in the sense that she would never have mutilated her own hair like that, but she knew the bizarre impression it gave was exactly what Lauren was going for, so the compliment was still somewhat genuine.

"Oh, thanks. I took Ariel to the salon with me and let him choose it. It was either this or a purple buzz cut. Then we both got manicures. Ariel, show Aunt Emily your fingernails."

"No!" Ariel shouted. His long pale blonde curls whipped from side to side as he shook his head with his arms crossed over his chest. He wore a blue T-shirt with a fire engine on it, along with a fluffy pink tutu and a pair of yellow floral rain boots.

"Ariel, do you need to pee?" Matt asked him, noticing how he was grabbing his crotch and dancing around.

"No!" Ariel said. "I'm just touching myself!" Matt shrugged and went to pour himself a glass of water.

"Ariel, I think that's for private time," Emily said.

"No, it's not," Lauren said. She patted Ariel on the head. "There's so much anti-masturbation stuff in the media nowadays, we may as well let him enjoy his own body while he's little enough not to understand shame."

"Is he wearing a...skirt?"

"Ariel dresses himself," Lauren gloated. "Some people say it's strange, but fuck them."

"Mommy, what's 'fuck them'?"

"Nothing, Ariel. I'm just speaking with Aunt Emily."

"You curse in front of him?" Emily asked, lowering her voice a bit.

"I like him to be present for adult conversations. It is ridiculous how people underestimate their kids and baby talk to them. You know, I take Ariel to work with me once a week. He needs the exposure to the adult world, especially in a female-positive, body-accepting space that recognizes and calls out his inherent privilege."

"Don't you work at a place called *Cunt Magazine*?"

"Yeah, but that doesn't matter to Ariel. Children are innocent. He loves his Fridays at *Cunt*. Don't you, Ariel?"

"I love *Cunt* day!" Ariel flailed his arms around and twirled.

"He isn't using it as a gendered slur, so as far as I'm concerned, he's just taking away the word's power," Lauren said. "I don't want to tell him to stop saying it. It might damage his self-esteem."

"Uh-oh, did I walk in on another debate about Photoshopping plus-size models to get rid of cellulite?" Emily's brother, Jason, stood in the doorway. Emily hadn't seen him since his divorce, and she was struck by his new single look. It had been a while since Jason qualified as attractive, and now that he was in his midthirties, balding could be added to the list of attributes that made him solidly average looking. However, he had slimmed down a bit, losing some weight in his face, and he had stopped wearing white Reebok sneakers with jeans unironically. Now he wore skinny jeans and an intentionally distressed Urban Outfitters T-shirt, dusty blue and paper-thin, with a faded image of a Fender Telecaster printed on it. He resembled the middle photo between "Before" and "After" on the LifeSpin progression board that was posted between the AeRate™ oxygen bar and the FloTate™ flotation chamber.

"Hey, Jason," Emily said. "Nice shirt. You look good!" She hugged him.

"You too, Em. Christina is coming by to drop Mia off later, by the way. She posted a picture of her on Facebook, and I have to say, she looks pretty cute in her flower girl dress. You're going to like it."

"Aw, I can't wait to see her."

"That makes one of us."

"Not Christina. Mia."

"Oh. Yeah, me too. Last time I saw her was three weeks ago. I miss my little girl. I had to miss our last weekend together for my friend Mike's bachelor party, and then Christina was too much of a bitch to give up the weekend after. Says it will 'ruin the schedule.'"

Marla strode over to them. "I couldn't help but overhear. Jason, have you heard from Christina yet?"

"Please refer to her by her proper name—Satan. And the answer to your question is that I haven't heard from Satan since last night when she said she'd be dropping Mia off today. Maybe she's been busy causing plagues in Africa or possessing the bodies of rural teenage girls."

"Hmm. Well, would you please ask her to give us an ETA?"

"Why would I ask her that? ETA for what? She's just dropping Mia off."

Marla turned to Emily. "He doesn't know. You told me you would tell him."

"I never said that."

"Well, he obviously doesn't know."

"What don't I know?" Emily would have taken his concern a lot more seriously if he hadn't been swiping through Tinder while expressing it.

"Emily invited Christina to the wedding," Marla said. "She also invited her to David's parents' barbecue. I told her it would cause problems, but she wanted her there. So now I'm just trying to avoid your constant drama, like always. Every *time* with you kids."

Jason looked up from his phone to glare at Emily. "Em! Dude! What the hell?"

"Look," she said, her heart beginning to race. "I didn't *want* her there. I invited her because it seemed really cruel to ask this woman—who I've known for years—to drop her kid off at my wedding and then drive away. I couldn't bring myself to do that."

Back when Jason and Christina were married, Christina had been the feminine, graceful older sister that Emily never had. She had given her fashion tips, and they had even gotten makeovers together at Macy's one Christmas. But with every loving, sisterly embrace came unsolicited advice, needless pep talks and confessions of problems that were actually brags, such as the fact that her butt was *too* round and made her look slutty if she wore white pants. Even so, as much as Emily was sometimes tempted to write Christina off as a delusional, self-important jerk, she couldn't. Christina had been the only person in her family to take her college social dramas seriously, or any of her mini crises, for that matter. When she was the only girl in her hall not to be accepted by a single sorority, Christina stayed on the phone with her for over an hour listening to her vent. Meanwhile, her father had only emailed her: Sororities are a waste of time and money anyway. Study. Love, Dad. Every time she worried about getting herpes from a toilet seat, Christina was armed and ready with her own handful of stories about herpes-afflicted friends and how none of them got it from a toilet seat. That made Emily feel better, and afterward she only Googled herpes for an hour.

"I can't *believe* you," Jason said. "Inviting my ex-wife when you know she's the worst person on Earth."

"You won't even have to see her. And this is my wedding anyway."

"Yeah, well, unfortunately she was at my wedding too. I'd like to go to a family wedding where this woman doesn't ruin it. Lauren, when are you getting married?"

"When same-sex marriage is legal in every country."

"Okay, so after Saudi Arabia is wiped off the face of the Earth by an alien invasion."

"That whole part of the world will be wiped off the face of the Earth anyway. Thanks to our corrupt government's white American imperial colonization."

"You are going to get married, though, right? If you honestly wait for gay marriage to be legal everywhere, it'll just never happen."

"So be it. I won't use any privilege that is only afforded to me because of my whiteness or straight-passing." Lauren picked up Ariel, as if to use him as a conversational shield.

"You're not straight?" Jason said. "You *only* ever date men."

"I'm pansexual and heteroromantic."

He blinked and turned back to Emily. "Did you *seriously* need to invite Christina to this stuff?"

"Jason, just relax about Christina," Marla said. "Don't let her rent space in your head for free. She never deserved you."

"She never deserved him?" Lauren said. "He cheated on her and emotionally abused her for years. You're blaming the wrong person, Mom."

"Abuse her!" Ariel said.

"Men can't help it," Jason said, quieter this time, as if to prevent Ariel from hearing him. "We're just not monogamous. We're always looking for the youngest, hottest thing around. Don't kill the messenger—it's just biology."

"Jason, that's ridiculous," Emily said. "Christina is beautiful."

"You're missing the point. Sure, she's hot, but she's only one woman. Would you tell a gay guy to stop being gay? I'm only attracted to hot, young women, and I can't be with one woman at a time. At least I admit it. You guys should be proud of my self-awareness." He smiled to himself, eagerly anticipating an argument. This was something he had been doing since he was a kid. In 1997 he told Marla he was a Republican just to get a rise out of her, and she cried for days after declaring she had failed as a mother.

Emily had heard enough. "You're not young *or* hot, Jason!"

"Women don't care about looks. They care about personality."

"Okay, well, you also have a shitty personality." It wasn't often that Emily sensed approval from her sister, but she knew Lauren agreed with that comment.

"Look, I know both of you are self-conscious about your looks or age or whatever," he said. "You shouldn't be. I'm not saying *all* men are like me. Obviously you're both with guys who are fine committing to a woman. I'm just of a different caliper."

"It's *caliber*, actually," Lauren said.

"Uh, where should I put these?"

Emily turned and saw David, still holding the two bags, his back against the wall. He looked like someone who had just seen a digitally remastered version of *The Exorcist* in the front row of a 3-D Imax theater. He always asked her why she tried to limit the time he spent with her family. Now he knew.

"The four horsemen of the apocalypse are here," Jason said, looking out the living room window as Christina's Audi pulled in to the driveway.

"Not your best," Emily said. "There aren't even four people, just two, and one of them is your three-year-old daughter."

Emily went outside to greet Christina. She saw Mia for the first time in a long time as Christina lifted her from her car seat. Mia had Jason's brown hair, cut into a clean little bob, and Christina's upturned nose as well as her sparkling gray-blue eyes. At times, Emily felt jealous of Mia, knowing that when she was old and unattractive, Mia would be young and pretty—prettier than she ever was. But she stopped herself. Her vanity had to have a limit, and being jealous of the future version of a three-year-old had to be that limit.

"Hey, sweetie." Emily hugged Mia.

"Mommy, is that a man or a lady?" Mia asked, her plump finger to her lips.

"I'm so sorry about her," Christina said, balancing Mia on her hip. "She's starting to figure out the difference between boys and girls and she's having a little trouble with it."

"No, I'm not," Mia protested.

"It's okay," Emily said. "She's hasn't actually seen me in person since she was tiny... I've been a pretty bad aunt."

"Nonsense. You do you." She leaned in to kiss Emily's cheek. Christina had changed her hair since she last saw her. It was blonder, straight and parted down the middle, stopping right above her shoulders. Christina had delicate, girlish features that always looked feminine and youthful even though her skin was freckled and lightly lined from years of tanning to a deep brown during her teenage summers in East Hampton. She seemed like the type of woman who would go for Botox, but her insistence on self-love and acceptance probably prevented her.

"I love your dress," Christina said. Emily knew she didn't really mean it. If she saw it in a store, she'd say it was cheap.

"Oh, thanks. It's probably all sweaty now. I should change."

"It is what it is. Never doubt yourself. You are a goddess. Just like me, and just like Mia. Every woman is a goddess. Aren't you a goddess, Mia?"

"No, I'm a princess. I'm Elsa."

"Are you coming to the barbecue at David's house?" Emily asked.

"Of course. I'm sure Jason will be a p-r-i-c-k about it, but then again, when is he not?"

"Yeah." Emily laughed a little. "I love your nail polish, by the way."

"Oh, thanks. It's one of those shellac manicures." It was clear and neutral, matching her flowing ivory silk top and gray skinny jeans. Such a simple manicure easily could have been done at home, but Christina usually chose the priciest option for anything. Even her toilet paper was organic. Everything about Christina was refined and subtle, expensive and tasteful. She came from Greenwich old money, and, as a result, had grace that Emily would never have, even if she became insanely rich overnight. On top of her family money, Christina worked at a New York ad agency and presumably was paid well there. Emily sometimes wondered if Jason had to pay alimony, or if Christina did, but she was afraid to ask. They both acted as though the divorce settlement was horribly unfair. No matter which one of them she spoke to, the story was one of gross injustice.

"So are you...dating?" Emily tried to get a feel for whether or not that question would offend Christina. But she didn't know what else to ask.

"Not in front of Mia," she whispered. "But...yes. I'm surprised at how well it's going. I am prouder and prouder of my decision every day." She pressed Mia's head to her chest and put another hand over her ear. "Between you and me, the only reason I'm fine with him having partial custody is that at least I have the occasional weekend to get a pedicure and go on a date. I honestly think he's a horrible father."

Emily wasn't sure what to say. "Anyway, we're going to the barbecue in a few hours. Come inside and we'll get you some coffee. Ariel is there in case Mia wants someone to play with."

Christina turned to Mia. "Mia, are you excited to see your cousin? Gosh, it's been too long! I don't think she remembers meeting him."

"Just a warning," Emily said. "If she's having trouble telling boys from girls, she's going to have a lot of trouble with him."

David's childhood home looked like a modern, more expensive version of a log cabin. In front there was a wraparound wooden deck, an expanse of freshly cut grass and a tire swing hanging from an old maple tree. A well-worn wooden play-house, painted red like a miniature barn, still stood out on the lawn. David's father had built it when he and his brother were little and later converted it into a shed for his tools. Nick was the type of manly-man father that Emily only saw on television. He had worked for years in risk arbitrage and was now retired. He was in his late fifties, and despite being able to afford to hire people to fix things around his home, he took pleasure in home improvement: building decks, fixing pipes, woodworking.

"Hello!" he called from the front door. Emily always marveled at how excited David seemed to see his father: no deep breathing to prepare, no nervous fidgeting, no anticipation of attacks, no deployment of prearranged conversational shutdowns. Nick gave David a long, effusive hug, as if it had been years since they last saw each other. Nick and his wife, Susan, had visited San Francisco just a few months earlier, and a similar hug had occurred then.

"Emily," Nick said, reaching out to hug her. He had a strong jaw like David's, the same blue eyes. He had a receding hairline, short brown hair sprinkled with gray, and freckles on his nose. Sometimes when Emily looked at Nick, she wondered if he was what David would grow up to be. She could do a lot worse.

"Emily, sweetheart!" David's stepmother, Susan, bounced over and hugged her. She was barely five feet, so Emily had to bend down. Susan had met Nick on eHarmony two years earlier. She had been living in Idaho, so they had a long-distance relationship for a year before she moved to Connecticut to marry him. She was plump with dyed blonde hair and hazel eyes. She liked to wear festive earrings that matched the season. Today she was wearing tiny dangling watermelons.

"Susan!" Emily said, giving her a hug. "You smell awesome, what is that?"

"You'll laugh," said Susan. "I went shopping with Maddyson and bought the latest Britney Spears perfume. I was worried she'd laugh at me for trying too hard, but apparently 'only older people like Britney Spears' anyway."

"That's crazy. I still love Britney Spears!"

"Well, Maddyson is eighteen so she thinks everyone is old. So how are things in *San Francisco*? See any great shows?"

Susan had very limited experience with big cities, other than the few times she and Nick had ventured into Manhattan to see the Rockettes or *The Lion King*. When they'd visited David in San Francisco, she had insisted on riding the cable cars everywhere.

"I don't really go to live shows very much," Emily said. "You mean music, right?"

"Any show!" Susan laughed. "You are so lucky. Young and in a big city!"

Steven and Marla approached. Emily tensed. Her parents had met Nick and Susan before, right after she and David got engaged. Emily had delayed that encounter as long as possible because she had a palpable fear that her parents would alienate Nick and Susan so much that they would advise David to break up with her. Once they got engaged, she felt a little more secure, and finally told her parents that David's parents lived close enough for them to meet up. Luckily for her, Marla and Steven only saw Susan and Nick for lunch once at a Mexican place called Cha Cha Cha Sombrero. Marla and Steven didn't make much of an effort to see them after that, despite Susan occasionally sending them invites to events they would obviously hate, like the Fairfield Pumpkin and Gourd Festival. Emily imagined the scene at the Mexican restaurant: Marla declining to order anything from the menu, instead producing a plum and a yogurt from her bag while regaling Nick and Susan with an exhaustive list of the anti-anxiety medications Emily was prescribed in high school. After the lunch, Marla called Emily to tell her that Nick and Susan were "nice people," which Emily knew was the real kiss of death for Marla. Later, Marla complained over the phone to Emily about a mass e card Susan had sent her for Easter, featuring pastel cartoon rabbits somehow hatching out of eggs, which she found offensive because "she should know we don't celebrate that."

"Well, if it isn't the most brilliant woman in the tri-state area!" Susan said, giving Marla a hug. "You look lovely!"

"Thank you, Susan. Such unique earrings." Marla hugged her, then gestured toward Susan's earrings as if she had just received an underwhelming piece of noodle art from a seven-year-old.

"Aw, thanks. There's this adorable little jewelry place I went to when Nick and I were visiting Beantown. I thought of you the whole time. What a kick it must have been to grow up there. All the shows!"

"It was nice."

"Do you get back there often?"

"Not that much. The last time I was there— God, I don't think I've been there since my last Harvard reunion."

Never misses a chance, Emily thought.

"*Ooooh*, Harvard! I forgot you went there!"

"Oh, let's not get into Harvard," Marla said, waving it off, a few bangles clinking against her narrow wrist.

"You know who you're like? JFK! Funny factoid, but he went there too."

Marla smiled weakly, and Emily could already see beads of sweat forming on her mother's freshly waxed upper lip. "Well, I don't think I'm that much like JFK, but I'll take the compliment." Marla had a distaste for Catholics that made little sense. It was an attitude more typical of lapsed Catholics with nightmarish memories of parochial school. Marla said her anger came from perfectly justifiable outrage over anti-Semitism, but Emily thought it seemed odd to single out Catholics for that. She was fairly certain that Marla's prejudice had more to do with a girl from her high school in Boston named Colleen Sweeney—a transfer from a Catholic girls' school—who in 1973 had won both the Latin award and the science award, two awards Marla believed she deserved. The Colleen story had been told to Emily various times over the course of her childhood, with a different moral each time. Once, the takeaway was that even if you fail at something when you are younger, you can always grow up to prove your critics wrong. (At the end of the story, Marla gleefully revealed that Colleen later turned out to be a stay-at-home mom.) Another time, she ended the story with the assertion that even if you are brilliant, if you don't work hard enough, some "idiot" with a better work ethic could beat you.

"So how is the psychiatry racket going?" Susan asked.

"Psychology, actually." It was a distinction that Marla wasn't proud of, and Emily was surprised she even owned up to it.

Susan turned to Emily. "What a kick, growing up with a mom who's a therapist! Did she ever diagnose *you* with anything?"

"Um, yes." Emily dug her heel into the lawn. "I mean, she diagnosed me with an anxiety disorder. And some other stuff that she later revised."

She regretted saying it as soon as the words left her mouth. Susan placed one hand over her freckled chest, another over her mouth, her eyes widening as if she'd just found out that Emily had a terminal illness.

"It's not a big deal," Emily said. "Honestly."

"Marla," Susan gasped. "I had no idea! I am so sorry."

"It's nothing to feel bad about," Marla said. "Emily has had her fair share of challenges, but it's very important to us that we strive to help her function as well as she possibly can."

"Mom, I'm literally right here."

"Well, this is nothing you don't know. I never wanted you to be treated differently because you struggle with anxiety. It was hard enough that you were profoundly gifted. Trying to help you assimilate socially proved challenging for me."

"Okay, I'm getting some food now." Emily took David's arm and waved goodbye to the four parents. She panicked for a moment, worrying that in her absence Marla would unleash embarrassing stories about her worst anxiety attacks—like the time when she was fourteen and she cried in a restaurant because she suspected a waiter had not washed his hands after using the bathroom and her parents made her eat her baked ziti anyway. But knowing Marla, she would try to keep her conversation with Susan as mercifully brief as possible.

"They'll be fine," David said, squeezing her hand.

Nick went to man the grill, donning an apron with a corny Mr. Good Lookin' is Cookin' slogan next to a cartoon of a goofy, big-eared and big-nosed barbecuing man with a head two times bigger than his body. Nick sometimes made Emily wistful; she couldn't help comparing him to her own father, who spent family dinners deriding other faculty members he was convinced were trying to sabotage his chances at tenure.

"My dad has already texted me since I've gotten here," David said, looking at his phone. "Why does he do this? This one just says, *Dave, so proud of you! You have really become a man!*"

"It's cute. He cares about you, and he still thinks texting is new and fun."

"Yeah, but I'm like ten feet away from him."

"I can't really blame him. When you come home it…well, I think it reminds him of your mom." Emily still felt uncomfortable approaching the topic of David's mother. No matter how angry she got with Marla, she didn't think she'd be able to go on if Marla died. She didn't understand how David didn't break down crying now and again. She liked to think he showed that people could bounce back from tragedy, but instead his calm attitude signified that she was just far too emotional compared to normal people, and that if and when her mother did die, she'd suddenly collapse and die too.

"I just don't need to hear how proud he is of me every time I eat a Hot Pocket," David said.

"At least he's proud of you."

"Yeah, well." He took a swig of beer. "I guess when my brother is the only other child he has to compare me to, I seem like Richard Branson meets Nelson Mandela."

She wondered if David ever felt that her praise and affection was too smothering. He never said so, but if he found it so irritating coming from Nick, he must occasionally feel the same way about her staring at him while he watched basketball, putting cute little notes on the bathroom mirror for him, and sending him heart emoji for no reason during the workday. She had tried to play hard-to-get when they were first dating, but it was so difficult not to fall off the wagon and start inundating him with kisses and compliments.

Emily looked over at the barbecue guests through the haze of smoke and flies. There was Jason, T-shirt slightly too small and revealing his belly, raising his arms in the air in what appeared to be a low-effort version of the Macarena. He was drunk.

"We are going to have an epic wedding week!" he cheered, raising his Heineken. He had finally stopped sulking about Christina's presence. It helped that she avoided him as much as possible. She had taken a liking to Joss, one of Susan's fifty-something granola-ish friends from the cat shelter where she volunteered, and the two of them were huddled in the corner having girl talk.

"You do you" Emily heard Christina say.

"Your brother is getting drunk," David said.

"No shit." Emily laughed. "Hey, where's *your* brother?"

"Hmm, I don't know. I assumed he'd be out of his cave by now." He looked for Nathan, and finally spotted him at the back door, half-hidden by a wooden column. He called out to him. "Nathan! Aren't you going to say hi?"

Nathan trudged over. He was only a few years younger than David, but Emily often thought of him as if he were a teenager because it was hard to remember he wasn't. He lived at home with Nick and Susan, and although he was usually eager to boast about his superior intelligence, he didn't have any work history or accomplishments to show for his self-evaluated IQ of 170. He was rotund, with flappy triangular man boobs outlined in sweat on his black T-shirt. His shoulder-length brown hair was gathered into a greasy ponytail. Growing along the underside of his double chin was an untrimmed beard with the texture of pubic hair. He was wearing his uniform: a faux leather trench coat, cargo shorts, white Nike sneakers, and a gray tweed dollar-store fedora.

"Salutations, David," he said. "Susan suggested I wear *le hat* for such a fancious occasion."

"Fancious?"

"It means fancy. I believe that it's a Middle English term but I could be wrong."

"Well, I'm really excited to have you as a part of our wedding," Emily said. She gave him an awkward hug, patting him on the back and trying to avoid the smell of his ponytail. She had met him once, last Thanksgiving—they had spent the holiday with David's family because Emily's parents were in the Vineyard—but hadn't spoken to him very much. He had spent the vast majority of the weekend playing *World of Warcraft* in his room, and at one point he proudly announced at the dinner table that he had made a thirteen-year-old cry after debating him online about atheism.

"So, Emily, do you have any fair ladies-in-waiting who would be pleased to make my acquaintance?" he asked. "Anyone looking for a gentleman?"

"Ladies-in-waiting?"

"Bridesmaids, as the plebeians say."

"Well, my friend Gabrielle is the maid of honor, but she's pregnant and married…"

"You didn't make your sister the maid of honor?" He looked horrified. Even someone as socially inept as Nathan knew how weird that was. Emily blushed.

"I just…it's a long story. She's kind of anti-wedding. I didn't think she'd do a good job at it."

"Cold, m'lady. But I remain intrigued. Prithee continue."

David frowned. Emily could tell it was taking all his restraint not to punch Nathan in the face.

"Oh, my other bridesmaids? Well, there's my friend Jennifer but she's…" She didn't know how to finish the sentence without saying "out of your league," so she just said, "a lot older than you."

"How old?"

"Twenty-nine."

"Hmm. Five years older than myself. That's pushing it, but I'll consider her if she enchants me. Women that age sometimes have a certain…je ne sais quoi."

David shook his head. "Nathan, don't. Just trust me when I say no."

"And well," Emily said, "the only other bridesmaid is…

Maddyson. But, ha-ha, since she's your stepsister that pretty much..." She trailed off, unsure of how to finish the sentence.

"Don't be so quick," David said. "Nathan has been hung up on her ever since Susan married our dad."

"What, really?"

"He's being oversimplificated," Nathan said. "I am not hung up on my stepsister. I merely admire a beauty such as she."

Emily involuntarily cringed.

"Dude," David said, "she's way too young for you. I am not doing this with you again."

"Eighteen is legal, for your information."

"Yeah, but it started when she was sixteen."

Nathan put his hand over his chest in a bad imitation of a pearl-clutching old lady. "Dear Lord! Sixteen! Reproductive age, legal in almost all of Europe and fully able to make her own choices! Whatever must we do with this pedophile?"

"I don't get why you can't just date girls your own age," David said.

"The older women get, the more demanding they become. If I were to approach a twenty-five-year-old, for example, she would be attractive but wouldn't have Maddyson's fertile, nubile looks. And to make matters more unsavory, she would look down on me for not having a so-called traditional job. Maddyson doesn't have a job, ipso facto, we are actually a good match. Moreover, if we lived just a few hundred years ago I would be the natural first choice to take her maidenhood—intelligent, wise, generous, successful—and in the same family line."

"How are you successful in any way?" David asked. "You just said you don't have a job."

"In days of yore, my good sir, I would have been successful. The trades in which I am highly skilled are not valued by our declining society. Sword fighting, for example."

Emily looked over at Maddyson, leaning against a column. She had wavy brown hair cut to her shoulders with a streak of pink. (Emily had objected to the dye job because Maddyson would be in the wedding party, but she wound up allowing it for fear of looking like a bridezilla.) She wore a pair of frayed acid-washed shorts, Converse sneakers and a large white T-shirt that looked intentionally splattered with green paint. She was looking at her iPhone with her eyes glazed over, giving a surly, slightly openmouthed expression to the screen. Emily noticed that Nathan had seen her staring at Maddyson, so she quickly averted her gaze.

"She's beautiful," he said with a knowing smile. "No shame in looking."

"I wasn't…"

"It's fine. All women are slightly bisexual."

"Nathan," David said. "That's enough."

Nathan shrugged. He was relatively immune to criticism. Emily couldn't tell if it came from abnormally low or abnormally high self-esteem. Either he was so used to negative feedback that it no longer affected him, or he was so delusional that he refused to believe that anything could be wrong with him. Perhaps she'd ask Marla to analyze him. She was sure there would be an interesting cavalcade of diagnoses on the ride home. All of Emily's ex-boyfriends had earned their places in the *Diagnostic and Statistical Manual of Mental Disorders*, from histrionic personality disorder to borderline personality disorder to chronic depression. Marla followed up each assessment with, "not that I've personally examined him or anything" as if trying to avoid liability. She had diagnosed Christina with narcissism back when she and Jason were dating, and Matt with compliant codependency. David was the only one who had evaded a diagnosis so far, probably because Emily had rigorously prevented him from spending too much time with her mother.

Jason

Jason was wasted, there was no way around it. He was mind-lessly peeling the label off his Heineken and glaring at Christina from behind glassy corneas. Why did everyone like her? Why did people respect her and not him? It was because she was a woman. The woman always got to play the victim and nobody asked any questions. He thought ruefully of Lauren's article in *Cunt Magazine*: "It Happened to Me: I Was the Victim of Grade-Shaming." It was an article devoted to the one time in high school when she got a C on an essay, and how it was not only an undeserved grade given to her purely because of sexism, but it also gave her lifelong brain-image issues. He had trolled the article briefly under the username Butthole_Dude_80 and told her she was a delusional bitch... and later felt bad about it briefly before finding it funny again.

That was when he saw her: the famed jailbait. Was it jailbait if they were eighteen? He had heard that David had a much younger stepsister, and there she was in all her slender, tanned glory. She was hanging around Nick's porch looking bored, as if she were afraid some friends at school would make fun of her for being too enthusiastic around her family. He had heard that girls her age—no, *women* her age, she was legal—absolutely loved older men because they saw them as confident, distinguished provider types. Jason wasn't at the sugar-daddy level quite yet, but that hardly mattered when it came to a one-night stand. The only problem was where they would do it. Certainly her room would be full of creepy childhood items, like teddy bears that said "I wuv you" when you pressed them, ballet participation certificates from elementary school, posters featuring those douchebags from One Direction and old haunted-looking Barbie dolls with tangled hair and rubbed-off eyes. Not to mention her bedroom was under the roof of her inevitably protective stepfather. Jason's room wasn't much better as it was under Marla and Steven's roof, with Lauren, the self-appointed Cockblocker-in-Chief, across the hall. He *did* have a car, though.

"Hello," he said, sidling up to Maddyson. She looked up from her phone, which displayed the Snapchat app. She met his stare, her eyes widening slightly. Either she was intimidated by his confidence and swagger, or creeped out. He was inclined to believe the former.

"Hey," she said, looking bored again. "Sorry, I didn't see you standing there."

"What's with the pink streak of hair?" Jason asked. "Is that a wig? You'd look better if you were Asian."

"Are you a friend of my dad's or something?"

"I'm going to pretend you didn't say that," he said with a smirk. He could never let comments like that get to him. Then he would be just as emotional and self-centered as Christina, or any other woman for that matter. He had to remain stone-cold and keep his alpha game tight.

"Oh, I'm sorry," she said. "I'm just trying to get through this party without having to talk to anyone."

"This attitude is going to stop being cute when you're older." He had to keep the smile on his face or else he'd just seem mean. The goal was to be *cheeky*—rude, maybe even arrogant and slimy, but never antagonistic. He felt a tap on his shoulder and a man's voice. "I implore you to leave her alone, good sir." The accent was vaguely British, like the generic old-fashioned accent used in gladiator movies.

He turned and saw an overweight man in his early twenties. He looked as if he were in a community theater production of *The Matrix*, complete with a shiny black trench coat lightly coated in sweat and giving off the fishy, chemical smell of synthetic leather.

"Who the fuck are you?"

"I am Nathan, good sir, brother of the groom."

"Wait, I heard about you. Are you the one who got banned from the live-action role-playing group for scaring those women with your sword?"

"Even LARPers can't always appreciate true historic accuracy," he said a little defensively. "In bygone days, females appreciated valiant warriors, and I never intended to fight a lady. In fact, I wasn't fighting anyone—merely displaying my sword-fighting skills for the womenfolk to behold. My plan was to throw my handkerchief to the most beautiful one once my performance was done...but next thing I knew, the police were there, and I was being asked not to return. Chivalry is dying in this society, verily."

"Damn," Jason said, taking another sip of beer. "You couldn't just talk to the girls?"

"Good sir. Do not try to debate *me* on the importance of chivalry. I implore you to step away from the lady."

Jason almost laughed but then realized he wasn't joking. "I'm sorry, I'm a friendly guy. I was just chatting with her."

"I am the protector of her innocence."

"Nathan," Maddyson groaned. "For the last time, I'm *not a virgin*! Both of you, go away!"

"Nonsense, milady." He turned to Jason. "You, sir. Be gone, unless you desire a duel in the arena of intellect. Care to discuss Descartes?"

"I don't want any trouble, buddy." He paused. An idea. "See that woman over there, man?"

He pointed to Christina, who had moved on from Joss and was now sipping some sauvignon blanc with Susan, laughing as she plopped a plastic ice cube into her glass. He could only hope she wasn't talking about him and his "constant infidelity" or "alcoholism." Women would complain to anyone who would listen, and Susan seemed like enough of a chump to fall for Christina's whole self-pitying routine.

"Yes," Nathan said. "The fair blonde lass."

"You want to intellectually duel someone? Duel her. She *loves* being told when she's wrong. Makes her hot."

Nathan smiled smugly, as if Jason had just made an embarrassingly basic grammar mistake.

"What?" Jason asked. "What is it now?"

"A gentleman cannot duel a lady. For if he did, he would no longer be a gentleman."

"Oh, brother. How about this? I promise to leave your sister alone if you—"

"*Step*sister."

"Okay. I promise to leave her alone for the entire night, if you go and talk to that blonde lass. I hereby beseech you to flirt with her, serenade her and defend her honor."

"But why? I don't know her."

"Look. I know her. She *loves* guys like you who are romantic and old-fashioned and whatnot. So if you're looking for a girlfriend, go talk to her."

"Intriguing." Nathan nodded and tipped his fedora. Then, with a whoosh of his trench coat, he headed for Christina. Jason sat back on one of the patio chairs, put his beer to his lips and prepared to enjoy the show.

Nathan

Nathan took a deep breath as he approached her. The closer he got, the older she looked, but she was still pretty. She reminded him of how he always imagined a miller's wife or tavern wench would look in the books he read—a bit weathered compared to her much more attractive eighteen-year-old counterparts, but comely still with clear blue eyes and flaxen

locks. Below her loose-fitting top he could make out a relatively ample bosom.

With all the aplomb he could muster, he bowed deeply, removing the fedora from his head with an elaborate flourish.
"Milady…" he said, staring at her feet. After sufficient time,
he straightened himself and made eye contact. She looked
frightened. Perhaps she had never met a true gentleman before.

"Um…hello," she said. His stepmother had vanished. For
all her faults, she always knew when to make herself scarce.

"What is your name, sweet lass?" he asked, taking her
hand. She had a dry, freckled palm like a farmhand, but her
fingers were small and delicate.

"Christina," she said, her voice shaking. "I'm the mother
of the flower girl. And you are…?"

"Nathan Porter. Best man and second in line to the country seat of Portershire."

She looked past him to where Jason was sitting. "Okay. Be
honest with me. Did my jackass of an ex-husband tell you to
come over here?"

"I know not the man of whom you speak."

"Okay. That's what I thought. Go back and tell Jason this
shit isn't funny, and if he wants to see his daughter at all this
week he's going to need to act like an adult."

"Milady, is it so difficult to believe that a gentleman of my
age would be interested in you? I value more than just looks,
you know, and besides, you're like a seven at least."

She sighed. "Go away. Tell Jason to quit it. Bye, Nathan."

He marched back to Jason, fixing his stare on the balding
slob, who was drinking beer before sundown like a tavern
drunkard. Nathan stood before him and put his hands on his
hips. "Jason," he said. "That woman is your ex-wife!"

"Yeah, guess I left that out. But hey, beggars can't be choos-
ers."

"She knew you sent me over. You have disrespected me in
mine own home. Now prepare for that duel."

Jason began to laugh. "Take it easy, buddy. I just wanted to have some fun. I didn't mean to hurt your feelings. I was trying to mess with her, not you."

That was more of an apology than Nathan had expected. Back in high school, the popular boys would play similar pranks on him, like the time they told him there was a sword fight tournament being hosted in Gym A, and Nathan didn't realize that was where the Womyn's Empowerment Club was having their "safe space" sexual assault discussion group. *He* was the one who got suspended for a week after that, all because he arrived brandishing a sword and wearing a Guy Fawkes mask. Some people took political correctness much too far.

"I appreciate your apology, good sir," Nathan said. "But I need assurance that you will not exploit me for your merriment again."

Jason got up from his seat, wobbling slightly. "Sorry if I took advantage of you. It was just such a perfect opportunity to piss off the ex. You know how it is."

Nathan nodded. He had never had a girlfriend, but that had not stopped him from plotting his revenge on other women. Already he had made one of his female tormentors cry on Twitter by calling her an imbecile for misspelling *lavender.* He smiled serenely to himself at the memory of that triumph.

"So you respect me?" Nathan asked.

"Sure. As much as I can respect a guy in a tweed fedora and sneakers."

"Do I have your gentleman's word?"

Jason threw his head back and laughed. "Yeah. My gentleman's word."

Emily

The air smelled of slightly burnt hot dogs, a childhood smell that filled Emily with nostalgia. She looked around and saw that the two families appeared to be mixing nicely, or at least being polite to each other. Marla and Susan were still talking. Marla was looking ever so slightly over Susan's head, her chin tilted upward, a very full glass of pinot noir in her hand. Emily heard Susan exclaim "So you've actually been to Madison Square Garden? In the Big Apple?"

Meanwhile, her father had cornered Nick by the grill. "I don't want to bore you with this, but the brutality of the Han Dynasty has been exaggerated by popular media. It was a topic I covered in one of my more famous articles. I'm not sure I would recommend it to you. If you're not in the field, you might consider it a bit dry."

"There you are, Emily!" She saw Marla waltzing over to her, her palazzo pants rippling in the wind. "I was looking all over for you. I'm calling a small family meeting outside. Wipe under your eyes, by the way, your mascara is melting."

"Calling a family meeting at another family's home?" Emily asked. "Come on, that's pretty rude."

Marla feigned pearl-clutching, which actually consisted of clutching her amber necklace, and appeared less satirical than she intended. "Oh no, Emily! Maybe they'll tell David not to marry you! The horror!"

"That's not—" Emily paused. She wouldn't pick this battle.

"If you must know, Emily, I'm doing this here because I fear you and your siblings would lash out at me if we were in private. Discussing this in a public setting makes it more likely that you'll all behave appropriately."

Emily wondered how Marla defined *appropriate*, but she decided not to say anything about it. Having done many "inappropriate" things in her childhood, which Marla still held up as examples of her missed social cues, she wanted to avoid having any of these failures paraded again. One incident in particular was a tantrum she threw at the age of eight when her mother refused to let her get a second candy bag at FAO Schweetz. She'd thought that, twenty years later, such a story would be merely funny or forgettable, but it still embarrassed her deeply, since Marla always made a point to relate all her modern-day anxieties to this one moment and harp on the fact that she was "much too old" to be getting so upset in public. "This is just like that time at FAO Schweetz," Marla would say, as Emily cried to her on the phone about a fear or hang-up that had nothing to do with candy. "You have problems handling a lack of control."

Emily followed Marla to a handmade wooden bench at the far end of the patio, where Lauren and Jason were already sitting. Matt sat at the end of the bench, looking like a startled deer. Marla glared at him.

"Matt," she said sharply, "this is a family meeting."

Matt nodded and slunk away. Emily took his seat on the bench.

"Mom, you didn't have to be so mean to Matt," Lauren said.

"He needs to stop following you everywhere. He's worse than Ariel."

"Actually, Ariel is profoundly independent. We still do skin-on-skin bonding, but he doesn't insist on it."

"I see." Marla turned to face the group. "Okay, I'm just going to say it. I want us to work together on what I think you'll all agree are some troubling issues facing our family."

"What issues?" Jason asked.

"It's no surprise that we aren't exactly close. As I get older, I want to spend time with my children, and while both you and Lauren live within driving distance, or a quick train ride on Metro-North, I rarely see you. And Emily, I know you live all the way in California, but we haven't seen you since two Christmases ago. I can't even remember the last time we saw you for Thanksgiving."

"You and Dad always go to the Vineyard on Thanksgiving."

"Yes, but only because we anticipate that you won't want to come home. Meanwhile, Lauren doesn't even celebrate Thanksgiving."

"That's because it should be called National Genocide Day," Lauren said. "Although to be fair, that's every day of American history." She leaned back as if waiting to collect high-fives.

"Look, I'm not here to blame any of you kids. It's not your fault that we aren't as close as we should be. I take full responsibility for being too trusting. I was silly to assume you would all want to stay in touch with me as I got old."

"Mom, don't do this," Emily said. "We just have our own lives—it doesn't mean we don't want to see you."

"Anyway," she continued, "since we're all together this week, I've decided that we should do a special family exercise. I think it will help us repair what has gone wrong."

"What is it, Mom?" Emily asked. She feared some kind of competitive team-building exercise, like the trip to Six Flags that ClearDrop organized, where everyone had to go on rides together in a group of thirty, and nobody could separate. But no, Marla was too cultured for something like that. Emily still recalled the disdain in her mother's voice when she found out that her friend Naomi's daughter got married at Disneyland with some guy dressed as the genie from *Aladdin* officiating.

"Well," Marla said, her voice cracking theatrically, "I sometimes feel that I have failed you as a mother, considering how none of you are particularly close. Lauren, when you were born, I was hoping you would become a best friend for Jason, and Emily…"

"I know I was an accident, Mom."

"Well, I did tell your father that the antibiotics I was taking might interfere with my birth control, but when he gets in the mood…anyway. Basically, what I'm trying to say is that we need to bring this family together before the wedding. If we've fought this much only a few hours in, just imagine how this week will be. This might be the last time we all see each other before I die."

"Are you sick, Mom?" Emily asked. Her throat tensed up.

"I could be," said Marla. "Many cancers are asymptomatic. But in terms of actual diagnoses, no. Nothing that I know of."

Lauren groaned. "Mom, you can't just say something like that to Emily."

"I apologize, Emily," Marla said. "But death is a reality, and I will die someday. And I don't want that to happen before we have all come to terms with our problems."

"So what's the plan?" Jason asked, frowning at his empty beer bottle.

Marla took a deep breath. "Family therapy."

Lauren looked incredulous. "Dad actually agreed to this?"

"Dad won't be involved. Just me. This is about you kids, not him."

"Then why would you be there?" Lauren asked.

"Because I'm going to be the therapist," Marla said triumphantly, as if revealing a stunning M. Night Shyamalan twist.

"You can't be the therapist for your own children," said Emily. "That's unethical."

"Ethics are important up to a point, but it's also important not to be too rigid about them," she said. That, at least, was true. Marla bravely resisted societal pressure to be ethical. "Frankly, Emily, when you call me unethical I think you're projecting. What you really fear is that your own moral flaws will be uncovered. Don't be afraid of that. This is for personal growth."

"And if I don't want to go to this?"

"Then I will cancel your wedding."

"What?"

"I'm serious."

Emily had a feeling she wasn't serious—after all, too many deposits had already been put down, the guests were all set to arrive, it would be a massive embarrassment—but why argue? If she didn't say yes to the therapy, she would have to deal with constant unpleasantness for the next six days. And perhaps it would be a good outlet to tell Jason and Lauren about all the times they had wronged her. She enjoyed complaining about other people, and if she could do it in an environment where nobody was allowed to yell at her for it, that would be even better.

"Okay, I'll do it," she finally said.

She turned to Lauren and Jason, who both reluctantly nodded. At first she wondered why they didn't put up more of a fight, and then she remembered that her parents paid for Lauren's rent and Jason's divorce lawyer.

NIGHT 1

Emily

"WHAT KIND OF BARS even exist in Westchester?" David's feet dangled from the tiny bed in Emily's childhood bedroom. Emily was curling her hair with a thick pink-handled curling iron. She wore a formfitting white dress and a gold key pendant necklace that he had given her for her birthday the previous year.

"Some place called Celebz. Jason says he's been there before." She finished the last step of her makeup routine—extra-thickening mascara—and put the mascara tube back into her makeup bag, full of the department-store splurges she had made specifically for her wedding week. She felt a twinge of shame when she saw the $50 Tom Ford lipstick in peach-pink, but she genuinely felt it was the only shade that didn't make her look haggard.

"You don't need to get all dressed up. It's just a bar. This is going to be the Zoogli barbecue all over again. Watching you run off screaming with barbecue sauce on your white skirt was pretty hilarious for me, but you were upset for days."

"That's because it was a Club Monaco skirt that I bought

at a sample sale and I never would have been able to afford it otherwise, smart-ass. My reaction was completely justified. Also, the Zoogli barbecue was in California, where everyone dresses like eighteen-year-old coders. New York is different. No hoodies and sneakers at clubs." She hoped he didn't take this as a critique of his usual night-out uniform of a white T-shirt and jeans. She thought it made him look like a Calvin Klein model, but her girlfriend Jennifer told her he had the same fashion acumen as Homer Simpson.

"Yeah, but Westchester? I don't want to trash your home county or anything, but all the bars I've seen so far look like pizza parlors."

"There have to be a few places that are heating up. It's Saturday. Jason will know a good place."

"Ready for the party countdown?" Jason was behind the wheel. "The British GPS bitch says we've got five more minutes." Emily sat in the back seat with Lauren and Matt, while David rode shotgun. Lauren had done her version of dolling up: bright blue eyeliner, red lipstick, a Ramones T-shirt that showed off her arm tattoos, too-long bootcut jeans that were frayed at the cuffs, and red Converse sneakers with doodles on them. "Ariel drew on my shoes," she boasted when she caught Emily looking. "That's just how little of a fuck I give about clothes."

"Are you sure this place is good?" Emily asked Jason.

"Pretty decent."

"Am I overdressed?"

"Nah. Well, maybe a little. But at least you didn't think it was sexy to dress like the guys from *Superbad* like Lauren."

"I didn't wear this to be sexy," Lauren said. "I wear what I fucking want. Just because I'm not as desperate for male approval as Emily—"

"Hey, I didn't even *say* anything!"

"Sorry. I didn't mean to insult you. I'm just used to getting judged. The hardest person to be in this world is a woman who dares to veer the tiniest bit outside Western standards of femininity."

"What about a disabled albino hermaphrodite in Rwanda?" Jason said.

"Actually, it's called intersex. And I'm not here to play the oppression Olympics."

"Well, no, unless you're the one winning. Hear ye, hear ye, the white woman in her thirties, whose parents pay her rent, is oppressed! May as well be straight out of a refugee camp."

"The only reason I even need Mom's money is because our patriarchal society devalues a gender studies degree. For women, receiving money from parents is actually a form of indentured servitude. If I were a man, society would be handing me money just for showing up, and Mom and Dad wouldn't have to. You're saying this from the lofty, privileged perspective of a white cis man."

"What's cis?" Jason seemed legitimately confused this time.

"It's what you are. But it's not my job to educate you, so Google that shit."

"How is it spelled, like *sissy*? How can I Google it if I don't know how to spell it?"

"Forget it. You have no interest in learning anyway. And like I said, it's not my job."

"Well, you don't have a job, Lauren."

"That's one thing we have in common then. But even if you refuse to give any credit to *Cunt*, it's at least more legitimate than WalkShare."

"What's WalkShare?" David asked, eager to change the subject.

Jason cleared his throat. "WalkShare is a revolutionary

mobile app that I'm releasing next month. It is what would happen if Tinder fucked Uber. For just ten dollars per person, we match you with up to five walking buddies from the two locations you select, with a fifty-fifty male-female ratio—unless you pay more for the RatioPremiere membership, in which case the ratio is on your side. Then—boom: walking to work just got sexy."

Lauren sighed and put her head in her hands. "It's ridiculous."

"You're not single," Jason said. "Never underestimate a man's drive to get laid."

"What about the women? Women spend their time specifically trying to avoid strange men following them home. I'm constantly avoiding men."

"Well, they don't need to use WalkShare when they're walking home, do they, Einstein?"

"I don't know about you, Emily," she said, "but even when I was single, when I wanted to do my groceries I just wanted to do them. I didn't want to turn it into a Pied Piper trail of perverts following me. No matter where I went, men harassed me, flirted with me and propositioned me. I would pay to *remove* that experience from my life."

Emily wondered for a second how Lauren got so much more male attention than any of the other women she knew, but she didn't say anything. Despite her anxieties about her looks, Emily was aware that she was at least a bit above average in attractiveness and yet the only times she got hit on were when she chose to wear dresses on her walk to work. And even then, most of the guys hitting on her were homeless, on drugs and old enough to be her father, not even bothering to flirt with her but preferring to shout sexual expletives in her direction. Sometimes she wondered if those men were her "league" all along. She knew she got lucky with David.

"I think WalkShare sounds like a cool idea," David said, humoring Jason. "You never know what'll go viral. Just look at Tinder—when that came out, I thought the only people using it would be creeps who actually call those late-night sex-chat numbers off the TV. But several of my buddies are actually *living* with women they met on Tinder. My boss Robert always tells me that a good product is ninety percent hunger."

"There we go," Jason said. "David thinks it's a cool idea. He'd be a great client. Tall, good-looking, prime age and future billionaire. Too bad he's about to be off the market."

"He's not *about* to be off the market," Emily said. "He's been off the market for three years."

"Emily, just because a guy is dating you doesn't mean he owes you exclusivity. Obviously David's a faithful dude, but technically exclusivity starts at marriage. Don't take this personally, but women demand so much of men."

"At least women don't rape!" Lauren snapped. Matt nodded solemnly.

"Point taken," Jason said. "Can we move on? It's going to ruin my game if we keep it up with the rape talk, and I can't have bad game because tonight I'll have my go at a heaping platter of Westchester poonani." He briefly affected an Ali G accent when he said *poonani*.

"They can go one of three ways: total JAP, Jersey Shore guidette or uptight Greenwich import." He paused, and looked at David. "No offense, dude."

"I'm actually from Fairfield," he said. "At least you didn't call me a spoiled frat bro. That's the real Fairfield stereotype, for the record. That or bow tie–wearing douchebag. Either way, I don't take offense."

"I take offense," Lauren said. "You can't classify women like that."

"Jason, seriously," Emily said. "If Lauren promises not to go on about rape, you need to stop saying stuff that's designed to piss her off."

"Thanks, but I can fight my own battles," Lauren said. "I deal with guys worse than Jason on my blog daily, like this dickweed named Butthole_Man_80 who keeps stalking my posts."

"Maybe we should all just save this for therapy with Mom tomorrow," Emily said.

"Oh, fuck," Lauren said. "I forgot about that." For just a moment, all three siblings fell quiet, collectively dreading therapy with Marla.

"I agree with Emily," Jason said. "Let's try to have a fun night. Sorry if I was too harsh, Lauren. You know I'm just teasing." He winked at her from the rearview mirror.

"Your teasing is built on centuries of white male supremacy. But I won't dwell on it tonight. We can wait for the therapy session."

"What's this therapy?" David asked.

"Oh, nothing," Emily said. "Just, Mom wants us to do some family therapy this week, with her as the therapist. Obviously it's one of her usual power trips, so we're just going to suffer through it and get it over with."

"What could be so bad about that?" All three siblings glared at him. "I mean, I know your mom is, well…your mom. But free therapy? Babe, you're always complaining about how pricey therapy is. You told me that you'd rather buy a dress for the cost of a therapy session, because at least you're guaranteed to have a result from a dress."

"My point still stands," she said. "But this isn't *really* therapy. It's just an excuse for her usual tornado of criticism."

"Enough about this," said Jason. "Here we are. Celebz. See? I told you this was the shit."

Celebz was wedged between an organic smoothie store and a hair salon in a strip mall whose glory days were long gone. All the parking spaces were empty, except for two minivans and an SUV.

"Is anyone even here?" Matt asked as Jason parked. It was a perfectly reasonable thing to ask, but because Matt was usually so quiet, it came off as weirdly abrasive.

"It's only ten," Jason said. "Give it some time."

The facade of Celebz was black with tinted windows, in an attempt to look like an upscale club—an illusion shattered by the flyers for dog-sitters and guitar lessons taped to the windows. There was no bouncer in front, only an open door next to an abandoned stool with a bunch of neon pink wristbands splayed across the seat. As Emily stepped out of the car, she made sure her cork wedge shoes didn't get scuffed. David put his arm around her waist and squeezed it slightly.

Celebz's decor was dated, although it was hard to pinpoint the year when it might have ever been up-to-date. Behind the bar, there was a ten-foot-wide painting of a pair of giant female breasts, with molten gold running down them and dripping off the nipples. On the opposite wall was a painting of a shiny red convertible with a pair of gold-embossed women's legs emerging from the front seat. The walls were adorned here and there with black-and-white celebrity photos, but without any autographs on them: Sarah Michelle Gellar, Renée Zellweger, Tyra Banks, Josh Hartnett and Matthew Perry. Kelly Clarkson's "Since U Been Gone" boomed from the speakers, while a television over the bar played a grainy Lil Wayne video with the sound muted. Lil Wayne's lips briefly synced up with Kelly Clarkson's words as he posed next to a woman's butt in leather panties.

The place was dead. A bartender in her early thirties wearing a nose ring and tank top presided over an empty bar and listlessly played with her phone. Of the fifteen or so tables in the club, only three were occupied: a group of leathery older men spoke Russian loudly and toasted each other with red wine; a silver fox dressed like a Republican senator in a blue suit and red tie was sharing a bottle of pinot grigio with a pearl-necklaced fiftysomething who had exfoliated one too many times; and, in a booth in the back, two women in their thirties, one East Asian and one blonde, were drinking frozen margaritas in a valiant attempt at a girls' night out.

Emily and the others settled at a table near the center of the room, across from the two women. "Good job, Jason," she said. "I can see this is really where the party is at."

"Things are just getting started. Just wait till midnight."

Lauren looked incredulous. "Midnight? I need to get to sleep or tomorrow is going to be a nightmare with Ariel. It's hard enough for him to be in a new house, let alone being in a new house and not having me and Matt in bed with him. These kinds of transitions could ruin his self-esteem."

"Dude," Jason said. "He's four. He needs to learn to sleep alone."

"Don't tell me how to raise my kid."

"How about I buy everyone a beer?" he said. "Huh? Huh? Anyone? Free beer, right here!"

"Grains," David said, waving him off.

"Say what?"

"Emily and I don't do grains. It's a LifeSpin thing. Thanks, though." He turned to Emily. "I'll get us vodka sodas."

"Wait—you don't *do* grains?" Jason asked, drawing out the word *do*.

"I know it sounds silly, but grains do serious damage to the gut's digestive flora."

"You're fucking kidding, right?"

"It's your wedding weekend," Lauren said. "Grains aren't

going to kill you. Also, this is a really dangerous philosophy to be marketed at vulnerable, mentally ill young women like Emily. LifeSpin? You may as well call it LifeAnorexia."

"That's…not exactly a good pun," Jason said.

"It wasn't meant to be a fucking pun."

"DeathSpin would have been better."

"Emily, do you seriously believe this stuff?" she asked.

"Uh, well—yeah, I mean—it's actually about health, not weight loss. You can be perfectly healthy without eating grains and sugar. I haven't even lost a pound since I started." Emily wished she was actually proud of this, instead of secretly resenting David for having lost fifteen pounds on Life-Spin, when she truly hadn't lost anything.

"I should hope you fucking didn't," Lauren said. "It's not just about you, it's about all the *other* impressionable women out there who look at you and see what you do. What if you have a daughter? Do you think it's healthy for her to see her mother eating fucking…green beans?"

"Beans are also a gut irritant, by the way," David said. "This stuff is actually pretty cool once you read about it—if you want to lose weight instead of just maintain, you just cut out all beans, grains, dairy and fruit, except for berries. We're just maintaining, so for us it's not as crazy, but my trainer Gillian lost fifty pounds last year with that method and she feels amazing."

"I'm sure *she's* a great role model for young girls, too." While Lauren usually prided herself on being an advocate for all womankind, women who successfully lost large amounts of weight really pissed her off. She had written a scathing post for *Cunt* after Jennifer Hudson lost eighty pounds through Weight Watchers, arguing that the actress was to blame for the bulimia epidemic. It was called "An Open Letter to Ms. Hudson" but wasn't written in the formal tone that title promised. Half the content was gifs of angry cats.

"It's not like that," David said. "First off, Gillian ran a 5K and she's super healthy. Second, the stuff on the LifeSpin FoodMatrix is way healthier than pretty much any popular diet you see these days. This woman at my office started on this diet where she could only eat cucumbers and dark chocolate, and she wound up fainting in the middle of a team-bonding golf trip."

Emily laughed. "Are you sure she didn't just fall asleep? Team-bonding golf? I'd give up all food for a month just to get out of that."

"This is exactly what I'm talking about," Lauren said. "Now Emily is talking about giving up food."

"Oh, come on," David said. "LifeSpin isn't about starving yourself until you look like Mary-Kate Olsen's ankle. It's just about being healthy and getting in shape."

Lauren raised her sharply painted eyebrows. *"In shape?"* she asked. "What's *in shape* to you? Am I not in shape? Does everyone need to look like a twelve-year-old boy to be in shape?"

"I thought you were anti–body shaming," Emily said. "Twelve-year-old boy. Nice."

"I'm just making a point." Lauren flared her nostrils at David. "What's *in shape*? You realize you can be healthy at any weight, right, so what's the point of being in shape other than to cater to your narrow-minded, white aesthetic preferences? Am I *in shape* enough for you?"

"Why do you even *care* if I think you're in shape?" he said. "You're engaged."

"That's right," she said, pulling Matt closer to her. "And he fucking *loves* how I look and would probably throw up if I lost weight. And even then, he's evolved enough not to care about the physical side of things. He loves my intelligence, my wit, my sense of humor and the taste of my vulva. So fuck you and your body policing." Emily involuntarily cringed at the word *vulva* and clenched David's hand. Matt smiled wanly and stroked Lauren's arm.

"David isn't saying all bigger people are unhealthy," Emily said. "He's just talking about healthy lifestyle choices. It's not about how you look—it's about how you feel. This girl Julia at my office is in LifeSpin too. She's a big girl, but she can lift way more than I can and she's in the advanced yoga class."

"Still," Lauren said. "I don't like how this whole LifeSpin thing conveniently started when you met David."

"Enough," Emily said. "You've made your point. Nobody should ever better themselves or eat well, especially if it's a man's idea. We get it, now drop it."

"I'll drop it if I see you drink a fucking beer. Both of you. Then let's see how poisonous all these grains are." She crossed her arms and smiled smugly, as if she had just presented them with an impossible *Sophie's Choice* dilemma.

Emily and David looked at each other.

"Are you guys getting beers or not?" Jason asked, standing up. "I really want the previous two minutes of my life back."

"Yes, we'll have beers," David said. "One for me and one for Emily. Oh, and a glass of hot water with lemon."

Lauren shot him a skeptical look. "Lemon water?"

"You should try it," Emily said. "It's great for your digestion if you know you're going to eat something inflammatory. I have low stomach acid."

Lauren was about to find fault with lemon water but couldn't seem to think of anything. "I'm glad it works for you, Emily."

Jason

The bartender saw Jason approaching and momentarily stopped playing with her phone, seemingly annoyed by the interruption. "Hey there," he said, his voice dropping half an octave in an effort to sound more masculine. "Let me get…four Stellas, and uh…one cup of hot water with lemon, please, for this gay guy in our group. Thanks, sweetheart." The bartender sighed, put her phone down, and began pouring the drinks.

"What time do you get off?" he asked, leaning against the bar.

"At the end of my shift," she said flatly.

Jason returned to the table sulkily. The bartender came over with the drinks. Everyone took a beer except Matt. Jason nudged him in the shoulder. "Gotta love the designated driver. Thanks, man."

"I don't drink anyway," Matt said. "Except for artisanal absinthe."

Jason handed some wrinkled cash to the bartender. "I would have tipped more if you had smiled. What's your problem, exactly? Bad breakup? You're too hot to be so rude."

She wedged the cash into the pocket on her apron. "This tip is fine, sir, thank you. Have a good night." She went back to the bar.

"Lesbian," Jason stage-whispered to David. He sipped his beer. "I know this isn't exactly the Meatpacking District, but we could definitely have fun here. For one, just look at those two hot girls over there." He nodded toward the two women with the frozen margaritas.

"I thought you didn't like women over thirty," Emily said.

"Look, the range of women I will sleep with is far wider than the range of women I would actually commit to. I would easily sleep with both of those women. The blonde is like, a six, which is fine, and the Asian is at least a seven. That's adjusted for age, but it's rare to see an Asian who's less than a seven. Adjusted for race, though, she's like a four."

"You are really gross," Lauren said.

"Yeah, you've made your point," he said. "You're the one who really needs a beer. Now let's go make some friends."

He stood up and swaggered over to the women's table, his shoulders swaying more than usual. The blonde pushed some hair behind her ears and fluttered her eyelashes as she gave him a little grin, while her friend zipped her jacket up to her neck.

"Hey, ladies," he said. "I couldn't help but notice you were alone. Want some company?"

"We're on a girls' night out," said the East Asian woman. She leaned forward to sip her margarita.

The blonde scooted over to make room for him. "Girls' night out is all about meeting new people, right? Feel free to join."

"Sweet," he said, sliding into their booth. "Looks like we both came here to make friends."

"Didn't you already show up with a big group of friends?" the East Asian woman asked.

"Oh, those aren't my friends. Those are my sisters. The one in the white dress—she's in town for her wedding, and—"

"Her wedding?" the blonde gushed. "Oh my gosh, that is so exciting! This is embarrassing, but I *love* weddings." She said it in a flirtatious whisper and Jason felt his confidence return. "I'm Sandy. This is Jeanine."

"I'm Jason." He reached across Sandy to shake Jeanine's hand.

Jeanine let out a smile so brief that it could have been mistaken for a small facial tic. "Nice to meet you," she said.

"So the million-dollar question," he said. "What are two single ladies doing out tonight without a swarm of dudes around them?"

Sandy laughed. "I don't know! Usually I have a bunch of creepers trying to buy me drinks. I seem to only attract losers and assholes! The only *good* man in my life is my best friend Bequon."

"And you, Miss Eastern Promises?" he asked Jeanine.

"Was that an Asian joke?" she asked. "*Eastern Promises* is about the Russian mob."

"Hey, we're all pink on the inside," he said. "So what's your story?"

"Married," she said curtly. She held up her left hand and wiggled her ring finger.

"Warning, ladies—a ring doesn't stop me, and it never has." He winked.

Sandy put her hands over her mouth in a half gasp, half laugh, while Jeanine checked her phone.

"I can see someone is fresh off the Buzzkill Boat," Jason said to Sandy, indicating Jeanine with his thumb.

"I can still hear you," Jeanine said. "And that's still incredibly racist."

"Oh, lighten up, girl," Sandy said. "He was just being funny—this is political correctness gone crazy. Jason, invite your sister over! I want to ask her about her dress!" He sighed and beckoned Emily and the others. Lauren reluctantly walked over, her sneakers squeaking against the linoleum floor.

"Sit with us, Em," he said. "See? I told you we'd make some friends."

Emily and Lauren slid into the booth. There was no room for David and Matt, so they remained standing, awkwardly facing the table.

"I heard you were getting married!" Sandy said to Emily. "What's your dress like? I'm Sandy, by the way."

"Um…well, it's white, of course, and strapless, which my mom was a total bitch about but she bought it anyway."

"Oh my gosh, your mom paid for your dress? My mom would never do that for me. That is so cool…most parents totally give up on paying for wedding stuff when their kids are our age."

"Our age? How old are you?"

"Thirty-six."

"Oh, um, I'm twenty-eight?" Her voice went up a little at the end, as if even she were starting to doubt her own age. Jason thought about lightening the mood with a joke about how if she was worried about looking old, she could always drop David and find a teenage boy with a cougar fetish, but he thought better of it when he realized a comment like that might actually make her cry.

Sandy looked momentarily taken aback at Emily's answer. "You are so lucky. It's because you're so mature and confident. I wish I was like you. Everyone looks at how goofy I am and assumes I'm still in college. I have my immature sense of humor to blame!"

"I feel you," Lauren said. "Everyone at work thinks I'm a college intern."

"Lauren," Emily said, "you've worked there for, like, three years."

"Well, obviously my boss knows my real age, I just mean people who are new to the magazine. They usually ask me to get them coffee and ask me what I'm majoring in."

"I assume this happens after a trail of men follow you home propositioning you?"

"Fuck you, Emily. Stop invalidating my experiences."

Emily

A few beers later, Jason had his arm around Sandy, and Jeanine was deep in conversation with Lauren. Jeanine was a stay-at-home mom, and luckily Lauren hadn't said anything judgmental about it being a form of slavery. Instead, she regaled her with tales of being harassed online because of things she had written for *Cunt*.

"I got PTSD after someone with the screen name Tittyman69 called me a fat bitch on Reddit."

"That's terrible. Did you get treatment for that?"

"Ha! I stopped trusting so-called medical professionals a *long* time ago."

"Wow, no doctors? So, like, you gave birth at home?"

"Of course. I'm not buying into the business of birthing. Did you see the Ricki Lake documentary about obstetricians? She fucked them up good. To have a baby, all you need is a good birthing stool, a kiddie pool and a net to get all the poop out."

"What about medical emergencies, though?"

"Nothing a midwife can't handle. Although my midwife was actually sex-negative, femme-fluid gendercritical and preferred to be called the Usher of Beginnings, due to the patriarchal implications of the term mid*wife*."

"Cool," Jeanine said, taking a long sip from her margarita while her eyes wandered. "So you're, like, really into women's rights?"

"Oh, not just women's rights. I work tirelessly to dismantle every single oppressive structure that exists. I don't know if you'd be into this, but I'm going to be doing a rally against the lingerie industry for fatphobia at the Galleria. Want to join? It's next week."

"Uh, what would it entail? I took some gender studies courses in college, but it's been a while."

"Basically we're going to be topless with duct tape over our nipples and we're going to chant, 'Kiss my fat ass.'"

Jeanine cocked her head to one side. "Are you saying I'm fat?"

"No, it's just the chant. It's to protest against them for

the unrealistic expectations they put on women's bodies and
how they shame women for how they look. I mean, all their
models look like gross ten-year-old boys! We were going to
throw a rally against them for being transphobic, but then
unfortunately they hired that trans model, so that had to be
scrapped. Those assholes are always one step ahead of us. And
wow, how progressive—a trans model who's tall, thin and
beautiful. Yawn."

"Oh, um, I'll think about it!" She picked up her phone again.

Jason was snuggling closer to Sandy. She was on her third
margarita and was having trouble sitting upright. She put her
head on Jason's shoulder and blew some hair out of her face.
As Emily watched them, she took a small amount of perverse
pleasure in seeing Sandy's mascara irrigate her crow's feet.
Sure, you look like you're in college. Right.

"Why is it so hard to meet good guys?" Sandy said, taking
a sip of Jason's fourth beer. "Every guy I've dated has been
such an asshole. Like, why me?"

"All guys are assholes at heart," he said. "But I was raised
to believe women liked nice guys. My ex-wife left me because I was too nice."

"She sounds like a bitch. How could anyone divorce you?"

"Well, I learned my lesson. Women like assholes, so I had
to become one. Even though I'm actually nice. I'm very complicated."

"I'm just as complicated. This is so lame, but sometimes
I just like sitting around and eating ice cream while I watch
Sex and the City. I'm such a dork."

Jason's grin widened and he licked his lips in a way that
looked far too intentional to Emily. "Well, I think that's
adorable. We all have our quirks and faults. Like I was saying, mine is that I'm just too nice. I give too much. In the
bedroom, and out." He winked.

"No, you're *perfect*! You're only thirty-five and you're the CEO of your own company? You're like...Mr. Big or something."

"It was important for me to become a self-made man," he said. "I didn't want to live off my grandfather's fame."

"Who's your grandfather?"

Jason hung his head in false humility. "Don't tell anyone, but...Arthur Berger."

"Who?"

"Arthur Berger...of Berger's Relish? *You can't have a burger without Berger's?*"

"Oh, Berger's Relish!" she said, her eyes lighting up. "Wait, so you're like *really* rich." She smiled deviously. "You're a real Christian Grey, aren't you?"

"In more ways than you think," he said, winking again. "So what's your plan for the rest of the night? Want to get out of here?"

"Jeanine drove me. I have to leave with her." She stuck out her lower lip and pouted, tracing an imaginary tear down her face with her French manicured finger.

"Forget Jeanine! She can take her own canoe home. My sister's fiancé is our designated driver, so we can take you home with us for the after party."

"After party? Fun! When I came out tonight, I had no idea I would meet someone like you. Wow."

DAY 2

David

"YOU'RE UP EARLY." Emily's dad, Steven, was in the kitchen making coffee. He was wearing a gray zip-up sweatshirt and a pair of too-short nylon gym shorts. The shorts displayed disproportionately skinny legs covered in gray hair, with veins like squiggly telephone cords bulging beneath the skin.

"Nine?" David said. "That's not so early."

Steven grabbed a mug from the cabinet. "Every time my kids stay here, they never get up before eleven, so forgive me when I say I'm surprised to see someone your age sentient before lunchtime."

"Yeah, I joke with Emily that she's nocturnal." David tended to wake up a few minutes before Emily every morning. He would make her a cup of green tea and leave it on her nightstand for her to find when she woke up. On the rare occasion that Emily woke up first, she made him breakfast and followed up with a massage, which she joked was her payment plan for all the tea. Women like Emily, as far as David could tell, didn't exist in modern day. Or if they did, they were uptight and unfunny, and voted for Ted Cruz.

"Technically Emily is not really nocturnal. It would be nocturnal if she actually fell asleep at dawn and woke up at dusk."

"Oh, I know. It's just a joke."

"I wake up at six. Marla gets up at five, but she goes out for her run and I usually don't see her until seven or so. She must still be out." He poured coffee into his mug. "The human body is actually designed to wake up at three in the morning, work for two hours, then go back to sleep until ten or so. But modern ideas of sleep and work prevent us from staying true to our internal clock."

Steven took out a white Harvard mug and motioned to David, who shook his head. "No coffee before food," David said. "Last time I did that I got nauseous."

"Oh, yes, feel free to pour yourself some cereal."

He thought about saying no, since cereal was chock-full of commercially processed grains, but he wasn't sure how Steven would react. "Actually, I'm not hungry yet." Steven shrugged and took a sip of coffee.

"Are you on your way to the gym or something?" He had never seen Steven in workout clothes before—only in khakis and button-downs.

"I am. I haven't been in a while, and it's time to get back on the horse. Marla pointed out that I'm looking a bit thick around the middle—it happens with age, you'll see soon enough. Your metabolism just goes on vacation and doesn't return. But it'll be good to get back to the gym. I got out of the habit because I was busy researching my next book. It's on Confucianism, which, contrary to popular belief, isn't something people just read about on fortune cookies." He smiled into his mug.

"Do most people believe that?" It was only after he asked the question that he realized Steven was attempting a joke.

"Oh, I hope not. But there are a lot of idiots in the world, so I wouldn't put it past them."

David wondered if he was being lumped with those idiots. Sometimes when he spoke to Steven, he felt as if he were in the middle of one of his recurring nightmares, in which he showed up for a class he had skipped for the entire semester only to discover he knew nothing on the final exam.

"You know," Steven said, "I have a gym pass if you want to come with me."

David weighed the question. He did want to work out. But he wasn't exactly dying to spend alone time with Steven. Finally, after what felt like an eternity went by, he knew he needed to respond. "Thanks, that would be great."

"Terrific. It'll give us some time to catch up. Plus, you'll absolutely love our gym."

Steven pulled into the parking lot, narrowly missing a garbage can with the nose of his car. The gym was in a low-rise stucco building painted Pepto-Bismol pink, with purple cursive letters above the door spelling *Barbelles*. David noticed a clutch of older women standing outside drinking protein shakes and wearing neon leotards and tracksuits. "This is an interesting place," he said. "It's uh…for women?"

"For the most part," Steven said, locking the car door. "It's Marla's gym. It caters to women, but they don't have a rule against male patrons. It was easier to just sign up for the BFF joint plan than have two completely different gym memberships. Plus we save hundreds of dollars a year."

David glanced at the women in their pastel clothing and headbands. He realized that as strange as it would be to work out in an all-female gym, at least he wouldn't have to worry about the kinds of men he sometimes ran into at LifeSpin. Women at the gym, as annoying as they could be when they sat on the hip abductor, mouth agape while checking their phones, were far less annoying than the men. There was one particular guy at LifeSpin named Lars, short and stocky with skin that looked like day-old oatmeal. His hands were always streaked with either chalk or protein powder, and he wore a weightlifting belt around his midsection that looked like a corset. He carried a clipboard with a detailed graph of all his reps and weight amounts, and he would regularly scribble away at his graph while cursing under his breath. David usually avoided him, but sometimes if Lars had his eye on the same machine David was already using, he would come over, puff his chest out and say, "Hey man, mind if I work in?" Trading off on a machine with Lars meant listening to his sharp and rhythmic "Fuck!"'s and getting secondhand protein powder and/or chalk residue on your hands. David would usually just stop working out at the machine, tell Lars he was almost done anyway, and do something else. One of his greatest fears was that Lars would eventually try to become gym buddies with him. He seemed like the kind of person who would shoot up the place if he had to wait for a machine.

David was guaranteed not to run into anyone like Lars at Barbelles. The interior was pale pink with bright purple hand weights arranged on a rack by a mirrored wall. Near the front desk were magazines like *Self* and *More*, and a shelf of skincare products, including some that were Barbelles' own brand. The gym smelled like air conditioning and fake chocolate—better than the rubber-and-ball-sweat stench of the LifeSpin weight room during peak hours. The front desk was U-shaped with a purple plastic counter. On the wall behind the desk was a poster of an ethnically diverse group of gray-haired women frolicking in a field, with the words *Sisters Push Each Other*.

The young receptionist had transparent eyelashes and waxy, pale blonde hair. She greeted Steven with a wide smile. "Have a great workout, Steven," she said. "And is this handsome young man your son?" David couldn't tell if she was complimenting him, hitting on him or commenting on his looks the way one would a three-year-old sitting in a car-shaped barber's chair.

"Actually, he's my son-in-law-to-be. My younger daughter is getting married this week."

"Wow, how exciting! You must be a *very* proud daddy." David then realized her slightly condescending tone wasn't reserved for him—she spoke like a volunteer at a retirement home to everyone.

"Would you two handsome gentlemen like a free soy smoothie?" she asked. "Or could I interest you in a calcium supplement? Our flavors today are Chocolate Sin and Macadamia Nut Felony."

"No thank you," Steven said. "I don't think we're going through menopause!" When she failed to laugh at his attempted joke, he added, "What I mean is, I'm not sure those nutrients would provide as many benefits to males."

"Pfft," she said. "That's just marketing. Soy and calcium are good for everyone. Osteoporosis is not just a women's disease." She wagged her finger at him.

"It does disproportionately affect women, actually," Steven said. "But if what you're referring to is low bone mass, point well taken."

The gym staff was all female, except for one skinny, redheaded teenage boy who was organizing the weight plates and wiping down a few sweaty machines. The staff wore purple slacks and candy-pink polo shirts. David wondered how the boy would try to explain that uniform to his friends. He probably told them he was working at Ben & Jerry's.

David began his workout on the treadmill, running at a steady pace with a slight incline. He ordinarily felt a little competitive with other members at LifeSpin, craning his neck to see how fast they were running and increasing his own speed to match. At Barbelles, he noticed other patrons staring at him as though he had magical powers because he had started his treadmill at level six.

As he ran, he inadvertently made eye contact with the woman on the treadmill next to him. She was in her seventies, wiry and short with a spiky pixie cut. She was walking slowly, but at an impressive incline, swinging her fists as she walked. When she saw he was looking, she smiled at him and kept on walking.

He wished his mother had been like her. With the hours she'd put in at her job, she never really had the time for a workout, or at least that was what she said. She'd stayed up late on business calls, finger-combing her ash-blond hair as she sipped coffee into the night. She'd also smoked, although she tried to hide it from the kids until they were old enough to identify the smell.

On the weekends, she would take the boys to pumpkin patches, apple orchards, amusement parks—even the Renaissance Faire once, at Nathan's request. (After eight-year-old Nathan scolded a man dressed as King Arthur because King Arthur was a Medieval figure, not a Renaissance figure, they never returned.) David never saw her take any time for herself. He wished he had urged her to relax a bit more, maybe see the doctor more often, or even just have a full night of sleep, but he'd been too young to know better. As a child, all he cared about was whether or not she would be able to leave work early enough to watch *All That* with him on Nickelodeon. More times than not, she couldn't.

He was about to head over to the bench press when he felt his phone vibrating. He sighed when he saw that it was his boss.

"Hey, Robert," David said.

"Just got back from surfing at Half Moon Bay. The waves were infuckingcredible."

Robert never missed an opportunity to talk about surfing. David suspected he had chosen this hobby to lend ruggedness and eccentricity to a personality that was otherwise entirely colorless. Employees who had actually gone surfing with Robert reported that he was strictly at the beginner level. His surfing consisted mainly of donning a wetsuit, lying prone on his board, and tentatively paddling out from shore.

"So what's up?" David asked.

"Do you have a minute?"

"Um, well, actually, it's my wedding week."

"Of course! I just thought I would ask you since you're always my go-to on this kind of thing. But I don't want to bother you, man. I could always ask Zach…"

He should have seen this coming. Zach, an executive David's age, had the same title as him, the same responsibilities, and the same role in Robert's ongoing science experiment of pitting them against each other.

"No, no, this is a good time, actually. What's up?"

"I have great news. We got the second round of funding from BluCapital."

"Wow, Robert, that's amazing."

"I need you to tweet about it. I know you're on vacation, but your social media style is great and the more tweets on this the better—we're trying to get TechCrunch to pick up this story."

"Sure, no problem."

"Thanks. I knew I could count on you. Between you and me, Zach isn't the best with social media. By far the best analytical mind in the office, though."

Kevin

Kevin was in baggage claim, looking for his driver. He scratched his chin. He needed a shave. When he was growing up he wished that he could grow a full beard, and he hadn't been able to until he was twenty-five. Now that he was twenty-eight, he couldn't go more than a day without shaving. He wasn't confident that he could pull off a beard. They worked better on guys who owned bars, or their own line of designer hoodies.

In the swarm of limo drivers holding cards with the names of passengers, he found one with the name *Hayes*. The driver was a short older man with frizzy gray hair and a jolly round nose. He looked as if he could have had a supporting role in *The Lord of the Rings*, but his black suit and tie ruined the illusion.

"That's me," Kevin said. He knew that a limo was kind of a splurge, but it wouldn't break him. He was smart about money. He bought his own tuxedo six years ago, and it had paid off—since then, he had been a groomsman in eight weddings. Besides, he liked the envious looks the other passengers gave him as they trod to the endless taxi line.

The driver looked at his phone. "So we're going to the Ritz Carlton in White Plains?"

"Oh my gosh, I'm sorry to interrupt, but you're going to the Ritz?" Kevin heard a high-pitched woman's voice behind him and turned. She was striking: nearly six feet tall and thin as a model, dressed in black from head to toe, with long, thick black hair. She had a narrow nose and brown eyes with long eyelashes. Her skin was light brown, and her lips were full and painted with dark berry lip gloss. She must have been around his age, but she had the bubbly voice of a college girl.

"Yeah, why do you ask?"

"I'm sorry if this is super weird, but my phone died and I can't get an Uber. Mind if I share with you? I will totally pay for half the ride."

"Don't worry about it. It'll be my treat. I'm Kevin."

"I'm Jennifer."

The driver led the way to the car. Kevin noticed she was carrying a large garment bag in addition to her mono-grammed suitcase. "Need help with that?" he asked. "Wait, this isn't your wedding dress, is it?" He flashed his winning smile, the one that always made women fiddle with their hair. She was no exception.

She giggled. "Absolutely not. Twenty-nine and single, don't rub it in. I'm a bridesmaid. Always the bridesmaid, never the bride!"

"That's something we have in common. I'm here for a wedding too, and I'm not the bride."

"Not your wedding?"

"No, definitely not mine. It's my friend's wedding."

He picked up her garment bag and caught a glimpse of the peach chiffon dress inside.

"So where are you from?" he asked.

"Oh, I get that all the time," she said, looking slightly ir-ritated. "I'm half Japanese and half Greek."

"Sorry, I didn't mean that. I just wanted to know where you flew in from. I just got in from DC."

"Oh! You're from DC? Unfortunately, I flew in all the way from San Francisco." She pointed behind her, like she was a human compass and knew exactly which way San Fran-cisco was.

"Why is that unfortunate? It's a cool city."

"Yeah. It is. I don't know why I said that. It's not unfor-tunate."

"I've only been out there once. It was great, except for this one guy dressed like a frog who tried to hump my leg out-side City Hall." Kevin smiled wistfully at the memory. That had made an amazing Twitter post back when it happened. Seventy-three retweets!

"What brought you to San Francisco?"

"To see a friend. He's actually the one getting married this weekend."

"Wait, this might be totally crazy, but is your friend David Porter?"

Kevin smiled. This was going better than he thought. "Yeah, he is."

"Oh my gosh! That's the wedding I'm going to, as well! You're a groomsman, I'm a bridesmaid—that is totally crazy! What are the chances?" She smiled. "What a hella small world. Aren't Emily and David literally the cutest?"

"I actually haven't met Emily yet. I know David from high school."

"They are *literally* adorable." She put her hands over her heart.

"Do you know anything about the other groomsmen? When I visited David in San Francisco, he was just settling in and hadn't made all these friends yet." He wasn't sure what kind of a group David had fallen in with out there. There was a chance that he had made friends with other fun-loving, ath-letic guys, like the kids they hung out with in high school. There was also the chance that he had gotten mixed up with suddenly wealthy tech guys—smart but socially idiotic—who used their new money in every appalling way possible to com-pensate for how little ass they got in high school.

"Oh, well, there's Mark. He is totally awesome. His wife, Gabrielle, who is one of my *best* friends, is pregnant. He's lit-erally a surgeon. Like, that inspires me. Honestly."

"Oh, well, that's cool."

"There's also Jason, that's Emily's brother. I don't know much about him but he's a little older than us. He just got divorced and his ex-wife is *gorge*. At least online. Some people look amazeballs online but shit in real life. I just look like a gremlin no matter where I go." Kevin knew she didn't really believe that. Jennifer was gorgeous, if not a bit too perfect, like those women on billboards who were more Photoshop than person. He imagined with five fewer pounds of makeup she'd look a bit better.

"What? No, you're…very attractive."

"Oh, you're just being nice. I weigh like five hundred pounds."

"Well, that's obviously not true." He usually didn't fall for these sorts of traps, but she was sweet and it wouldn't kill him to say something that made her happy. "So back to the other groomsmen. Have you ever met Nathan?"

"Oh, right. David's brother. I've never met him either, but I've seen him in pictures and, no offense to him, he seems like kind of a loser." She put her hands on the side of her face, as though she felt bad about calling Nathan a loser but also wanted to look adorable while feeling bad.

"I knew him in school. He's…interesting."

"Aw, you weren't mean to him, were you?"

Kevin smiled. "I probably could have been a little easier on him, but…oh, you'll see what I mean. He really asks for it. When he was in tenth grade, he tried to sniff this girl's sweatshirt hood in class because he wanted to see what her head smelled like. Apparently he'd had a crush on her for, like, a year, but he had never even talked to her. He even started writing these weird-ass letters to her and pasting them on her locker. When she stopped responding he got pissed. I think he called her a 'treacherous harpy' or something like that. So a bunch of my friends started writing him letters 'from her' saying she was in love with him all along, you know, and he totally bought it."

"That's super mean!" She punched him in the shoulder.

"Yeah, not my finest moment, but you can't coddle people like that. Life will kick their asses if you don't do it first, you know? I can only hope he's changed. I would feel bad for him if he didn't make it *so damn easy* to laugh at him."

"Maybe you can teach him your ways."

"My...ways?"

"I don't know, you seem like you know how to put yourself together."

"Oh, thanks." Kevin didn't think he looked especially put-together that day. He was just wearing jeans, a white T-shirt and a pair of Adidas sneakers. "So what do you do?" he asked.

"I'm a dermatologist. That's actually how I met Emily. I work at the same hospital as Mark, and Mark is David's best friend, so I came with Mark and his wife, Gabrielle, to a party at David's house and totally fell in love with Emily. She is hella sweet."

He raised his eyebrows involuntarily. She didn't seem stupid, per se, but he imagined that a person with a medical degree would sound a little less like a sorority girl.

"Wow," he said. "So can you tell me if the freckles on my face are okay?"

"They all look amazing," she said, laughing. "I mean, I wasn't looking that closely. I would need to do a full examination." Kevin couldn't tell if she was speaking factually or offering to get naked with him, the way a fake dermatologist would at the beginning of a porno. It wouldn't have been the first time a girl shamelessly came on to him. He once shared an Uber with a woman who didn't say anything to him for the entire ride but, when they arrived at her destination, slipped a piece of paper with her phone number into his jacket pocket and ran off.

"Oh my gosh!" Jennifer laughed, a little too loudly. "You thought I was hitting on you! I'm so sorry, I totally wasn't. I just don't want you to sue me or something if I say you don't have some skin condition and then you do. Just ignore me." She laughed again, covering her berry-stained lips with her hand. "So what do you do?"

"I manage political campaigns."

"That is literally amazing."

Emily

The three Glass siblings sat on the beige suede couch in Marla's office in order of birth—Jason closest to the window, Lauren in the middle and Emily closest to the door. There were fake plants on the windowsill that had been there so long that, through discoloration and damage, they had begun to resemble real plants. The room smelled like cinnamon and blood orange, thanks to Marla's Anthropologie scent diffuser. Abstract paintings on the walls looked like rectangles of rust and gold. The tan carpet rivaled the beige walls and sofa for blandness. It was noon and bright outside, but the shades had been lowered and the room was dim.

Marla's office was ten miles from the house, on the first floor of a brick office building. Dr. Abe Leibowitz, a psychiatrist, shared the suite of offices with Marla. She sent him patients who needed medication; he was the one who had prescribed Ritalin to all three Glass kids in the late nineties. Emily always suspected that Dr. Leibowitz just rubber-stamped Marla's diagnoses, such as their debilitating ADHD, which prevented them from taking the SATs in the standard amount of time, or her assessment of all three children as "profoundly gifted."

When they were little, they would sometimes sit in Marla's waiting room after school and do their homework. They would stare at the people who were waiting to see their mother and speculate about what was wrong with them. Marla's patients became cautionary public service announcements for the kids, her own version of *Grimm's Fairy Tales*. Emily assumed that all the stories were true when she was little, but by the time she was a teenager, she started questioning their veracity. There was Evelyn, the eighteen-year-old who had sex in high school and eventually wound up becoming bulimic because of her low self-worth. There was Rose, the woman whose son died when he smoked weed at a party and jumped off the roof because he thought he could fly. There was Marissa, who disobeyed her parents' wish for her to go to college and wound up being homeless (Marla never elaborated on how she discovered Marissa was homeless years after her therapy ended). There was Katie, the girl who sent her boyfriend a sexy email of her masturbating with a zucchini, and when he sent it around school, the principal punished her by forcing her to watch the video with her parents. Katie's story was echoed in a series of urban myths around Emily's school and online—sometimes the item was a broom, sometimes a hairbrush, sometimes a plunger—except in the plunger story, she slipped and the plunger impaled her and came out through her mouth.

"So, Jason," Marla said, crossing her legs. She was wearing a long patterned hippie skirt with a pair of thick-soled sandals. "Why don't you start—oldest first?"

He cleared his throat. "Well, um, Mom, I don't really know what to say. I haven't done this before."

"You were in therapy with me as a child. And with Dr. Leibowitz."

"Well, yeah, but that wasn't a group session."

"We're all here to support each other. Don't be afraid of judgment."

"I'm not afraid, I just don't really know what I would even have to say. Can you at least kick this off?"

"That's fair. I'm so glad you all agreed to do this. I guess I'll start by saying I have noticed a pattern of all three of you feeling…uncomfortable expressing gratitude toward me and your father for all that we have done for you. I can't help but think you have some residual anger at us, and I want to help you come to terms with that anger."

"Mom, we're not mad at you," Emily said. "And I don't even see how we're ungrateful."

"Speak for yourself," Lauren said. "I have a lot of residual anger at Mom and Dad. As for gratitude, it's a nonissue. Nothing they have given me is beyond the realm of basic living expenses."

"Lauren, your father and I pay your rent, and for Ariel's preschool. We also paid for your graduate degree in gender studies, not to mention your college tuition. And we bailed you out of jail." Marla laughed incredulously at her last sentence.

"You're acting like I stole something. I just protested. If you really think I should have just written a strongly worded essay instead, then you're tone policing. Riot is the language of the oppressed."

"What the hell were you protesting against?" Jason asked, laughing and holding his veiny forehead in his hand. "Nobody ever told me about this. Why does nobody tell me anything?"

Lauren pursed her lips. "For your information, I was protesting against a local toy store in Poughkeepsie. They had aisles that said Boys' Toys and Girls' Toys. I refuse to tolerate the concept of gendered toys, so in the middle of the night my friend and I broke in and spray painted Gender Is a Fucking Social Construct in both aisles."

"Seems legit."

"Jason, don't mock your sister," Marla said. "And we're running far afield from my point. What I was trying to say, Lauren, was that we have paid for a whole lot more than basic living expenses. Now, we support all of those things as well as your job at *Cunt* because we applaud creativity. But you cannot accept all this money from us, and still write articles like, 'I Suffered Abuse at the Hands of My Narcissistic Parents.' At the very least, you could have spoken to me first, so that I didn't have to find out about it from the five friends who emailed it to me."

Jason looked impressed. "Five? I didn't know *Cunt* got that kind of traffic. Good job."

"I did suffer abuse, Mom. Writing about my trauma is the best way to handle it. Sometimes speaking directly with your abuser is the worst thing you can do because then you have to relive what happened to you all over again."

"Come off it," Jason said. "You weren't traumatized. If I wasn't traumatized, you definitely weren't. Mom made me watch the video of my birth when she thought I was going to have sex. You want trauma? Watch your head crown out of mom's '80s bush vag. No offense, Mom, but that's trauma."

"Oh, boo-hoo," Lauren said. "You had to see a *real* human vagina pushing out a *real* human being—I feel so *bad* for you! That's nothing. Mom and Dad never came to my performance art show *My Clit Is a Sword*, my senior year of high school, and that left me with intense feelings of low self-worth. And that's just one of the many times they made me feel like shit. I've never told you this before, but watching Mom diet throughout my childhood gave me anorexia and I still suffer from it."

Jason looked at her. "Um…it isn't working that well."

"Fucking educate yourself. The fact that you think food has anything to do with what size you are is just so fucking ignorant."

"Wait, you're saying food *doesn't* have anything to do with weight?"

"Yes, that is what I'm saying."

"Lauren, that's absurd," Marla said. "You are extremely intelligent—profoundly gifted, in fact. You should know better than anyone that body fat is directly connected to the calories you consume."

"First off, you're a psychologist, not a nutritionist, and I don't trust doctors anyway. Plus, while we're on the topic of ungratefulness, why don't you have a go at Jason and Emily? They get money from you and they're not even using it to make the world a better place."

"Are you kidding?" Emily said, shocked to hear her voice for the first time after the constant argumental ping-ponging between Lauren, Marla and Jason. "How are you making the world a better place?"

Lauren opened her mouth to talk and Jason pulled out his phone to access Tinder. "By working for *Cunt*," Lauren said. "By paying my rent, Mom and Dad are enabling me to do something truly important. But the stuff you get from them is just pointless. Mom and Dad are paying for your wedding. You didn't need such an expensive dress, but heteronormative celebrations are so important to you that you want Mom and Dad to fork over two thousand dollars for a dress that allows you to objectify yourself and celebrate the loss of your individual identity. Do you realize all of that money could go to homeless shelters for former sex workers?"

"Trust me, from personal experience," Jason said, swiping right without even looking at the screen. "Hookers have enough money."

"This is not what your grandfather would have wanted," Marla said. "His money nearly tore the family apart once already, with Aunt Lisa and that whole ordeal. I thought at the very least, I could use it to unite mine. I am not about to repeat my father's mistakes and allow my children to attack each other—and me—over something as meaningless as family money."

"Hey, family money isn't meaningless," Jason said. "Grandpa went from a small-town deli owner in Brookline to the fourth-largest relish manufacturer in the country. If his family money isn't meaningful, I don't know what is."

"Whatever," Emily said, turning back to Lauren. "So you would never spend money on anything that doesn't benefit the greater good? We all know you and Matt aren't going to get married, but if you were, you'd want a nice dress too." After saying that, she realized Lauren probably wouldn't want a dress at all—too oppressive—but she would want something else. Fancy sneakers?

"You know I almost never wear dresses. I'm not trying to garment-shame you or anything, but your wedding dress is a gross, distasteful display of your white classist privilege."

"And you wonder why you aren't my maid of honor!" Emily said, a little louder than she intended. Marla pursed her lips as if she were watching a movie that just got interesting.

"I just want to point out to Lauren," Marla said, "that Emily has severe anxiety. People with her level of neurosis can often make decisions that to the rest of us might appear irrational or even cruel, but her intentions aren't malicious."

"Mom, I'm not a maniac. I didn't make Lauren my maid of honor exactly because of this stuff. Gabrielle actually likes weddings and doesn't criticize me for wanting a nice dress or a pretty color combination."

"I didn't say your color combination was bad," Lauren said.

"I just said you were unnecessarily pandering to gendered ideas of female and male colors. There is no reason why the tuxedo for the ring bearer has to be blue. Pink is Ariel's favorite color."

"Gee, I'm sure nobody influenced that," Jason said, with one hand to the side of his mouth like he intended this comment to be secret.

Emily sighed. "Mom, you can see what I'm dealing with. Would you have made her *your* maid of honor?"

"Family comes first. I would have considered my sister's feelings."

"Mom," Jason groaned. "You haven't spoken to Aunt Lisa in twenty years."

"That's because Aunt Lisa is toxic."

"It's not just Aunt Lisa. You don't talk to *anyone* in your family, or Dad's family. When Grandma died, you said, 'One down, one to go.'"

"I said that because I was grieving for your father's loss of his mother. And my emotions got the better of me because my relationship with her was very complex. It just so happens that there are a lot of toxic people in my family and your father's. Many, many people in our families happen to suffer from narcissism and sociopathy. It's remarkable that the only person in this nuclear family with any mental issues is Emily, to be honest. The point is, Emily, you should have at least discussed your decision to leave Lauren out of your wedding before just going ahead with it."

"I didn't leave her out. She's still in the wedding party, which, might I add, she resisted agreeing to at first because she felt it was *too gendered*."

"I'm just saying," Lauren said. "If I ever get married to Matt, it wouldn't be a *wedding* per se, because I hate weddings, and most of our wedding party won't even have defined genders to begin with, let alone assigned gender roles. There won't be 'bridesmaids' and 'groomsmen,' just people there to witness our union. No vows to 'God,' not even a promise that marriage will last forever because sometimes the happiest relationships, shockingly, aren't the ones that end in death. And I wouldn't make *anyone* wear a dress. One of my friends, XXX, identifies as glitterbutch-girlboy-curious so xhe would wear a dress, but that's xher choice." She sat back and smiled smugly.

"Why do you even want to be my maid of honor, Lauren?" Emily asked. "You hate weddings! Meanwhile, Gabrielle has been reading wedding magazines since before she even *met* her husband. She's a professional event planner, for crying out loud."

"Not to butt in," Marla said, "but, Emily, I'm getting the sense, and I believe Lauren is too, that you're acting from a place of entitlement. This is classic Aunt Lisa behavior."

"Emily," Jason ventured, "just my two cents, but I think you're too young to be getting married. I got married in my twenties and I regretted it."

Emily felt her throat tightening as if she were about to cry. "Oh, great fucking idea, Jason! I'll just cancel my wedding! Then I won't have any reason to be blackmailed into these bogus sessions. Awesome!"

"Jason, you're not helping," Marla said. "Emily, I think what Lauren is trying to say is that you are not grateful enough for the money we are spending on the wedding."

"Mom, Lauren literally didn't even come *close* to saying that. She's just bitching about not being maid of honor."

"Okay, just a warning," Lauren said, her voice rising. "If you use another gendered slur, I am walking out and I won't even be coming to the wedding."

"Oh, for fuck's sake." Jason put his head in his hands.

"Is FuckSake your next start-up, dumbass?" Lauren said.

"Emily, I believe your sister has brought up some interesting points," Marla said. "The money I spent on your dress was, by and large, unnecessary. What would really show growth and maturity would be if you paid me back." She brought her hands together and closed her eyes as though she were finishing a profound prayer.

"Mom, you can't do that."

"Yes, I can. I'm not saying you *have* to pay me back. I would just be very disappointed by your immaturity if you didn't."

"Mom!" Emily felt on the verge of tears again. "I wouldn't have asked for a dress that expensive if I knew you'd ask me to pay you back for it. You said it was your gift to me! You even discouraged me from getting a cheaper one because you said it was tacky!"

Marla paused. "What I'm hearing is that you are all realizing that you have issues with gratitude and are working on those complex emotions toward your father and me. I'm so glad we decided to do this."

NIGHT 2
Emily

EMILY'S BOSS, LINDA, had made her life a living hell in many different and inventive ways, but she had to give her credit for one thing: if Emily had not been working for Linda, she might never have met David.

Three years earlier, Emily and Linda represented Clear-Drop at SourceCon, a start-up expo in San Francisco. At Linda's request, Emily stood at the ClearDrop booth for four hours in her uncomfortable beige heels and pencil skirt. Linda sat on a swivel chair behind her, chatting on her Bluetooth with a friend, who, she claimed to Emily, was also a prospective client.

Linda gave Emily an hour-long lunch break, which meant she was feeling especially generous or happy that day. As soon as Emily found out she'd be getting an hour for lunch, she started checking her phone every few seconds to see if time had started going by faster. She could feel her stomach gurgling under her skirt. Luckily nobody else could hear it. The room was abuzz with chitchat, as well as the loud laser-blasting sound coming from a virtual-reality booth.

Emily had been instructed to speak to every single person who came by, even if they seemed irrelevant or weren't interested in PR. That meant she spent about twenty minutes talking to a visor-wearing German tourist who seemed to speak minimal English, but was inexplicably interested in ClearDrop's history. A few people drifted by, looked at the booth's logo, stole a few mints from a bowl on the table and briefly made eye contact with Emily before walking away.

It was so easy for her to feel horrible about herself at these events. Most of the companies had hired "booth babes"— attractive young women in heavy smoky makeup, minidresses (or alternatively, irrelevant sexy nurse costumes). They were hired to stand in front of a company's booth to lure the type of men who believed they had a chance with women who were paid to stand there and talk to them. Emily couldn't tell why she was so jealous of these girls—it wasn't as if she had applied to become a booth babe and been turned away. The requirements weren't even that strict: young, thin, long straight hair. By those standards, she qualified. She envied them nonetheless. Maybe she envied how confident they all seemed. If she were paid to look good all day and lure weirdos to a cloud-computing booth, there was no way she could ever doubt her attractiveness again.

When noon finally arrived, she waved goodbye to Linda, who was too deeply involved in her conversation about newborn Harper's math abilities to really notice. Emily walked away from the ClearDrop booth toward the neon-green Life-Spin booth, where techno music played, and where she suspected they were handing out free food or drinks. If she could get a free snack and not have to shell out thirteen dollars for a tiny sandwich at the expo café, she'd feel slightly better about the entire experience.

That was when she saw a man who stood out in the sea

of people—handsome, brown-haired and bright-eyed in his blue button-down shirt and slim-fit jeans. His ears were a bit too big for his face, which made him just approachable enough. He had his hands in his pockets as he talked to a waxy-looking, muscled male trainer at the LifeSpin booth. The trainer, whose name tag read Zxon, was showing him a bottle of NaturBuzz, turning it over to the ingredients label.

"You see, man, NaturBuzz is all natural. That's why we call it NaturBuzz. These ingredients are so pure you could inject them. Not only does it provide energy without the crash, but it helps build muscles better than a protein shake. And all of this for just ten calories a bottle."

"I'm skeptical," the man said, smiling and bringing the bottle closer to read the ingredients. "I've been a protein shake guy for the past…oh, I don't know, ever since high school."

"Never too late to make a switch," Zxon said. "Believe it or not, I used to eat *lectins.*"

The man looked up from the bottle and saw Emily, unflatteringly standing next to a LifeSpin booth babe. The babe was wearing stretchy, lime-green microshorts and a black sports bra with beat-up black leather pumps. She had an extremely dark tan and black hair that went down to her waist.

"Can I help you?" Zxon asked, turning to Emily.

"Oh, sure. Are you handing out energy drinks…Zee-son?"

"It's pronounced 'John,'" he said. "And I sure am! I was just giving a demo to David, here. It's David, right?"

David nodded.

"Come on over, *girl!*" Zxon squealed. He handed her a bottle of NaturBuzz.

"This bottle is ergonomically designed. Did you know that with ordinary water bottles, your hand begins to develop tears in its ligaments and muscles, and it can actually impede your lifting?"

"Oh, I don't lift," she said.

"You're about to start. Judging by your booty, or lack thereof, you could really benefit from my PowerSquat class. Here's my card. I can do a free training session and body-fat measurement." Emily winced, but took his card.

"You don't need a body-fat measurement," David said. "You're probably, like, seventeen percent."

She smiled. "Very precise. Is that good?"

"It's in the athlete range. For women. For men, you want to be between five and ten percent."

"And what are you?"

"A lady never tells," said David, in a goofy high-pitched voice. She laughed. It wasn't that funny, but he was cute.

"So—" Zxon looked for Emily's name badge "—*Emily*. If I told you that you could have a three-month free membership to LifeSpin, would you take it?"

"Totally free?"

"Totally free. All you have to do is spin our wheel, and if your arrow lands on 'Three Month Free Membership,' we'll see you at LifeSpin!" Zxon pointed to a large carnival wheel with different sections of the wheel indicating different prizes, including "One Free Bottle of NaturBuzz" and "One Free Week of ColonWipe."

"David failed the challenge," Zxon said. "Maybe you'll have more luck. But even if you don't, $150 per month is a steal for what we offer at LifeSpin."

"That's a little much for me," she said.

"That's why you're spinning the wheel! Give it your best shot!"

She wasn't sure how important it was for her to be part of such a trendy gym. Her at-home yoga videos seemed to be doing the job just fine. But, as her freshman roommate Maria had reminded her, she had a "white girl ass." Maybe it was time for something a little more intense. She remembered, with some nostalgia, when people were satisfied just pressuring women to be thin. Now they had to have giant asses, too?

Emily spun the arrow, watching it go past the "Three Free Months" section again and again. Finally, it landed on the orange section entitled "Fifty Squats."

"What's that?" she asked.

"It means y'all gotta do *fifty squats, giiiiirl!*"

"For what reason?"

"Just for…fun!"

"I thought all the sections were things you win."

"Maybe you can give her a deal on a membership," David said. "I'd sign up too, if I could get a lower membership fee. Is the price negotiable?"

Where were all the men like David hiding? Places like LifeSpin, she supposed. Suddenly, cost barely mattered anymore. She would be seeing this handsome stranger every day. All of her single friends complained that they had to move to another city to rid themselves of San Francisco's horrible "man problem." The stereotype was that men were either good-looking douchebags, engineers who didn't bathe or stoner losers. Maybe David would turn out to have his own skeletons—Madonna-whore complex, micropenis, balloon fetish—but for now, he was perfect. She had to make sure they both joined LifeSpin.

"Look," Zxon said. "I like both of you guys, so I'm going to cut you a special deal. If you both sign up now, it'll be just a hundred dollars a month each." David smiled at her.

"We'll do it," he said.

"We will?"

"Sure. I'll be your workout buddy if you want. And besides, it comes with five free bottles of NaturBuzz." He took one of the sample bottles at the desk and tossed it to her. Thankfully, she caught it. She was so terrible at sports, she was shocked she was even able to catch a bottle from a few feet away.

"How much do they cost normally?"

"Nine bucks a bottle," Zxon said. "But let me tell you, NaturBuzz replaces your coffee, your toxic energy drinks and even your protein shake. So it's actually ridiculously cheap for what it is."

Minutes later they were signing the gym membership agreement on an iPad, and Emily was plugging her phone number onto the screen.

"You actually need to type your number again," David said.

"What, did it not go through?"

"No, I'd just like it if you typed your number into my phone too. So we can be workout buddies."

She laughed. "Smooth."

"Wait, I'm not being creepy, am I?" he asked.

"No, of course not. Well, a little. Appropriately creepy."

"That's what I was going for."

"I'm just saying, you can't compare the basketball David and I played to your team in San Mateo, Mark. It's public versus private, East versus West. Apples and oranges." Kevin put down his plastic fork, which was coated in General Tso's sauce. The Glass family had ordered in Chinese food to celebrate the arrival of more wedding party members: Kevin, Mark and Gabrielle. Jennifer was invited too, but had declined because she had just applied self-tanner and it was supposed to rain that night.

"Sorry, man, I just can't take Connecticut basketball seriously," Mark said, shaking his head. "Connecticut doesn't even have an NBA team. The Bay Area has the Golden State fucking Warriors! You're telling me there's a baller in Connecticut who holds a candle to Steph Curry?"

Emily couldn't help but notice how attractive all of David's friends were. Was it just a coincidence? They were all good-looking in different ways, of course. Kevin was blond and boyish, David was dark-haired and chiseled, and Mark was black with a shaved head, a few inches of height on both the other men, and modelesque bone structure accented by a sharp pair of hipster glasses. She wondered if her friends' appearances were a good way to gauge her own attractiveness. She hoped so, since she thought Jennifer and Gabrielle were quite pretty, but she also felt she had too few friends to have a reliable sample size. The only reason David had just two friends in his groomsmen party was that Emily *only* had two girlfriends and didn't want the bridal and groomsmen parties to be embarrassingly uneven, further highlighting her social ineptitude.

"There are plenty of great tri-state area ballers!" Kevin insisted. "And fuck San Francisco—at least we have seasons."

"You guys," David said. "Jesus."

"You have a very oppositional streak, Mark," Marla said, with a slightly flirtatious smile. "No wonder you're a lawyer."

"He's a doctor," Emily said.

"What do you do, Mrs. Glass?" Mark asked.

"Dr. Glass, dear. I'm a psychologist."

"Oh, right! I think David told me. And you, Mr. Glass?"

"Also Dr. Glass. I'm a professor."

"Oh. What's your field?"

"Asian history and religion. By the way, when you mentioned the Golden State Warriors, that reminded me of the Golden Warrior of Almaty in Kazakhstan. Are you familiar with it?"

"No, not really."

"It's a statue of a Scythian warrior that was recovered from a kurgan, or burial mound. It's sometimes known by its Russian name, Zolotoi Chelovek. I wrote one of my more famous articles about it. If you'd like to know more, I should have a copy of it around here somewhere—"

"Dad," Emily interrupted. "Why don't you tell Mark and Kevin about how you used to play basketball in high school? They'd love to hear about that."

"Oh, it was nothing," Steven said, taking a bite of chicken, oblivious to the sauce dripping down his chin. "I was on the team, but I never got to play. I'm five foot nine—there wasn't much demand for me."

"How tall are you, man?" Mark asked Kevin.

"Six-two, you?"

"Six-three. How about we find a court around here and play sometime this weekend? East versus West, the ultimate showdown."

"Sweetheart," Gabrielle said, putting her hand on Mark's. "Not now. I don't want a repeat of the 'Pluto isn't a planet' disaster."

"Pluto isn't a planet," Steven said.

"Oh yes, we know," Gabrielle said. "My mother, unfortunately, didn't believe us, and the first time Mark met her, he debated her about it until she stormed out of the room."

"Oh, come on, babe, she didn't storm out. And that's not at all the same thing as a friendly competitive game of basketball."

"For you, 'friendly' and 'competitive' are often mutually exclusive. You get way too worked up and you need to win everything."

"Emily used to have a thing about planets," Marla said, a smile creeping across her face. "Has she ever told you guys? When she was sixteen she saw some alien movie and she was convinced that they were planning an invasion. She said, 'Just because there's no proof of aliens doesn't mean they don't exist.' I mean, I always knew she struggled with her fair share of irrational fears, but I was afraid she was going full-on tin-foil hat!"

"Yes," Steven said. "*That's* crazy but all the people in the world who think a giant bearded man controls their lives are totally normal."

Gabrielle giggled. "Emily, is that true? Did you really believe in aliens?"

Emily tried to hide her annoyance. "Mom, I think I heard Ariel calling for you upstairs."

"I thought he was asleep."

"He was, but on the baby monitor I kept hearing, 'I want Grandma!'"

"Really? He has severe stranger anxiety and has resisted spending time alone with me. How long ago was this?"

"Just now."

"Mom," Lauren said. "He actually has very normal levels of caution around strangers. Although I've noticed he can sometimes be uncomfortable around new white people. I try my best to expose him to as many people of color as possible, and he's growing up with a very healthy fear of whiteness."

"Sounds healthy," Jason said.

Marla rushed upstairs. Steven put his plastic fork down. "American Chinese food isn't really Chinese in any sense. It's all sugary American versions of things most people in China never even eat."

No one responded. Emily tried a new subject. "So, Kevin, Jennifer texted me and said she ran into you at the airport."

"Yeah. We wound up sharing a car. She's gorgeous, by the way."

Bringing up Jennifer was a mistake. She wanted the conversation to end before people started raving about Jennifer's looks. It was tiring to hear the inevitable cascade of compliments about Jennifer's beauty every time she came up in conversation.

"Ooh, a bridesmaid," Jason said, digging into the greasy beef lo mein and plopping it on his plate. "She's the hot one, right?"

"No offense taken," Gabrielle said, rolling her eyes in unison with Lauren.

"You're married and pregnant," Jason said. "You weren't even included in the ranking."

"Wow, there was a ranking!" Gabrielle laughed. "The more you know."

Lauren cleared her throat. "I want to push back against women of color such as Gabrielle being excluded from this so-called ranking."

"Oh, fuck off," Jason said. "Besides, I'm pretty sure Jennifer is Indian."

"She's not Indian," Emily said, not sure why that was what she chose to take issue with.

"What is she then?"

"You're fetishizing, Jason," Lauren groaned, serving herself some tofu. "She's a human being, not a commodity." Emily nodded, although she was less concerned with Jason objectifying Jennifer than about having to field further questions about her hotness.

"Seriously, though," Jason said to Emily. "What is she?"

"She's half Greek and half Japanese."

"Hot. Is she single?"

"Yes, but you're not her type. She's really picky. She likes super tall, rich guys her own age. Being a bald, divorced guy with a kid doesn't strengthen your case."

"Tons of women don't think I'm their type, but I turn it around."

"You turn what around?" Marla was back downstairs. "Ariel was not happy to see me, Emily. He started shouting uncontrollably as if he were having a night terror. Are you sure he actually called for me?"

"Maybe I'm hearing things."

"No, you aren't. You're neurotic, not psychotic. You diagnose yourself with enough diseases you don't have, please don't add auditory hallucinations to the list."

"Your mom is hilarious!" Kevin said to Emily.

"Yeah, she's really subtle with it. So many people can't tell she's joking."

"I want to hear more about this Jason-Kevin-Jennifer love triangle," Mark said.

"It's not a love triangle," Jason said. "Kevin shared a cab with her but I've been watching her social media posts for months. Good luck catching up, kid." He winked at Kevin.

"Ooh, it's heating up!" Mark rubbed his hands.

"Stop trying to make everything a competition," Gabrielle said snippily. She then softened her face and smiled at Kevin. "Frankly, Kevin, I think you'd be a great match for Jennifer."

"And not me?" Jason asked, in a tone that fell somewhere between "genuinely offended" and "only joking."

"Well, um… I…"

"I don't think you guys realize how malleable a woman's attraction is," Jason said. "How does Hugh Hefner get all these babes?" He reached out his hands to gesture "all these babes" but he inadvertently looked like he was referencing Lauren and Marla.

"Money," Emily said. "They're basically sleeping with him for money."

"Wrong. Game. He's alpha as shit. And that's my strategy

too—sure, I'm not the best-looking guy ever but I game women." His pointer finger collided with the surface of the table for emphasis.

"You mean manipulate women?" Lauren said, her mouth full of rice. "Or are you just drugging them?"

"You'll never catch me drugging anyone. I just game women better than they expect to be gamed." He crossed his arms and sat back.

"Sure, we'll never *catch* you." Lauren motioned to Emily as if asking for backup.

"What about Sandy last night?" Emily said, temporarily much more annoyed with Jason than with Lauren, a feeling she knew would change within the hour. "You got her so drunk, she would have slept with anyone. That's not game. If you had game, these women would be sober when they had sex with you." She turned to Kevin. "We always joke around like this, don't let it freak you out."

Kevin smiled. "My parents live in a Bermuda co-op for over-sixty swingers. I don't think your family is going to freak me out."

"Whoa, is that a real thing?" Mark asked.

"It is," David said. "They have a branch in San Francisco with great Yelp reviews."

"Sandy and I didn't have sex anyway," Jason said to Emily quietly. "I went down on her and she fell asleep halfway through." He gave her an irrationally self-satisfied smile.

"Who's Sandy?" Marla said. "Who's going down on whom?" Emily recognized the pesky tone in Marla's voice from when she was younger and Marla would go through Emily's AIM buddy list asking her to identify screen names: *Who is 2sexxy4maishirt? Who is yankeesrock33? Who is hottie-babe87? Who is blow_jay88? Who is gwenstefanifan8_08? Who is ieatpoop?*

"Jason brought some girl home last night," said Lauren. "Some drunk girl from the bar."

"Jason, this is my home," Marla said. "You do not bring street women into my home."

"To be fair, Mom," Emily said, "she was just a normal drunk woman, not a prostitute. He didn't bring a 'street woman' home."

"Still, I have some accent pieces from Chico's and Peruvian Connection and I don't want them to get stolen."

"This food is amazing," Kevin said, attempting to ease the tension. "Thanks so much for having us." Emily recognized something in Kevin that she'd seen in David the first day he arrived in Westchester—the eagerness, the willingness to please, the excessive politeness. It would all dissipate in time once the novelty of Marla's free food and hospitality faded and her criticisms and dramatic declarations became more abundant. Emily gave Kevin two days with constant exposure to Marla before he stopped being so polite, or four days with occasional exposure.

"So, Jason, what do you do?" Kevin asked. Emily wasn't sure whether to be annoyed in anticipation of Jason's inevitable WalkShare pitch, or to be relieved that Kevin had asked Jason about his career, and not Lauren. A *Cunt Magazine* pitch might be even worse.

"Thanks for asking," Jason said, swallowing a chunk of beef. "I run a social networking start-up called WalkShare. It's sort of like Meetup on-the-go."

"That's cool," Kevin said. "What stage are you at?"

"Right now we only have a small amount of angel funding, but I know you rub elbows with some of the fat cats in DC, and—"

"Jason, the government doesn't fund dating start-ups," Emily said.

"I know that. But Kevin is a well-connected dude regardless. I've seen his LinkedIn. Kevin, I don't know what your situation is, but a small investment of just three thousand dollars could turn into a return of *three hundred million dollars*."

"I'll think about it," Kevin said as if he were talking to a college-aged Greenpeace canvasser.

"My buddy Evan already got in on it."

"Nice, getting your first investor must be tough."

"Well, he hasn't invested any quote-unquote 'money' yet. He promised he would invest twenty thousand in WalkShare if I invested a mere five thousand in his company. So once he has the money, I'm getting my money back and then some."

Kevin's eyebrows rose. "What's Evan's company?"

"Beardster."

"Beardster?"

"It's like Pinterest but for beards. It's all photos, all beards, all the time. Over forty-seven downloads so far."

"Nice. Good luck to him. And to you too."

"We're actually thinking of merging Beardster and Walk-Share to create the next Grindr—a location-based dating app for gay bearded men. We might call it BearShare. The gays are an untapped market for this industry because there's no restriction on sex. And you know why? No women. Women hold the key to sex and if you're hetero, men have to climb Mount Everest to get to the pussy."

"Jason!" Marla said.

"I've just got so many ideas, man," he said. "They're all just…flowing. All the time. I'm like a windmill, and the wind is all my ideas."

The phone in the kitchen rang. Marla got up, shaking her head. "So rude to call after eight, honestly. I have grandchildren sleeping upstairs! It's probably the fucking Jehovah's Witnesses. They have a points system, you know, and converting a Jew is the highest achievement for them."

"Do Jehovah's Witnesses actually call you?" Mark asked. "I thought they just knocked on the door."

Marla waved her hand around. "They haven't called *yet*, but clearly they're getting more tech-savvy every day because that's definitely them. Two of those maniacs were at our door just last month—this is their sick follow-up." She walked into the kitchen and answered the phone.

"Oh, Lisa. Hi! Well, yes, we're all quite busy with Emily's wedding… Oh, no offense taken, I'm aware you would be too busy to attend, that's why I didn't invite you. I didn't want to make you feel obligated when I knew you had so much going on with those adorable antiques shows, and really, we had to keep it intimate, close family and friends only. I'm sure you understand. How has that—oh? Okay… really! And you call me about this at *night*? I have grandchildren upstairs, who, might I add, you've never met. Oh, okay. Right. Well, Lisa, this was terrible timing on your part. You really couldn't wait until the wedding was over? Oh, well, of course, it's what Mom would have wanted. Easy for you to say that when Mom is in an urn, how convenient for you. You know what, Lisa? I have to go. I'm with my family. I'll call you tomorrow."

Marla walked back into the dining room. Her expression instantly changed from annoyance to deep devastation. "Pardon me, all," she said, in an unnecessarily formal tone. "My beloved aunt Ellen, who was more of a mother to me than my own mother, who I'll admit was a narcissist but that's beside the point…she has…sadly…passed on." She hung her head.

"Oh my gosh, I'm so sorry!" Gabrielle said, getting up to hug Marla's stiff board of a body. "I went through this when my aunt died last year. Trust me, she's in a better place."

"She's in a morgue, most likely," Steven said. "The afterlife is a nice story, but let's not insult Marla's intelligence here."

Gabrielle, perplexed, looked around, unsure as to why nobody else seemed to care about Aunt Ellen as much as she did.

"Mom, sit down," Jason said.

"I don't want to be rude," Mark said to Jason in a low voice, "but isn't this kind of a big deal? She said this woman was like a mother to her. Maybe you should try to be a little more——"

"Mom hated Aunt Ellen," Jason said. "She stopped speaking to her more than thirty years ago. I've never even met her."

"That's not true at all, Jason," Marla said. "Aunt Ellen met you when you were a baby. She probably wouldn't remember it any better than you do, though. She was a raving alcoholic and nearly dropped you on your head because she was so sloshed, but that's beside the point."

"How was she like a mother to you?" Emily asked. "You told me a few years ago that she was your inspiration to go into psychology because she was such a—and I quote—'pathetic failure of a woman' and you 'wanted to have a real life that went beyond slaving away for offspring all day.'"

"Aunt Ellen was absolutely a failure of a woman," Marla said. "But that doesn't mean she wasn't important to me. If it wasn't for her, I'd be some complacent stay-at-home mom in Massachusetts with a worthless degree in anthropology."

Steven looked prickled. "To be fair, Marla, degrees aren't ever useless."

"Not for professors," she shot back. "Check with your students in ten years and see what they think is useless. Anyway, this conversation has reeled entirely off topic. I need to grieve for my aunt. Emily, I'm sorry to say this, but I need to fly up to Boston."

"What?" Emily got up from her seat. "For how long? You're going to miss my wedding?"

"No, I'll probably come back the morning of. You'll be fine, trust me, it's really time for you to be an adult and showing some empathy here would be great personal growth."

"Mom," Lauren said. "I don't mean to grief-shame you, but I have to agree with Emily and Jason that you barely even liked this woman, let alone loved her. When exactly is the funeral?"

"She isn't having one," Marla said. "They're just cremating her and her kids are hosting a small get-together for close friends and family at cousin Hannah's house. I'm not sure how they're going to fit everyone, though. Hannah's house is far too small last I checked, just a dinky split-level covered in those tacky cat decorations, it's really quite absurd. And honestly, I don't even need to go to that, I just want to go up there and pay my respects."

David turned to Emily. "Why are none of these relatives coming to the wedding? I assumed they were all dead."

"Dead to her," Emily said.

David was a great cuddler. Emily didn't know that someone could be good or bad at cuddling until she met him. He was just so warm, and his body fit perfectly with hers. They snuggled up in bed after Mark, Gabrielle and Kevin went back to the Ritz. It took a few minutes of making out with David for Emily's family to fade from her thoughts. Every time she closed her eyes, all she could think about was her mother pursing her lips and shaking her head in disapproval. She would probably have thought the lingerie Emily was wearing right now was tacky because it was red and lacy, and not...what kind of lingerie did Marla wear anyway? Did she *wear* lingerie? Emily didn't know why she did this to herself. She was making out with the sexiest guy she knew and thinking about her mother's panties.

She racked her brain for a fantasy, anything to get her mind to a better place. She envied men—they didn't have to think about anything, it seemed. Men could reach orgasm with women they didn't even find attractive. Jason loved to remind her of this when she was in college. That was back when she was hooking up with cute guys for the first time, squeezing in with them on twin-sized college beds with pilly sheets, beer seeping from the pores of their sweaty bodies. No sex, of course—she didn't want to get syphilis. But making out with a cute boy was fairly harmless, and the validation outweighed her small risk of getting mono. "It's not a compliment that they're fucking you," Jason had said, assuming any guy Emily kissed had also rawdogged her. "Men fuck anything. It just means they think you're at least a five." She wondered if that was his way of being a protective big brother. She knew he would never be sentimental enough to admit he actually cared about her safety.

She really had to stop thinking of her family. Finally she pictured David as a sexy high school teacher in a tweed jacket and unbuttoned white shirt, and herself as the misbehaving schoolgirl in pigtails and a pleated skirt. In this fantasy, she also had clearer skin. David's hand stroked up her right thigh and she felt shivers. His other hand fell on her left breast gently.

"I like your boobs," David said.

He was never the best at dirty talking. She sometimes felt he just said things because he thought he should say something. He had a few go-to lines he strategically sprinkled in depending on the situation, but this was a little too seventh-grade, even for him.

"Shh," she said, holding back giggles. "My sister is going to hear you. You're off dirty-talk duty for tonight."

"That's good, because 'I like your boobs' was all I had."

"We're not going to have sex less when we get married, right?"

"Of course not, why?"

"I don't know, I just… I look at Jason and the stuff he says about Christina, and the stuff Christina says about Jason and I just wonder if that's how all couples turn out eventually. And Lauren is pretty tight-lipped about sex with Matt but… come on, can you imagine them *ever* doing it?"

"Jason has always been an asshole." He kissed her again.

"The gloves are coming off."

"Yep. They'll come all the way off when I'm officially your husband."

"I can't wait."

Matt

Matt came out of the bathroom after brushing his teeth. Lauren was in bed, breastfeeding Ariel, who wore only his tutu and a pair of Cinderella underpants. She had promised Matt that the breastfeeding would stop the year before. She had also told him, at other times, that she liked that it was a natural form of birth control, and that she wouldn't stop until Ariel wanted to stop. The best form of birth control was, of course, abstinence, and she seemed to be practicing that fairly well. Matt wanted to say something, but he didn't want her to think he was disapproving of her bodily autonomy. The last thing he wanted was a repeat of the pube dye fiasco.

"Hey, sweetheart," he said. "Is he going to bed soon?"

"He's asleep now, I think." Ariel's mouth was open. His cheek was squashed against her nipple, filmy white milk dripping down his chin. "I don't want to move him. Look how adorable he is."

"It'd be nice to get some Mommy-Daddy time," he said, giving her a flirty smile.

Lauren smiled back. "Let's give this a try." She gingerly picked up Ariel, her shirt still pulled up over her breasts. He began to stir and started rubbing his eyes.

"Mommy, are we all going to bed now?"

Lauren looked at Matt with big eyes. "He wants to co-sleep tonight."

"How about I put him to bed across the hall with Mia, and you sit here and relax... I'll come back and give you a nice foot massage. How does that sound?"

"Matt, I can't reject him like that. If he wants to sleep with us, I'm not going to banish him."

It wasn't worth a fight. This had been the routine almost daily since Ariel was born. It had gotten to the point where Matt often had to schedule sex with Lauren days ahead of time, although she seldom kept the commitment. Ariel always needed her in some way or another. On the rare occasions that she agreed to put Ariel to bed in a different room, there was still no guarantee of sex. Usually Matt would massage her, go down on her for about twenty minutes, pulling out all the tricks that he knew—that was the only way she could orgasm, she claimed. After she finished, she would tell him she was too tight and sore for sex, and he would have to jerk off in the bathroom. She was abnormally tiny down there, she'd say—she was just smaller than the average woman. Nothing to do with him. Matt once asked her how this was possible when she had vaginally delivered Ariel, and Lauren yelled at him for purporting to know her body better than she did.

"It's fine," he said with a long sigh. "Ariel can sleep in bed with us."

"Aw, thanks, sweetheart." She pulled her shirt back down and pulled the covers over Ariel, kissing his forehead before yawning and falling asleep in seconds.

Matt had heard David and Emily having sex through the walls when he was showering. It began with the unmistakable rhythmic bed-squeaking noise and ended with moaning. He and Lauren hadn't been like that even before Ariel was born. He once read an article about how some marriages fail due to mismatched sex drives, but Lauren didn't have a low sex drive. She had three brightly colored, glittery vibrators the size of bear penises. She had even released a vlog on YouTube for *Cunt Magazine* about masturbation techniques in which she described herself as a "high-drive woman."

He exhaled deeply, put a T-shirt on that read Women Poop Too, and climbed into bed, giving his son a kiss on the cheek before falling asleep.

DAY 3

Emily

"SO WHAT ARE we looking at here?" the hairdresser asked. Emily sat in the swivel chair, an unflattering black cape draped over her body. She looked like one of those dolls with a life-like plastic head and a mismatched cloth body, but no arms. It was creepy.

"Well, it's a trial run for my wedding. I want my hair to look full, curly and long."

On the walls of the salon were posters of hairstyles that Emily assumed had been cutting-edge fifteen years ago— angry-looking women with heavy black eyeliner and short, choppy hair with stripy highlights. The photos made her worry that this Westchester salon wouldn't be able to do anything modern, but Eva, the hairdresser, had great reviews online.

"Emily, are you sure you don't want an updo?" Gabrielle asked.

Gabrielle almost seemed more excited about the hair trial run than Emily. When she picked Emily up that morning she had stuck her head out the window of the car and honked

the horn, shouting, "Toot, toot! The beauty train is here!"
She brought an unenthused Jennifer with her.

Gabrielle was an event planner and could turn the most
commonplace task into an event that required planning. For
the salon visit, she had brought a two-inch binder full of
magazine cutouts showing a variety of makeup and hairstyles.
Emily couldn't tell if Gabrielle's pregnancy hormones were
responsible, but she had somehow become even more energetic and organized than usual. However, this was nothing
compared to one of Gabrielle's Pinterest boards, entirely devoted to garter ideas for Emily.

Emily had invited Lauren to the hair trial run too, solely
out of a sense of obligation. Although Lauren claimed that
she didn't mind being passed over for maid of honor, Emily
felt guilty about it. Still, having invited her to the salon, she
hoped Lauren wouldn't come because she didn't want to deal
with her inevitable comments about the unrealistic beauty
standards on parade in the women's magazines in the waiting area. Luckily Lauren had declined because she wanted
to take Ariel to the playground, but said she would pick up
Emily to take her to the meeting with the caterer afterward.
Sure enough, when Emily arrived at the salon, there was an
issue of *Glamour* sitting there at reception with the headline
Shrink Those Thighs!

Eva raised an eyebrow. "Honey, I don't think you are going
to get much volume no matter what we do," she said, in her
low, Eastern European voice. She was a tall, slender woman
in her midthirties with the clothing style of an angsty teenager, a lip ring and white bleached hair in a choppy bob that
covered one eye.

"Well, whatever you can do. If it needs to be straight,
that's fine too."

"That's not going to work either. Either you do updo, or we cut."

"Cut? I really don't want it short. I spent the past year growing it out."

"And highlighting it and styling it, right? Yeah, I thought so. Your hair is damaged. There nothing for us to do but trim it."

"I'd go for it," Gabrielle said, putting her hands on Emily's shoulders and inspecting her in the mirror. "You're already paying for the salon appointment. You might as well get a good trim while you're at it." Emily felt awkward looking at herself in the mirror, baggy-eyed and tired, next to Gabrielle. Gabrielle insisted Emily was more beautiful because Emily was a size two while Gabrielle wore an eight. But Emily envied Gabrielle's youthful, feminine face and perfect skin. Gabrielle was older than Emily and was repeatedly mistaken for the younger of the two. Gabrielle got told she looked like Kerry Washington all the time (a comparison Gabrielle felt was more racist than flattering because she didn't think they looked much alike), and Emily once got told she looked like Camilla Parker Bowles (a comparison she hoped was just racism, but couldn't be). Emily liked Gabrielle in spite of all of this.

"What do you think, Jennifer?" Emily asked.

Jennifer had been staring at herself in a different mirror but turned around quickly, embarrassed. "I think you would look totally cute with anything."

"No, I wouldn't. I wouldn't look cute with a shaved head."

Jennifer shrugged. "What about Natalie Portman? She looked hot."

"Yeah, but that's because she's Natalie Portman. She still looked better with long hair."

"Everyone, stop freaking out," Gabrielle said. "Nobody is

getting a buzz cut. Emily, it's just a trim. I think you should go for it. You do seem to have some split ends." She took Emily's hair between two fingers and rubbed them back and forth.

"Your pregnant friend is right," Eva said, matter-of-factly. "She smart lady. Like my Yaya used to say, when you carrying baby, you absorb its brain."

"Fine," Emily said, "but just remove whatever is damaged, nothing else. I still want it to be long." She clutched her hair, both frizzy and straight at the same time. It was like a corpse on her head. Yes, all hair was dead, but hers was rotting. Still, it was the only thing keeping her feeling remotely feminine-looking.

"Of course," Eva said, in an almost offended tone. "Why cut what you don't want cut? You think I want you to be unhappy?"

"No—I've just spent a really long time growing it out and I don't want that to go to waste."

"Nonsense. I will cut what is dead, nothing more. Your hair cannot grow if it damaged." She grabbed Emily's hair in her fist and began twirling it around, displaying her ends and fanning them for emphasis.

"Fine, I'll do it," Emily said.

"You do nothing. I do the cut." Emily reached for a *Cosmopolitan* with the headline, The Sexy Issue. *Isn't every issue the sexy issue?* she wondered. She flipped to the back where all the sex stuff was. She wondered if she could write in to *Cosmo* about the hand job on the plane. It might make it into the Cosmo Confessions column, although she had started to wonder whether most of those stories were made up. The one about the military wife having her mother-in-law walk in on her double-penetrating herself with a giant purple double-sided dildo seemed a little farfetched.

She flipped to this month's confessions. The page was dog-eared already—thank goodness she wasn't the only one who read this stuff. There was a separate page for male submissions. One man, a firefighter from Kansas, told a story of how he fingered a girl on an exhilarating Ferris wheel ride. The story was juxtaposed with an image of a shirtless male model, apparently meant to represent the Ferris wheel did-dler. Another man, identified only as Aaron, age twenty-nine, proudly regaled the *Cosmo* editors with a story of how he had sex with his side chick who left her underwear at his place, only to have them discovered later by his girlfriend, who just assumed they were hers and wore them. Then, after she was done with the panties, he kept them and sniffed them because they now had the scents of two women on them. Emily gagged a bit while reading it. She had already been a little nauseous that day—probably from taking her LifeSpin VytaPack on an empty stomach—and that story didn't help.

Emily thought that Jason was like Aaron, age twenty-nine. She had spoken to him only sporadically over the past few years, but even before Christina left him, Emily knew about some of his unfaithful episodes. To call them "affairs" would be giving Jason too much credit, assigning romance and drama to something that was only heartbreaking and gross. Of course, the details emerged once Christina left. None of his sexual exploits were romantic, and that, paradox-ically, became his defense after he was found out by Chris-tina's private investigator. He insisted women were secretly aroused by promiscuous, unfaithful men, as long as their in-terest in other women never became emotional.

Emily wanted to say that assessment was ridiculous—and the arousal part was, at least for her—but she would have been far more devastated if David had one emotional affair than a series of meaningless flings. Whenever she saw an attractive woman, she imagined David on a date with her, laughing and having fun, or even announcing their wedding or the birth of their child. That upset her more than imagining David having sex with them. It also disturbed her how easy it was for her to imagine any of those scenarios. What if all men had it in them to be like Jason? Maybe they just didn't realize it until the opportunities presented themselves.

"You look so cute," Gabrielle said, pointing to the mirror. Emily looked up from the magazine for the first time and saw her reflection. Eva had finished cutting and was blow-drying, pressing the hairdryer to the round brush she was using to style her hair. Emily could not believe what she saw in the mirror. Her hair had been cut from her midback to her shoulders.

"What?" she shrieked, dropping the *Cosmo* on the floor, now covered in blond hair. "You cut it so short!"

Eva shrugged. "You say cut off the dead parts. I cut off dead hair. It go up to shoulder."

"There is no way my hair needed to be cut this short!" Emily shouted, feeling tears well up in her eyes. "I look like Barbra Streisand! I look like a mom!" She worried at first that she might offend the pregnant Gabrielle, who was not only a mom-to-be but also a Barbra Streisand fan. Instead, Gabrielle put her arms around her from behind and smiled.

"You look beautiful," she said, "and your hair is so thick and healthy now!"

"Why didn't you stop her?" Emily asked.

"Stop who?" Jennifer asked, briefly looking up from her phone.

"When you said you didn't want it short, I thought you meant boy short," Gabrielle said. Her hair was relaxed and polished, curled slightly under her chin. Easy for Gabrielle to say short hair looked good—she had poreless brown skin, full cheeks and a delicate heart-shaped jaw line. Gabrielle didn't know the struggle of doing whatever she could to avoid looking like an elderly male horse.

"My wedding is in four days!" Emily cried, wiping tears from her eyes. "I look so old now. Like a soccer mom."

"This not mom hairstyle," Eva protested. "This normal hair. Mom style is to ear."

"It makes my nose look huge!"

"So what? You have big nose. So does lady from *Sex in the City*."

"Sarah Jessica Parker?" Emily sniffled. "Are you telling me I look like fucking Sarah Jessica Parker? She's over fifty!"

"I meant young *Sex in the City* lady. Young version."

Gabrielle tapped Eva on the shoulder and said, "You're not helping. She's having a moment."

"I'm not having a moment, I just got ugly! I was at least sort of pretty when I got here. Now I'm a solid four. I look middle-aged. I look like Sarah Jessica Parker!"

"Sarah Jessica Parker is gorgeous," Gabrielle said.

Emily rolled her eyes. "No, she isn't. She's one of those older female celebrities who women claim is gorgeous just because she's successful. Like Meryl Streep, Helen Mirren or Anjelica Huston being 'gorgeous.' None of them are."

"That's totally not fair," Gabrielle said. "And Helen Mirren is extremely sexy."

"Really? You really think Helen Mirren is sexy?"

"Of course. And Anjelica Huston is smoking hot."

"Now you're just being ridiculous. None of these women are hot in their current iterations. There are no men jerking off to Angelica Huston." She could tell Eva was snickering in the corner but she didn't care. At least Jennifer was too involved in her phone to be judging her.

"You shouldn't measure beauty that way," Gabrielle said.

"It's about grace and strength. That's what makes those women so sexy."

"Only a woman would say that. On a purely physical level, men don't find any of the women I listed attractive. Including Sarah Jessica Parker."

"Emily, I don't think you look like her. I'm just saying that's not an insult, since she's drop-dead gorgeous."

"She really isn't. Next you're going to say Cloris Leachman is gorgeous."

"She is, though! In her own way. She's very distinguished." Emily knew she was trying to be nice, but was furious at how Gabrielle insisted on these platitudes. She remembered how Gabrielle reacted earlier that year when Emily gained five pounds and casually mentioned wanting to lose it. She was afraid Gabrielle would be offended since she was the heavier of the two, but instead she just insisted "weight didn't matter" because "just look at Oprah and Rosie O'Donnell—they've done well for themselves." Emily tried to explain that this was more insulting than just agreeing that Emily needed to lose the weight, but Gabrielle didn't seem to see why.

"I think your haircut looks cute," Jennifer said, looking up from her phone. "But worst-case scenario, we can get some extensions if you absolutely need them."

Emily wiped her nose. "Good extensions are expensive and I can't afford them. And the last thing I want to do is ask my parents for money. Also, David doesn't like fake hair. He says it reminds him of rodents."

"Oh, I think I know what this is about," Gabrielle said, rubbing Emily's back. "This is your version of grief. This is about your great aunt Ellen."

Emily nearly laughed, despite the tears building up in her eyes. "Oh, I completely forgot about Aunt Ellen!" Emily said, wiping her nose. "But fuck, thanks for reminding me. I need to make sure my mom isn't running off to Boston."

"Who's Aunt Ellen?" Jennifer asked.

"I don't know any more than you do," Emily said. She briefly felt guilty for being more upset about her hair than about someone dying, but people died every day. There were probably more deaths per day, especially among eighty-five-year-olds like Aunt Ellen, than there were bad haircuts just days before a wedding. Emily allowed herself to have this moment.

The caterers, Fiddle & Jam, occupied a small storefront in a twee Scarsdale shopping center, sandwiched between a high-end pet salon called Frou and a luxury children's clothing store called Winklepea, which Emily once ventured into, just to see how expensive it was (it turned out to be selling a $160 cashmere cardigan made for three-month-olds).

Fiddle & Jam was trying very hard to look like a colonial-style house, with red-shuttered windows and white wooden siding. Inside, it was pure white: white tiles, white walls, white wooden Federal-style chairs around little white tables. A few enlarged photos of gourmet food adorned the walls. As Emily arrived with Lauren, she looked at the display case full of ready-made dishes. Everything seemed to be loaded with saffron.

"Ah, there you are," said Marla. She was standing by the counter, talking with the caterer, Kelly, a pink-cheeked, chubby woman in her thirties with a tight bun and a permanent smile.

Marla looked at Emily. "Your hair is…different. It suits you. Much more mature."

"Yeah, I didn't want it this short. I'm pissed off about it, so let's just talk about something else. I've already cried over it."

"You cried over your hair?" Lauren asked, slightly amused.

"Seriously, Lauren, not helping. Some of us actually want to be attractive."

"I am attractive. I'm really fucking attractive because I'm attractive to myself. My ideals of beauty aren't ruled by what men think." She angrily motioned through the window to a frail-looking old man feeding squirrels out in the courtyard.

"Look, let's not do this. I just wanted my hair to look feminine for my wedding."

"Hair length has nothing to do with femininity. Are you telling me Natalie Portman wasn't feminine with a buzz cut?"

"Yeah, because Natalie Portman is gorgeous already. Most men aren't huge fans of buzz cuts on women, *shockingly*."

"Seriously, why are you so obsessed with what men think?" Lauren threw her head back.

"Because I want to be attractive to men, specifically the man I'm marrying. And guess what? That's most women. We want to be hot. We want to be pretty. So yeah, ideals of beauty are directly related to what men think. Just like men wanting to look good for women. Do you berate men for working out?"

"I pity you. You spend so much time trying to be more attractive. With the amount of daily sexual harassment I receive, if anything, I'd want to be *less* attractive."

"Sweetheart," said Marla, mildly amused, "I doubt that so many men are harassing you. This is classic paranoia."

"Uh, yes, they are. I get hit on daily. Usually by guys in high school. And by pretty much every male coworker I've ever had."

"Where do you go that you meet high school boys daily?" Emily asked.

"None of your business."

"If I may," Kelly said in a high-pitched, wobbly voice. "I think now would be a good time to review the menu."

"Of course," Marla said. "Apologies, we're all a bit stressed out. My mother died last night."

"Oh, I'm so sorry!" Kelly said. "That must be hard."

"She's your mother now?" Lauren asked. "Come on, Mom, at least be honest."

"The closest thing I had to a mother anyway," Marla said. She zoomed in on Kelly's name tag. "*Kelly*, you must understand where I'm coming from. I was raised by clinical narcissists and the only person in my life who showed me any kindness was my aunt Ellen, and that's who died. Granted, her kindness was probably due to a very meek, passive personality, exacerbated by the fact that she was drunk 24/7, and as a result I didn't have much respect for her, but that's why it's so complicated for me. It's really bringing up a lot of emotions in regards to my own success and all the times I've felt the need to make myself smaller to make way for men in my industry. I'm a psychologist, by the way."

"Wow, Mom," Lauren said, putting her hands on her hips. "Are you done now?"

Marla gave a belabored sigh. "Yes, I suppose I am. I thought you of all people would be tolerant about this."

"I am, but don't talk to me about sexism in your workplace when you're a privileged, educated white woman and you work alone anyway. You should be sitting down and listening while trans women of color talk about their experiences instead of hogging the space and making it all about you."

Despite her sadness, real or imagined, Marla began to laugh hysterically, laying her hand down on the catering counter as her laughter grew so intense it made no more noise. Finally, she composed herself. "Very good point, Lauren, I'll just sit here waiting around until a trans woman of color walks in to Fiddle & Jam to tell her story instead." She turned back to Kelly. "You seem like the only reasonable millennial here."

"Oh, I'm not a millennial," Kelly said. "I'm actually thirty-seven but everyone thinks I'm twenty. It's so annoying!"

Marla and Lauren instinctively turned to Emily, who was gritting her teeth.

"So let's chat about food!" Kelly said in a chipper tone. "For the hors d'oeuvres, we're having the steak and cheese puff pastries, the ham croquettes and the watermelon slices with olive oil and mint."

"Can we add something else?" Marla asked.

"Of course. What did you have in mind?" Kelly took out a small notebook and pen by the register.

"Mom, why do we need something else?" Emily asked.

Marla finger-combed her black hair back and closed her eyes in frustration. "I'm kicking myself right now for this, but it just occurred to me that we never made any effort to include enough kosher options. I mean, we've got the watermelon thing, but that's clearly just the vegan option, it doesn't look like it was a specifically kosher choice. And what is everyone going to think when they arrive at a Jewish wedding and ham is being served? I know it's too late to cancel the ham now, but at least let's add kichel or something."

"Mom, this isn't a Jewish wedding," Emily said.

"This is news to me! I knew your officiant was some secular person you found off Yelp, but I didn't realize you were going full shiksa."

"In Emily's defense," Lauren said, "you haven't been to temple since the seventies."

"It's about paying respect to your culture," Marla said. "Emily, please tell me David is at least willing to wear a yarmulke, or I swear on Aunt Ellen's grave, this wedding will be a disaster."

"David is Catholic. He isn't going to wear a yarmulke."

"Oh, right. I'm sure his parents would have *quite* an issue with that. They probably think he'll grow horns." She raised her pointer fingers to the side of her head to illustrate her point and Kelly put her notebook away.

"Mom, come on."

"I may not be the best Jew in the world, but there are a few things I know. First of all, weddings are the time to honor your ancestors and your culture. How do you think I'm going to be perceived if my friends show up and David is wearing some giant cross?"

Emily shifted her weight from one aching foot to the other. "First of all, there won't be any crosses, and second of all, I'm pretty sure your friends are expecting a secular wedding, if they even care at all."

"That isn't true. Judy Stein actually asked me why the wedding wasn't being held in a temple, and I didn't have the heart to tell her the truth."

"The truth is that it's a secular wedding and it's being held at the Ritz Carlton. Also, who's Judy Stein?"

"Oh, she's the saleswoman at Neiman's who helps me find good deals. She found me a great pair of Stuart Weitzman boots the other week, because they were—"

"I love Stuart Weitzman!" Kelly piped up cheerfully.

Emily ignored Kelly. "Wait, Mom, are you seriously just inviting random people now? I don't even know this woman."

"I have no family, Emily. That's the truth. I'm all alone in this world. Unlike you, my parents are dead, and your aunt Lisa, well, enough said. Aunt Ellen was all I had, and now she's dead too. Judy Stein is my family now. It's horribly unfair to say that David's father can invite his family and I can't invite anyone because my family of origin is toxic. You're punishing me for being born into a family of narcissists."

"Can you just let me know who else you're inviting?"

"Nobody you don't know, other than Judy. And trust me, you're going to love her."

Kelly spoke up. "Getting back to the topic at hand, we can always add another appetizer. We have plenty of kosher options. What about spinach pies?"

Marla winced. "It's a bit Greek, but okay."

"Okay, thank goodness," Emily said. "Guess the wedding won't be a disaster after all."

"Well, since we're talking about wedding stuff," Lauren said, "there's something I need to tell you." She clasped her hands together.

"After my hair and this kosher festival, I don't know what news could piss me off further. Just go for it." Emily took a seat in one of the wrought iron chairs near the window.

"Ariel won't be able to perform as the ring bearer. And frankly, I feel the need to push back against that gender-normative decision on your part."

"What?" She almost didn't believe what Lauren was saying. It was as if Lauren were doing an impression of herself. "He's the only little boy I know. Of course he's the ring bearer. We don't have anyone else to do it."

"What about Mia?"

"She's the flower girl. Look, we just don't know enough kids for them to have their pick of the roles, okay?"

"Well, Ariel wants to be the flower person."

"What?"

"He wants to wear the dress and walk down the aisle with the flowers."

"It's Mia's dress. Christina ordered it six months ago, and it's too small for him, so they can't just switch."

"Ariel can wear his tutu. And he doesn't need to wear a shirt—that'll be so cute! People will really love how different it is." Kelly had stopped listening and appeared to be playing a game on her phone instead.

"Fuck. I am not having that at my wedding. I'm anxious enough about everything already and this is not helping."

"Emily," Marla said, "why do you think your sister doesn't have your same level of...well, all this stress and anxiety?"

"Because she's delusional!" Emily said, her voice rising. "You obviously used some different parenting book when you raised her and Jason, and because I came along so much later, you changed the rules for me. I've never once heard Jason or Lauren doubt themselves. I doubt myself every day. And as much as I want to write that off as me being crazy, I think *they're* crazy to think so highly of themselves when everyone else knows they're losers!"

"*Oy vey,*" Marla muttered.

"I'm a loser?" Lauren said. "I'm an activist. When was the last time you changed anything for women?"

Emily wanted to cry. And then she felt angry for wanting to cry. Why did she want to cry? Everyone else got to say what they wanted. Everyone else got to criticize her. So why was it so horrible when she spoke the truth? Surely someone would say it wasn't the truth at all. There was always some alternative explanation, some diagnosis, some reason why everything she felt was fake.

"You look upset," Marla finally said.

"Well, yeah, of course I do. It's my wedding week and Lauren won't quit criticizing me. And now, my hair..."

"Well, I think we're all done here," Kelly said.

"What I'm sensing," Marla said, ignoring Kelly, "is that you lash out at the ones you love when your own sense of self-worth has been downgraded—this time by a haircut. Your own looks mean so much to you that they cause you to antagonize those who love you."

"You guys don't love me," Emily said. "And if you do, you
do a great job of hiding it."

Suddenly, overcome by an unexpected wave of nausea, she
threw up on the bleached wooden floor, the hot, sharp chunks
rushing through her esophagus and splashing onto the floor.

"Emily!" Marla gasped. "Are you okay?"

"No, I'm not okay, I just threw up everywhere. Kelly, I'm
so sorry!"

"Did you have too much to drink last night?" Marla asked.

"I didn't drink anything. I think I'm getting sick." With
that, she bent over and expelled what felt like another gal-
lon of vomit, splashing Lauren's checkered Vans. Lauren, in
a rare moment of fashion-consciousness, squeamishly backed
away and checked her shoes for stains.

The two sisters drove home in silence. Emily had been
afraid of another confrontation, another thorough autopsy
of her mental failures, but instead Lauren was quiet. Emily
couldn't tell whether she should be relieved, or apprehensive
about what was coming.

"You should drink some ginger tea," Lauren finally said. "I
had terrible morning sickness when I was pregnant with Ariel.
Ginger tea was the only safe thing that helped." She said this
clinically, as if to avoid any danger of seeming sympathetic.

"Morning sickness?" Emily felt like she might throw up
again, this time strictly from the dread of potentially being
pregnant. She hadn't really worried about an unplanned pregnancy since college, given that terrorist attacks and drive-by
shootings were so much scarier. But now that it was a possibility, she wanted to kick her old self for abandoning pregnancy anxiety in favor of worrying about hypothetical serial
killers who targeted fake blondes.

Lauren continued. "It came on a bit suddenly, around my

second month. And it's not always in the morning—that's a misnomer. Sometimes I'd throw up at night or in the afternoon. One night Matt asked if we could have sex and I threw up all over him."

"We need to go to CVS," Emily said. "I need to get a pregnancy test."

"That's ridiculous. I was just telling you that story to make you feel better, Emily. Not everything applies to you. You can't be pregnant. You're on birth control."

"Mom got pregnant on birth control—that's how I was born! And I did take antibiotics two months ago, now that I think about it. I thought I had a staph infection so I got Mark to write a prescription for me, but it turned out to be acne. The pharmacist told me the meds wouldn't interact, but maybe she was wrong, I mean, she was wearing braces, she could have been some Doogie Howser impersonator. Oh, fuck."

"Relax. We'll go to CVS, but you're not pregnant. You always worry about this stupid one-percent-chance stuff. The brain tumors, the STDs from toilet seats…"

"I'm serious."

"Okay, well, when was your last period?"

"I can't even remember. I stopped getting it regularly last year, now it just comes a few times a year. It's common with some pills and my doctor told me not to worry."

"Just because you need to calm the fuck down, we'll go to CVS. My guess is that you just ate something bad this morning." Lauren made a sharp left turn to drive back to the CVS they had passed five minutes ago, and the motion made Emily throw up again, this time out the window of Lauren's car.

Back at the house, they sat in the mint-tiled bathroom, Lauren on the edge of the tub and Emily on the toilet. The

pregnancy test, placed gingerly on the sink, still had two minutes to develop. At first Emily had been timid about taking
down her panties in front of Lauren to pee, not because she
was uncomfortable with nudity but because she had a feeling
Lauren would criticize her choice to remove her pubic hair.
She got a fleeting stare of judgment but luckily nothing more.

Looking at Lauren perched on the edge of the tub made
Emily think of the old days, back when they still looked like
sisters—both brown-haired, peachy-pale and girlish, before
self-expression and experience changed their appearances—
before either of them had a "style." It was easier to feel like
sisters back then. Emily used to look at Lauren and see an
older version of herself, or a female ally against Jason's taunting and Nerf gun attacks.

"Worst case scenario?" Lauren said, noticing that Emily
was staring at her. "Speaking as someone who's been pregnant, it's not the end of the world."

"But you wanted a kid."

"I was pregnant before Ariel. I had a few abortions in college."

"A few?"

"Don't judge me. It's no different from using a condom or
getting your period. Just more cells going down the drain."

"You weren't sad at all?"

"Pfffft," Lauren said. "Fuck no. It's no big deal. The media
makes it out to be so scary and sad just because they don't
want women getting them. But the truth is, if men could
get abortions, the government would be handing them out.
In Russia, the average woman has had five abortions before
the age of thirty."

"Well, that sounds like a real utopia."

"Minus the homophobia and all the other stuff, it is. Abortions shouldn't be seen as anything scary or sad. It's like going

to the DMV. It's not fun, but everyone does it and the worst part is the wait."

"What if it really is scary and sad for some people? If I turn out to be, you know…it would make me sad to get an abortion."

"So keep it then," she said flippantly, as if discussing whether to order pizza or Chinese takeout.

"It would make me sad to keep it too. I'm not sure if I'm ready to be a parent. Wait, did I say not sure? I meant definitely. And I can't imagine David is ready. He never even wants to talk about kids. The one time we discussed it, he said he wanted to wait until his midthirties. If I kept the baby, he might resent me forever, then maybe he'd leave me, and I'd be a single mom, and…"

She stopped talking when she noticed Lauren staring at the pregnancy stick on the sink.

NIGHT 3

Jason

IF JASON HAD to hear the song "Let It Go" one more time, he would jump out the window. He had spent the evening alone with Mia—his first in a long time—while Christina went out with friends. He had tried to show her some old toys from his childhood, his beloved G.I. Joe and Hot Wheels, but she had cried and demanded he play *Frozen* on his laptop. She watched it before falling asleep on the sofa, her little arm dangling off the edge. He picked her up and got her dressed for bed, hoping she'd wake up during the process and want to spend time with him, but she slept soundly even when he pulled the pajama top over her head.

Women, it seemed, had a built-in advantage with parenting. Mia was attached to Christina from the moment she popped out. Jason had to work so much harder to get any reaction from her, and now that Christina had gotten her addicted to mobile devices, he had to compete with technology too.

He tried not to dwell too long on his relationship—or lack thereof—with his daughter, realizing that this at least gave him an opportunity to have fun. With Mia asleep and at home with her grandparents, Jason was pumped for another night out. This time, it wouldn't be at Celebz.

He looked at himself in the mirror after his shower. His towel was tied around his hips, his small beer belly protruding slightly, wiry hair covering his fleshy torso. The hair on the sides of his head was still thick and dark but had gotten too long, which made him look as if he were trying to distract people from his receding hairline and bald spot in the back. He knew it didn't really matter—women loved older men even if they were bald, which was why Patrick Stewart's wife was so hot. That was at least what his favorite pick-up-artist blogs told him: men were attractive because they were confident and charming, regardless of looks, while women were attractive solely because they were young and pretty, regardless of their personalities. Balding and aging sucked, sure, but it sucked worse to be a woman.

When he was at Colgate, losing his hair was the last thing on his mind. He didn't think they were his glory days at the time. He thought they were the beginning of something better. Every weekend, at the dilapidated white colonial that housed Delta Xi Tau, he and his fraternity brothers would host a party and invite the girls from the two hottest sororities. The girls from the slightly uglier sororities would invariably wind up coming too. A few times there were some hidden gems in there, or at least girls with big boobs and self-esteem issues. The Delts would set out the liquor on the table, and in a matter of hours the bottles would be empty and placed on the mantel if they were particularly impressive, like a jumbo bottle of Jack Daniels. The girls would arrive, already drunk from their own pregaming and ready to dance. He'd crank up "Californication" by the Red Hot Chili Peppers, and, more times than not, any girl he approached would be his.

Except Christina. The senior alpha female of Sigma Theta, she would sit in a corner with her friends, sipping on her drink delicately, laughing as if she were at a debutante ball and not inches away from an empty Coors Light box full of vomit.

One night, he approached her after he had a few too many shots of Jack. "Why is it that I've seen you so many times, and you've never said hi?" he asked, breaching the wall of sorority girls that surrounded her. "It's pretty rude to drink a stranger's drinks and not even introduce yourself." He smiled, to make sure she knew he wasn't actually angry. Normally, such a pickup line would work with women. He believed in the semiconfrontational approach to flirting.

She took a sip from her red Solo cup of Franzia sauvignon blanc. "Because I have a boyfriend?" He tried to focus on the light bouncing off her Tiffany charm bracelet. He knew if he didn't, he'd be looking at her perky chest, her blue eyes or her perfect lips.

He normally ignored girls with boyfriends because there were so many other willing girls who were single. But he couldn't get Christina out of his mind. She looked like a Victoria's Secret model who required no retouching. It was like a tragic Greek myth: someone had created his perfect woman and then made her unavailable to him.

He asked her sorority sisters and discovered that Christina's boyfriend went to Stanford, and they saw each other only a few times a year. He considered waiting it out until they broke up but didn't feel like taking the risk that she would be the one-in-a-million girl who actually stayed with a long-distance boyfriend. He had to take action.

Knowing that girls like Christina would never refuse an opportunity to dress up and go somewhere fancy, he organized a fraternity winter formal that would blow all previous formals out of the water. He put pledges to work organizing it from top to bottom, making sure everyone pitched in their money to get the best venue. Geography limited him to the Utica Radisson, but that was better than all the previous formals held in the school annex. He made formal wear mandatory and told the pledges they had to rent tuxedos or stay away.

When he asked her to be his date—only as a friend—she bit her glossed lip and looked down at the floor. "Only as a friend."

The night of the formal, Jason and his friends rented a stretch limo to pick up the girls at the sorority house. Christina emerged in a sequined floor-length ice-blue gown that hugged her hourglass body. She picked up the hem so that it wouldn't get wet in the snow and climbed into the limo next to Jason. When he scooted closer to her, she edged away slightly but smiled at him.

"How would Mr. Stanford feel about you sitting so close to me?" he asked with a wink.

"He wouldn't care because he knows we're just friends."

"He knows about me?"

"No, but…you know what I mean."

At the Radisson, Jason requested that the DJ play TLC, Christina's favorite group. He handed her a martini, which became two, which became three. Without her usual entourage of best friends—he had instructed his brothers not to invite any of them—she found herself in conversation with Jason and only Jason. As the two of them drank more and more, Jason told her about the amazing job he had lined up at IBM after graduation. This wasn't true at all, but Christina's eyes lit up.

Westlife's "If I Let You Go" began playing. He asked her to dance. Her hands rested on his shoulders, but she laid her head on his chest, so he let his hands migrate to her butt.

Later that night she told him that she didn't think things were going to work out with her boyfriend after all.

That first night with Christina was probably the best sex Jason ever had—probably, because, having drunk so much, he couldn't remember the details. But he remembered waking up the next morning next to the most beautiful woman he had ever seen, wondering how on Earth she got there and feeling a deep sense of panic as he realized he would need to find a job at IBM as soon as possible before graduation.

The story he later told Christina was that he had been promised the job but at the last second they gave it to one of the senior executives' sons instead. Much to his relief, she understood, and even better, consoled him with sex. Crisis averted. As the days ticked off to graduation, he sent his résumé to dozens of tech companies. He wound up at a junior sales job at a third-tier computer hardware company called PushComp.

They moved to New York City together after graduation, where Christina began her career in marketing. He wasn't making that much, but what he made he spent on her: clubbing in the Meatpacking District, designer clothes, towers of sushi.

Four years into their relationship, Jason began finding bridal websites in Christina's search history. At one point she had been the perfect woman, but by now he had seen her with a stomach bug and without makeup, and he knew how the bathroom smelled after she used it. Little signs of her tanning addiction were starting to show on her young face. He had become a senior sales associate at PushComp. If he hadn't moved in with his college girlfriend, who knows what kind of women he might have met? Perhaps ones who continued to give blow jobs after the first six months—something Christina insisted was gross and degrading.

He dragged his feet on the proposal while he created anonymous accounts on dating websites with no photograph and
no bio. When she was out or asleep, he scrolled, surveying
the single women in New York at his disposal. He resisted
messaging. But he started taking a stand with Christina. At
one point he even told her that he believed marriage was a
sexist institution and that, as a woman, she shouldn't be interested in it. This gambit did nothing to forestall her ultimatum
and, when it came, he panicked at the thought of losing her.
He told himself that, perhaps, his doubts were temporary: he
was only twenty-six, so of course he was afraid of marriage.
Things would work out. He spent a year's worth of commis-
sion to buy her an engagement ring at Tiffany.

When their sex dwindled from every other day to once
a week, then once every two weeks, she told him she just
didn't have as high a sex drive as he did. She still smiled and
giggled when he took her to dinner at expensive restaurants,
but when they were home she spent most of her time flipping
through *Architectural Digest*, watching HGTV and shopping
online at west elm. When he tried to touch her, she recoiled
as if her entire body were ticklish. One day he overheard her
on the phone telling her mother that Mr. Stanford had become a VP at Google.

He wished he had listened to his brothers when they told
him not to mess with a girl who had a boyfriend. As his hair
thinned and his metabolism slowed, the handsome, smiling
frat boy in old photographs became his nemesis, taunting
him about his lost youth. He was determined to turn back
the clock. He logged on to one of his anonymous dating accounts and added a photo. He began taking off his wedding
ring whenever he was out with friends. The girls didn't quite
fall into his lap as he had hoped, but with hard work and per-
severance, he did find a fling here and there: an aspiring "TV

personality" working as a Hooters waitress, a single mother in her midthirties who genuinely believed he wanted to be her boyfriend, a married woman on his sales team who was just as discreet as he was and as many erotic masseuses as he could afford.

And suddenly Christina was pregnant.

He pretended to be happy about it, went to all her doctor's appointments and held her hand, but all the while he was thinking about the Thai massage place around the corner from PushComp, the strip club on the West Side Highway and his hot coworker Jill in Compliance.

In spite of all his ambivalence, once Mia was born, the DNA kicked in and Jason found himself falling completely in love with his daughter. Mia, on the other hand, preferred Christina from day one, and Christina was just so much better with her than he was. Jason found himself jealous of both of them, they were so close. Christina loved Mia more than she had ever loved him, and Mia loved Christina more than she could ever love him. The only advantage of this was that Mia kept Christina so busy, she no longer had time to monitor Jason's actions. She was taking Mia to Mommy and Me classes, to Gymboree, to a music class called Little Chopin where parents paid one hundred dollars a session for their toddlers to sit in a circle and suck on dirty plastic flutes. Jason had more time to himself than ever, and he spent it doing what he loved most, without guilt. Why should he feel guilty? Their whole marriage began with infidelity. Was she really any better than he was? If she really wanted him to be faithful, she would have sex with him more often. Besides, it wasn't as if he fell in love with the other women he was with. It was only sex—he might as well have been masturbating.

When Mia was five months old, he was laid off from Push-Comp. Going to job interviews was intimidating and demoralizing. He thought his work in sales had prepared him for rejection, but he hadn't expected to be blown off so many times by email. When the subject line included the words *thank you* he knew what was coming. On the rare occasions that he tried to express his frustration to Christina, she claimed that there were jobs out there—he just wasn't looking hard enough. The boyish charm and good looks that once seemed to get him everything he wanted had deserted him. He was in his thirties with no job, no sex life and a daughter who cried whenever he held her.

It was only a matter of time before Christina found out about the other women. He had expected a fight, maybe even a few cut-up Oxford shirts strewn across the living room floor in revenge, but as it turned out, Christina had no qualms about pawning her engagement ring, changing the locks and filing for divorce.

The first time he had slept with Christina, that night of the winter formal, it had been the best night of his life. Thirteen years later, despite hundreds of attempts to top it, it still was.

Jason got dressed. He had already asked David if he wanted to go out that night, but he was going to dinner with his dad and stepmom. Emily had been sleeping ever since the afternoon. Lauren and Matt were spending the night in watching Netflix. The house was quiet with the kids asleep. He went on Facebook. He had friended all of the wedding party, even people he hadn't met yet, and everyone had accepted his friend request, even Jennifer. He had flipped through her pictures a few times, evaluating just how much effort he would exert to sleep with her. He had gotten to the point where sex was less about his own pleasure, and more about how big a high-five he would receive from telling people. Jennifer was sexy, tall and svelte, but she was twenty-nine. She was probably full of baggage and desperation but still hot enough to bang. A man would have to be insane not to at least try.

When Jason opened his chat window, he noticed Nathan was online. Nathan's profile picture was a webcam selfie in which he gave an overly serious glare to the camera while tipping his hat. The collar of his leather trench coat was turned up, like a fat male version of Carmen Sandiego.

He found Maddyson's profile. Her profile pic was an iPhone selfie, the default for girls her age. She wore a black tattoo choker and made a face that looked artificially surprised. He saw the green dot next to her name on Messenger—she was online too.

Hey, what are you up to? he typed. If she didn't recognize him or thought he was being creepy, he could always claim he meant to message someone else.

"Nothing. Hanging out at home."

"Same."

"Wanna come over?"

This was a stunning development. Could it be that he had entered a new prime in his life? His early thirties hadn't been the pussy festival of his early twenties, but maybe thirty-five was the beginning of a new era. If he was right, he was looking at a second Golden Age!

Sounds good to me ;) he typed. I'll bring the liquor.

David

"I think it's time for a toast," Nick said.

"Dad, you made two toasts already."

"No, no, hear me out. To the next Steve Jobs!" David cringed as the couple at the next table turned and looked at them. He overheard the wife asking the husband if he recognized David and then saw the husband shake his head, perplexed.

Susan giggled and raised her wineglass, and David slowly lifted his up to meet theirs.

"I'm not done," Nick said. "And may his compassion, intelligence and empathy serve him well. In business, in marriage and in life."

Susan got her phone from her sequined clutch purse. "I have an idea! Let me take a selfie of my two handsome men! Lean in together, you two."

David smiled weakly. "Susan, it's not a selfie if you're taking it of other people. A selfie is a picture you take of yourself."

Susan's eyes widened. She turned to Nick. "Can you believe this? All up with the tech lingo! He'll be running Silicon Valley in no time!"

"Speaking of lingo, David," Nick said, "I've been meaning to ask you—what's *twerk*?"

"What?"

"Is it some sort of computer thing?"

"No, it's, um, it's a dance."

Susan laughed. "I am so glad I have you kids! Without you, I'd never know any of the hip words!"

David thought about correcting her use of the nearly obsolete word *hip* but decided against it. Susan took a photo of him and Nick. He felt his phone buzzing with a call. He checked it. It was Robert.

"I have to get this. It's my boss."

"Ooh, it's Bill Gates at work!" Nick said. He took out his own phone and snapped a too-close candid of David with the flash on.

"Hey, Robert, what's up?" He heard Nick mutter "Ugh, it's too blurry" as he looked at his phone.

"How's your wedding week going?" Robert said on the other end.

"It's good. I'm actually at dinner with my family right now."

"Oh, right, the time difference! I just came back from Pacific Beach. Man, the waves down there. Unbefuckinglievable."

"Cool, cool. So—what's up?"

"So I'm looking at your Twitter feed now and I'm not seeing any tweets about the BluCapital thing."

"Oh, no, I'm so sorry. I totally forgot. It's been kind of crazy—"

"I get it. You're getting married. No problem, man! I'll make sure Zach does it tonight."

"No, it's okay, I'll do it right now!"

"Okay. Because Zach is more than willing to help out if you're feeling slammed."

"It's fine. I'll do it. Thanks, Robert."

"Cool. Say hi to your family for me!"

"I will, thanks."

He turned off his phone. He looked up and saw that Nick's eyes were moist.

"That was amazing," his dad said.

Jason

"Good evening, gentle sir."

Jason had knocked on the front door of the Porters' expecting Maddyson to answer it. Instead, there was Nathan, wearing his signature leather trench coat, his fedora tipped rakishly over one eye and no shoes. Maddyson stood behind him, twirling her pink strand of hair around her fingertips, flipping through her phone again. It was astonishing how terribly young women dressed, Jason thought. Jennifer might have been older than Maddyson, but she at least put some effort into doing her makeup properly, getting a decent manicure and wearing heels. Maddyson wore a large boxy sweatshirt that looked not only unflattering, but uncomfortable in the summer weather, along with a pair of high-waisted denim shorts that made whatever butt she had look long and deflated. As for makeup, she appeared to be wearing nothing except for dark purple metallic lipstick—something Jason assumed was a trend among girls her age. It didn't look good, so he focused on her smooth, slender legs.

"Hey, guys, I brought some vodka," he said. "Nathan… I didn't realize you'd be home."

"I heard that you would be joining my dear stepsister for a night of merriment. What kind of gentleman would I be if I left her unattended?"

Jason shrugged. He should have seen this coming. "Well, I'm happy to see you, man. We haven't gotten to spend much time together, and I think it's time we got to know each other a little better."

"'Tis a pity indeed, good sir, that so many men become so embroiled with the pursuit of females that they forsake the intellectual pleasures to be found with other like-minded courtiers."

"Okay, I'm going to be straight up with you. I have no idea what you just said."

"Perhaps we can watch a film. Or otherwise, play *Skyrim*."

"Not again with the *Skyrim*," Maddyson said, her head craning back.

"Your parents still out with David?" Jason asked as he walked into the house and perused the family photos on the walls. He wanted to make sure it would be a while before Nick and Susan returned.

"Yeah," replied Maddyson. "It's a little private congratulations thingy since he's getting married and all."

"More like marching to the gallows," Jason said. "I was married once. Never again." Normally that line piqued women's interest, or at least made them wonder what his story was. But Maddyson just scrolled through her phone as if she were listening to one of her dad's friends talk about his 401k.

"Why don't we start drinking?" Jason asked. "Nathan, you can pick a movie."

"I know a great deal about cinema," he said, speaking to him but looking at Maddyson. "But I fear my tastes could be a bit...*refined* compared to what you normally watch. Plebeian taste confounds me."

"How about a classic?" Jason said. *"American Pie."*

"We have the DVD," Nathan said. "That was my brother's favorite movie in high school. A bit blue to watch in front of the lady, though."

"Nathan, I've seen it before," Maddyson said. "It's just that old movie with the guy from *Orange Is the New Black*, right?"

Nathan went over to the DVD player to put the movie on, groaning slightly when he bent over to insert the disk. He motioned to Maddyson to sit on the sofa. With an effeminate flourish of his hand, he took off his trench coat and laid it on the carpet in front of the couch, bowing and removing his hat to reveal his greasy scalp. Tonight he had gone without a ponytail and just let his oily hair hang free as if he were a villainous lord on *Game of Thrones*.

"After you, milady," he said, encouraging her to walk across his coat.

"Dude," Jason said, patting him on the shoulder. "This really only works if there's a puddle or something. I'm sure she can walk on the floor herself."

"'Twas merely a joke!" Nathan said.

"With you, it's hard to tell."

Maddyson ignored the coat on the floor and walked to the other side of the sofa where she sat down with her arms crossed in front of her chest. Nathan took a seat several feet away from her.

Jason went into the kitchen to make some drinks, looking over his shoulder as he left to make sure Nathan wasn't making any new moves on Maddyson. Nathan appeared to be frozen, staring at his stepsister with his hat shading his face, but unable to say or do anything. He looked like a giant garden gnome.

The Porters' kitchen was decorated in a rustic style. There were a pine table and chairs and a glass vase with white daffodils as a centerpiece. The walls were covered in blue-and-white tiles with little roosters on them. There was a photo calendar on the fridge. The photograph representing June featured a slightly younger Nathan sitting on a patio chair at a cookout, clad in his trench coat and fedora, surrounded by happy and chatting middle-aged people in their bright summer clothes. He was glaring at the camera with one hand on his chin and the other tipping the brim of his hat. The picture was framed with cheerful little cartoon images of umbrellas and flip-flops.

Jason quickly mixed some of his vodka with Susan's no-pulp orange juice and carried all three glasses into the living room. *American Pie* had started. Nathan had edged slightly closer to Maddyson on the sofa, but he was still a good three feet away. Jason placed the glasses on the coffee table and sat down between them.

"You're really into your phone, huh?" he asked Maddyson.

"I guess. Why do you care?" He peeked over to see her phone screen but couldn't get a good look.

"Well, you may or may not know this, but I'm the CEO

of a revolutionary transportation-based start-up called Walk-Share. And I'm soon to be the cofounder of Beardster."

"What?"

"It's kind of like, Tinder meets Uber, but…"

"I'm on Tinder right now." She finally revealed her phone screen, where she was flipping through different men, all between the ages of eighteen and twenty-three.

"I can't allow that," he said. "You can't use my competitor." He smiled in a way he hoped was sexily arrogant, not just arrogant.

"Is your app on the market yet?"

"No, I mean, we still need to get an engineer to actually build it, but—"

"Then Tinder isn't your competitor." She continued to scroll, swiping right at most of the men she saw.

"I thought you would be pickier than this."

"Oh, I'm not using this to meet guys. It's a social experiment where, once we connect, I ask them what they think of slut-shaming and see how they respond. Then I post it all to my Snapchat story. It's for my final project."

"I don't shame sluts. I love sluts. It helps that I am one." He thought of winking, but that would be too much. Instead, he flicked her shoulder playfully. She turned to look at him like he was an irritating mosquito.

"*Slut* is a word to shame women. Not men. So when you call yourself that, it's different. Men created the word *slut* to keep girls like me down. Men like you are the ones enforcing dress codes, for example. Did you know that I led a protest at my high school over their ban on crop tops and booty shorts? That day, we all came to school in crop tops and booty shorts."

"So this is what's going on in high school now. Nobody cared about dress codes when I was younger." He wondered if maybe Lauren was the future of America—billions of Laurens walking around getting angry over booty shorts. It had infected the *cute* girls now.

"I think it's generational," she said. "People in my generation care passionately. We want to change the world. Your generation...no offense... I mean, baby boomers are pretty much responsible for all the problems my generation faces."

"Baby boomers? I'm not sixty."

"Whatever. You know what I mean."

He paused, wondering how he would recover. He shouldn't have drawn attention to their age difference since that was the one thing stopping him from gaming her. He changed the subject. "So when you said the word *slut* exists to shame women like you, do you mean that you're promiscuous?"

"I guess," she said. "Depending on your definition."

"You two!" Nathan whispered from the edge of the sofa. "Keep it down, I am trying to watch the film."

"Yeah," said Jason. "Nathan doesn't want the subtleties of the tongue tornado scene ruined for him."

"I know this movie is subpar and classless," he shot back. "I put it on for *your* enjoyment as I am a good host and a gentleman. If you want to simply talk throughout it, I would be happy to watch an atheism documentary instead."

"No need for that, buddy," Jason said. "I don't want to be a bad guest. I was just chatting with your sister. Surely that's okay with you."

"Stepsister. So any sexual relations we might enjoy would be legal. But yes, by all means, talk with her."

"Ew, Nathan," she said. "Why do you *always* go there?"

"I am just speaking the truth. Now, if you both want to continue watching *American Pie*, I am happy to regale you with my thoughts on this film's representation of decaying Western society—a society plagued by feminism, and superstition known as *religion*, where free thinking is no longer practiced, where women willingly give themselves away to the alpha males, where truly intelligent thinkers are not rewarded with sex but punished with virginity, where chivalry and decency are dead, where—"

"Dude," Jason said. "You're bumming everyone out."

Nathan took a sip from his screwdriver and went back to the movie. Hopefully if he got drunk enough, he'd just fall asleep, Jason thought. He didn't seem like a big drinker.

"That reminds me," Jason said, taking a sip from his own drink. "Maddyson?"

"Oh, right." She gulped down the lion's share of her screwdriver without wincing the way other eighteen-year-old girls might. He remembered how girls drank when he was a Delt. They claimed to be drunker than they were, and they claimed to like whiskey and football just to impress him, when in reality they had mini-fridges stocked with Smirnoff Vanilla and cranberry juice and spent their weekends at outlet malls. They would pretend to be innocent or promiscuous, whatever they thought would impress him. He would tease them about their hair as an excuse to touch it, and he would show them his football trophies in his bedroom, where he kept cold tequila and limes in his own mini-fridge. He remembered very little of the actual sex. Usually by then he was blacked out.

And there he was, on the sofa with Maddyson, plying her with a screwdriver while she ignored him for her Tinder social experiment. How had it come to this?

"Actually, Jason," she said. "While I've got you, could you answer a few questions for me?"

"Sure."

She opened her laptop and began typing as she talked. "Back when you were young, was it normal for a woman to have multiple partners?"

"Uh…well, I'm not that old now. What's this for?"

"We'll get back to that question. Would you say that attitudes toward female promiscuity are more lax or less lax now than they were when you were young?"

"How old do you think I am?"

"Can you just answer the question?"

"Wait, is this for some kind of college assignment?" He took another sip of his drink. He needed to drink more to get through this.

"I won't use your name, don't worry. Okay, would you say that slut-shaming behavior between women was more or less common in the eighties than it is now?"

"I wasn't an adult in the eighties."

She closed her laptop. "This isn't working. I'll just ask my friend's dad instead. See you guys. I'm going to go hang out at Chelsea's house."

"No!" Nathan protested. "You are too inebriated to be behind the wheel of a vehicle!"

"She lives down the street. I'm walking."

"Dressed in such a tempting manner at night, by yourself?"

"Fuck off, Nathan."

Maddyson put on her Chuck Taylors and left. Jason turned to Nathan, who was slumped over on the sofa, sadly staring into his screwdriver.

"Nathan, drink more."

"A gentleman never becomes three sheets to the wind."

"Yes, they do. I do, at least."

"Well, you, my good sir," he said, taking another dainty sip, "are not a gentleman."

When the end credits of *American Pie* rolled, Nathan was still awake and alert, having had had only one drink. Jason was on his fifth.

"You should be ashamed," Nathan said.

"Of what?" Jason knew he was slurring his words.

"I know why you came here. You're recently divorced, and after your heart was trampled upon by the fair Christina, you thought you were free to take my stepsister's innocence right in my manor."

"Okay. First off, Maddyson isn't a virgin. Second, this isn't a manor and it's not yours."

Nathan checked his steampunk-inspired bronze watch, with visible gears. "Maddyson does not seem to be returning from that wench Chelsea's house. I suppose it is just us gentle sirs now."

"I should be going then."

"Nonsense. I shan't allow it. You are too deep in your cups to drive safely, and as much as I disdain your predatory posture toward my stepsister's delicate flower, I will not see my brother's wedding marred by your untimely demise."

"Well, thanks." He got up and stretched, allowing his belly to show when he raised his arms. Who cared, it wasn't like Maddyson was still around. "Fuck, why did I even *come* here?"

"Only you can answer that. Here. Prithee follow me to the guest quarters. *World of Warcraft* awaits."

"Ugh, anything but that."

"Perhaps you'd prefer that I tell my father and stepmother that you came here to get Maddyson drunk," he said, his eyes dancing mischievously. "They'd love to hear about that."

"Fine, whatever. I'll be your weird fucking video game buddy."

Nathan steadied him as they went upstairs, past a series of photographs of Nathan and David as little boys. It was strange to imagine Nathan as a child. How did he become this?

"You looked different as a kid." He missed a step and almost fell into Nathan.

"Ah, yes. My innocent days. Before I learned about the treachery of romance."

"You *really* hate women, don't you? And you think I'm the scumbag?"

"To the contrary. I adore women. I adore everything about them—their slim waists, their long hair, their full lips, their… heavenly girlhoods. But I have become resentful, for these females want nothing to do with the likes of me. You appear to have the same problem."

"Fuck no," he blurted, accidentally spitting in Nathan's face. "I'm not a virgin like you. I was married. And before that, during that *and* after that, I've fucked *tons* of women."

"Yes. But you are unhappy nonetheless. Is it a particular female that plagues you so, my brother?"

"What? No. I'm just drunk. Stop it."

"As you wish." He opened the door to the guest room and Jason flopped on the bed, his face pressing against the quilted floral duvet. Vodka-scented drool trickled from his mouth. He felt the bed's weight shift dramatically, as though some kind of gravitational force were pushing him off. His dizziness didn't help. When he rolled over and opened his eyes, he saw that Nathan was seated at the foot of his bed.

"You really want a friend, don't you?" Jason said. "Why are you still here?"

"I may *want* a friend. But you, my good sir, *need* a friend. You have nothing, is that not the truth? The females did this to you."

"Women aren't aliens, dude. Fuck, no wonder you've never had a girlfriend. What the hell did women do to you to make you this way?"

As if he had been waiting a lifetime for that question, Nathan took a deep breath and prepared to speak. He removed his fedora and placed it on his lap. "I was once innocent. I

once believed that in order to attract a female for sexual pleasure and companionship, my only course of action would be
to be nice to her. To do her favors. To tell her how beautiful she was."

"Well, no. That's called being a spineless weirdo."

"I did not know that at the time. My mother, may she rest
in peace, taught me that women would see me for who I am
inside. And what happened? The females flocked to my taller,
more handsome brother, and ignored me. And so I came to
realize the true nature of the females."

"And you seriously wonder why women don't want you?"
he asked. "You're ridiculously bitter."

"One particular female germinated my worldview." Nathan took a deep breath in, staring straight ahead at the wall
instead of Jason, as if he were performing in a dramatic play.
"When I was in ninth grade, a lass by the name of Sophia
caught my eye. She was stunningly beautiful, with long blond
hair and the face of a mystical warrior wizard. The female
kind, obviously. I became friends with her, called her every
night and whispered sweet nothings to her. I became her best
friend, her confidant. However, I was never good enough for
her to date. I was her friend through every breakup, every
crush, every devastating fight fueled by her girlish fury and
his brutish lack of sophistication. And she never once realized that the only true gentleman who would treat her like
a lady was standing right in front of her."

Jason raised his eyebrows. "You realize you just described
every teen romantic comedy ever, right? Is your life this
much of a cliché, or is that just how you like to view it? Either way, it's very sad."

Nathan turned to look at him sternly. "It is a trope because art imitates life."

Jason sat up, shaking his head. "You get that there are tons of reasons a woman wouldn't date you, other than you being too nice, right? I mean, for one, you don't seem to bathe more than once a week."

"I believed Sophia was deeper than that."

"So one girl didn't like you. Did you ever tell her you liked her?"

"No. I simply left a bouquet of wilted black roses by her locker with a note reading 'From your masked guardian, lurking in the shadows in passionate silence.'"

Jason lay back down and rolled onto his bloated belly. "Dude," he said. "That's fucking terrifying."

"She never figured out it was me. She asked me many times if I knew anyone who was watching her from afar. I said no."

"Well, no wonder she wasn't into you. You did creepy shit, and then never admitted you were into her. How was she even supposed to know?"

"Females have remarkable intuition. It makes up for their subpar logical skills and inferior upper-body strength. Oh, she knew, she knew. But she delighted in tormenting me. For four whole years I was forced into a platonic servitude that brought me nothing but misery. It is thanks to Sophia that I am the tortured soul I am today."

"Yeah, okay."

"I experienced something similar in college," he said, just as Jason was beginning to hope that he was wrapping things up. "There was a woman in my philosophy class. She was slender, brunette and petite with the milky white legs of a…" He paused, as if he was trying to think of a good comparison. "Of a stool," he finally said. "A stool that's white."

"Got it. Stool legs." Jason smirked.

"But comely. Anyway, I never could work up the courage to speak to her. So instead, I became her guardian in the dark. I followed her home each day, making sure nobody harassed her or touched her. You have no idea how many creeps are out there. I friended her on le social media—it meant but a pittance to her, since she friended everyone—and then used that to find out which events she attended. I would attend those events, as well, my eyes glued to her, ready to swoop in with my katana the minute any lesser male thought he could impress my fair lady."

"Your *katana*? You brought a katana?"

"No. My figurative katana. Otherwise known as my mind. I would intellectually eviscerate any male who came close to her. But she never seemed to notice or care. One time, she just told her low-grade suitor that I was 'some drunk ass-hole.' I had imbibed nothing that night! Eventually I became resentful. I had been protecting her and caring for her and all for what?" Nathan's voice had grown higher and louder. Jason was worried he might cry, so he put his hand on Nathan's shoulder.

"Buddy, you never spoke to her. Your whole strategy is flawed. Women don't notice their 'guardians in the darkness.'"

"Exactly. This is why I cannot trust them to be true, to be genuine...to be *ladies*."

"No. Look, I'd be the first to say I don't have a great track record for respecting women, but if you want to get laid, you need to actually *talk* to them. Not follow them home."

"Is that any better than getting my stepsister drunk with the expectation of sexual intercourse? Shame on you."

"Yeah, shame on me. I get it, I'm a pervert."

Nathan turned to meet his eyes. "You may be. But tonight you have done something very few other men have done, and for that I commend you."

"Oh yeah, what's that?"

"You talked to me."

DAY 4

Emily

Hey there, just found out I am pregnant but haven't gone to the doctor yet to determine how far along. Obviously unplanned. I've been on birth control and didn't know I was pregnant so I have been drinking. Just want to make sure I haven't harmed the baby. I barely ever get periods anyway because of my pill so I don't know how long since my last period. Did any of you not show at all in the first trimester?

DAVID LAY SNORING beside her as she typed. She always marveled at his ability to sleep while she was awake and tossing. Normally when she was trying to sleep, she worried about the latest gang initiation method only half debunked on Snopes or wild stories on BuzzFeed about women whose faces rotted off after sharing makeup brushes. If, by some miracle, she wasn't worried about anything in particular, her brain would put on a slideshow of all the worst things she had ever done. A memory that made a regular appearance was the time she got diarrhea at camp and clogged the toilets with so much toilet paper that maintenance had to be called, and she could overhear the plumbers talking about how "they had no idea so much shit could come out of ten-year-old girls."

Moments after she typed her query to the pregnancy forum, she got her first response.

"Omg if u hve been drinking durin the first three months sorry but ur baby might be retarded or something...i didnt drink at all when i was pregnant why wud u do that to ur kid???? shame on u."

She replied, I didn't know I was pregnant. If I had known, I wouldn't have drunk anything.

Another message came in:

"To answer your question, when I was preggers with my little Kayden I didn't show at all until six months. My waist was 23" before pregnancy, and it was only 25" at my fourth month! People had no idea I was pregnant even into my second trimester because my waist was so tiny! (I think all the baby fat went to my big Kim K butt and 28H bewbs lol) I had no clue I was pregnant at all! But I don't drink so I had nothing to worry about. Good luck!"

And another:

"This didn't happen to me but I heard somewhere that if you aren't showing in the first trimester your baby is probably seriously ill. Go to the ER now. What the fuck is wrong with you asking about this online? This is an emergency. SEE A DOCTOR."

Of course, see a doctor. That would obviously be her first course of action as soon as she returned to San Francisco, thanks to ClearDrop's bullshit HMO, which wouldn't cover nonemergency costs outside of California. At least if she hid this from David long enough to marry him, she'd get on Zoogli's better health plan.

"You have to tell him." Emily and Lauren were having tea in the kitchen while the rest of the house slept. Lauren put her mug down and put one hand on her hip. Only Lauren could intimidate Emily this much when apparently trying to help her. Why did she even bother saying anything? For a split second, Emily wished Lauren hadn't been the one to take her to get the pregnancy test. If only she'd learned how to drive twelve years ago like a normal person.

"I know," Emily said.

"So when?"

"I don't know."

"Are you just going to pop it out one day and be like, 'Oh, I didn't know this was there?'" Lauren pantomimed a baby coming out between her legs, using her hands to form the head.

"Well, I could be like one of those women on *I Didn't Know I Was Pregnant*." David would have found that remark funny, if the context had been different. He and Emily loved that show, especially the dramatic reenactments with slightly hotter actors.

"Seriously—"

"It's our wedding week. You know? I'm really stressed out and—I'll wait until after, all right?"

"Matt and I don't keep secrets from each other."

"Thank you, Lauren. Thanks for taking time out of my crisis to humblebrag about your pseudomarriage for the nine thousandth time."

Lauren put her mug in the sink. "Matt and I trust each

other. If I were you, I'd think about that before you walk down the aisle."

Maybe I should call it off, Emily thought. As much as the thought terrified her, it would be somewhat fulfilling to blow Lauren's whole "flower person" plan out of the water.

David

David sat across from Nathan at Jojo's, their favorite ice cream parlor. It had been a treat when they were little, a place their mother would take them when she wanted to spoil them, complete with the pink-and-white-striped awning, retro posters of ice cream trucks and the same classic flavors throughout the years, including a "blue mystery" flavor that was Jojo's trademark, despite literally being vanilla with blue food coloring. As much as David and Nathan both liked Susan, they were disappointed that she preferred gelato (due to it being Italian and therefore exotic) and didn't see the appeal of Jojo's. Jojo's had become a place for David and Nathan to go alone, and they hadn't been in years.

"Thank you for the ice cream," Nathan said, gingerly taking a bite of dark chocolate ice cream in a bowl. "I must say, however, as I grow more mature, I develop less and less of a sweet tooth."

David rolled his eyes. "Right. You're so mature and refined that you rely only on fine cuisine for nourishment: Doritos and soda."

Nathan failed to come up with a retort.

As much as David wanted to savor his favorite childhood treat—the teddy bear ice cream sundae—he couldn't let himself slip up like that. He knew his family and friends didn't understand his commitment—some might say obsession—with eating healthy. But he would never forget the image of his mother at the end, lying in her hospital bed, looking decades older than her forty-eight years. He'd vowed he would never end up like that. Emily was the first person who really understood his fear of death. It was one of the reasons he loved her the most. She got it. Unlike his exes, she never complained about his repetitive workouts and electrolyte smoothies. She didn't pressure him to eat greasy wings and "act like a real man." Sometimes the two of them would stay up all night talking about mercury levels in fish.

So no, no teddy bear sundae. Instead, he had ordered a smoothie made with Greek yogurt and organic blueberries, a new addition to the menu. He requested no sugar and was not prepared for how bad it would taste. Still, he was at Jojo's, and the nostalgia sweetened the entire experience.

"So did you and Maddyson have fun last night?" David asked. He regretted saying this as soon as the words left his mouth. The last thing he wanted was another argument about the ethics of sleeping with stepsiblings.

"Not particularly," Nathan said. "She left to go to her friend's house. But I forgot to tell you. Jason showed up. Most likely in a pathetic attempt to deflower Maddyson, but after she left he and I spent some time together. We played video games until two in the morning and he fell asleep in the guest room."

David couldn't help but laugh. Some smoothie almost got into his nose and stung his nostrils. "No way! What the fuck?"

"Do keep your language appropriate, dear brother. There are ladies here."

David looked behind him to see a group of high school girls sharing one giant sundae. "I wouldn't exactly call them ladies, Nathan. More like children. But all the more reason to be appropriate."

"They were looking at you," Nathan said sullenly. "They always look at you, never me."

David rolled his eyes. "I'm not doing this with you again. There is so much you could do to get a girlfriend and you refuse to do it. Step one—get a job. Also, all of those girls are way too young for you."

"Don't you see? I want to meet a woman who likes me the way I am, not some perfected version of me. I don't want to have to lose weight to meet a girl. I don't want to have to make money. Why can't someone love me the way Emily loves you?"

"Emily probably wouldn't have been attracted to me in the first place if I still lived with my parents and never stepped foot outside the house."

Nathan stared up at the ceiling, trying to think of something profound to say. "Then her love shan't be pure."

David snorted. "Oh, come the fuck on."

"Language!"

"I'm sorry. But think about it—what would Mom say? Mom loved us unconditionally, but she wasn't afraid to tell us where we were fu—messing up. Do you think Mom would want you to be freeloading off Dad and Susan?"

"Such a comment is irrelevant," Nathan said. "Mom is dead, and there is no afterlife. Thus, you are an idiot."

"Come on, man, I'm trying to help you. Regardless of where Mom is or isn't, she was a person you respected, right? And her philosophy wasn't about being complacent and bitching and moaning. She would want you to better yourself!"

"And eat disgusting smoothies when I could eat ice cream?" Nathan asked incredulously, pointing to David's unsatisfying, pale mixture. "No thank you."

David furrowed his brow and lowered his voice. "Don't you realize that if Mom had eaten like this, she might be alive today? Breast cancer now happens to one in eight women, and that's not even getting into the heart problems and cancers that affect men. Are you really going to give me shit for trying not to die young?"

Nathan looked into his ice cream. "Of course you want to live a long life. Your life is one worth living."

"Finally, I get to see David's game!" Mark shouted. They were playing basketball at a playground near the Glasses' house. "Look at you, Draymond Green, back at it again with the flagrant foul."

"Whoa, David," Kevin said. "Take it easy."

"I like it!" Mark said. "Connecticut ballin'. Bring it on!"

David dribbled to the top of the key, pulling out Kevin to guard him. He took a hard dribble to the right, bullying past Kevin, accelerating to the hoop at top speed. He leaped with all his might, cocking the ball back, only to feel the rim rejecting him at the point of contact. The adrenaline surged through his veins, and for a split second he felt like he was flying. Then he fell backward, his body parallel to the ground, and then—*crack*.

It all happened so fast—one minute he was looking at the rim and the clear blue sky, and the next minute all he could see was the ground and Mark's and Kevin's dirty sneakers. He breathed in the all-too-familiar stench of rubber and tarmac. It hurt more than anything he had ever experienced, an excruciating pain right in his ass.

"Are you okay, man?" Kevin asked, coming over. He reached to help him up, but David tried to get up on his own. It was no use—the pain was agonizing. He lay back down.

"Oh, fuck. It hurts like hell."

Mark bent down over him. "You landed on your tailbone. Let me see…"

David recoiled as Mark touched his butt.

"Dude, I'm a doctor. I need to examine your tailbone."

In a gesture more humiliating than David would have preferred, he rolled over to one side while Mark rubbed his butt crack carefully, making sure to apply pressure to his tailbone. David shrieked in pain. The only thing that would have made the situation worse would have been Kevin laughing. Luckily, Kevin managed to keep a straight face, but David knew it was a struggle.

"Stop touching my ass!" he cried out to Mark, who had begun stroking his backside too lovingly for his taste.

"We've got to get you to the hospital. This looks like a bruised coccyx."

"Bruised what?"

"That's the medical term for tailbone."

"You could have just said *tailbone*."

Emily

Sitting on the couch in Marla's office, Emily kept imagining the baby inside her. There were so many things to worry about, she could barely focus on one at a time. All morning she had thought about the various ways in which David could divorce her and leave town once he found out she was pregnant. How would she date as a single mom? Already she feared her premature worry lines would make her completely undesirable if she wound up single, and she could only imagine how brutal it would be if she also had saggy boobs, loose skin around her bellybutton and a baby.

Even if David did stay with her, and even if the pregnancy completely overjoyed him, so much could go wrong. There was the drinking, the birth control pills, the soft cheese and half a sushi boat that she ate in June when they were celebrating their impending wedding. If her baby had any chance at survival, it might still be born with three eyes, or no eyes at all. How would she deal with a baby with no eyes? And fuck, it wasn't just the eyes that could go wrong.

She took a deep breath in but it was no use. What if the baby was a jerk? Not just a petulant toddler for a few years, but a full-blown asshole, and nothing she or David did would change things? Jason was ample evidence that her family carried the asshole gene. What if her baby grew up to be a serial killer or a guy who wore Ed Hardy tank tops with John Deere trucker hats?

"You seem distracted, Emily," Marla said.

"I'm just a little nauseous. It's nerves."

"I was quite nervous before my wedding too. I didn't throw up, but given your anxiety, it's hardly shocking. You're not freaking out about diseases, are you? Don't go to Dr. WebMD. I don't think anyone here wants a repeat of the porphyria disaster."

"That's the thing that makes you have purple shits and turns you into a vampire, right?" Jason asked.

"Yeah, and it can strike anyone, for the record," Emily said. "It's not even that rare. But anyway, no, I wasn't worrying about diseases. I'm just not feeling well. And it's just WebMD. Not Dr. WebMD."

"Jason, you don't look so good," Marla said. "Are you coming down with something?"

"I was out last night, Mom. Hung out with David's weird brother, something nobody else is willing to do. That's right, I'm a good person." He crossed his arms and gave everyone a satisfied nod.

"You two probably went out to pick up random girls," Emily said. "Don't act like you were there on a charity mission."

"We didn't go out to pick up girls, actually, but so what if we did? I'm not even dating anyone."

"Yeah, but it wouldn't matter to you if you were," Lauren said. "I'm all for polyamory but that's when all parties are on board. As long as we're doing this therapy, you need to at least come to terms with why you always cheat on women."

"None of you understand what it's like. You're all women. Imagine that you only got to eat mashed potatoes for the rest of your life, no salt and no butter. And all around you there are burritos and ice cream sundaes and roast chickens. Eventually you're going to slip up."

"Then why don't all men do what you do?" Marla asked. "Why has your father been faithful to me?"

"Because he doesn't have the options. I don't want to be disrespectful because obviously I love Dad, but he's a total fucking beta."

"I don't know how anyone expects me to trust men when this is the kind of stuff I have to listen to," Emily said, her head collapsing into her hands.

"Interesting," Lauren said. "You have a hard time trusting people. So this means that other people should trust you, right? That you're always honest about everything?"

"Oh, just stop it. You know I'm not feeling well today, hassle Jason or Mom about something instead."

"I'm just saying that people who lie, even by omission, aren't to be trusted, so if you're going to distrust other people, maybe you should look at your own behavior?"

"What are you talking about?" Marla asked. "Did Emily lie to you about something?"

"While we're on this," Jason said, "Lauren, when are you going to be honest with Matt about not really being attracted to him?"

"Classic projection," Lauren said.

"What, I'm saying you're not attracted to Matt because, in reality, I'm not attracted to Matt? That's true, I guess."

"Mom, he's being ridiculous, get him to stop."

"This is a safe space," Marla said. "You may not like what he's saying, but I can't tell him what he can and can't say. Personally, I think honesty is a very good topic for today. Especially since you've probably all lied to me more than anyone else you've lied to."

"Mom, what have I ever lied to you about?" Jason asked.

"That job at IBM you supposedly got before even graduating. That one was so obviously ridiculous, I don't know why I fell for it."

"I only told you that because I lied to Christina about it, and you called me while I was hanging out with her."

"Ah," Lauren said. "Kill two birds with one lie."

"Don't be so quick to criticize, Lauren," Marla said. "I still remember a certain someone denying that she was related to Arthur Berger during her Communism phase. You'll take the money, no problem, but you don't want to be associated with it."

"That was in college, Mom. And I didn't claim not to be related to him, I just never mentioned it. I don't have to announce to everyone I'm related to the Berger's Relish guy."

"I thought lies of omission were just as bad," Emily said.

"Mine didn't hurt anyone."

"It hurt me," Marla said. "It was hard enough for me to grow up in that strange world of money and privilege. How do you think it feels to suffer through that, only to have your own children deny it?"

"How on earth is it hard to grow up with money?" Lauren asked.

"This is the reason I'm careful not to give you kids too much. My father's money was like a prison. I was never free to be...motivated the way other kids were. If I hadn't been getting an allowance from my father, maybe I would have gotten my medical degree. I could have accomplished so much more if he hadn't coddled me."

"Well, Mom," Jason said. "If you don't care about money, why aren't you speaking to Aunt Lisa?"

Marla stiffened. "That was not about money. That was about your grandfather writing his will in such a confusing way that it was bound to create conflict."

"His will was pretty clear," he said. "Half to Grandma, one-quarter to you and one-quarter to Aunt Lisa." He karate chopped the air in front of him to illustrate the fractions.

"Yes, but Aunt Lisa doesn't have kids, and she lives in Brookline. Her cost of living is significantly lower than mine, and she didn't have the decency to split up the estate fairly between us. What does a childless woman need millions of dollars for? New shoes? Besides, your grandfather left Aunt Lisa the grand piano because she enjoyed playing it, but that was twenty thousand dollars in her pocket instead of mine. I never got a grand piano. I didn't even get a painting! Aunt Lisa got two Chagalls."

"Hey, Glass kids!"

Outside Marla's office, the three Glass siblings saw an older man pouring himself a cup of coffee in the waiting room. It had been more than ten years since Emily last saw Dr. Abe Leibowitz. He had been attractive when she was in high school in that "older man" way—barrel chest, tortoiseshell glasses, tweed jacket and a full, well-groomed brown beard. Now in his midsixties, he had gray hair and a paunch, but he still held himself with as much confidence as he always did, like a Jewish Sean Connery.

"Emily!" he said, hugging her. "You look exactly the

same." Emily didn't know whether to be flattered because it meant she hadn't aged since she was a teenager, or insulted because the last time he saw her she was gawky and pimply.

"Hey, Dr. Leibowitz," Jason said. "Any chance of a refill on that Adderall prescription?"

Leibowitz laughed. "I don't think I can ethically refill a prescription that is over twenty years old."

"I'm just messing with you, man. How are you?"

"Outstanding. Just returned from Machu Picchu. I nearly passed out from the high elevation and a sherpa had to revive me with indigenous herbs. You really haven't lived until you've traveled outside of your safe zone."

"Everywhere is outside of my safe zone," Emily said.

"I always liked your sense of humor, Emily. Where are you going on your honeymoon?"

"Probably Cabo, but not right away. I need to accrue more PTO."

"Got it. Well, I am looking forward to meeting the lucky groom on Saturday."

It took a moment for this to sink in. It would be awkward having the man who used to prescribe her Zoloft at her wedding, but apparently that had not stopped Marla from inviting him. She tried to hide her surprise. "Um, you're coming?"

"Wouldn't miss it for the world."

Later at home, Emily lay on her bed, attempting the deep breathing exercises she learned two therapists ago. She could hear Ariel and Mia playing in their makeshift nursery down the hall. As guilty as it made her feel, she couldn't stand their high-pitched squeals. How on earth could she be a good mother when the sound of children playing made her want to rip her hair out? She closed her eyes tightly and tried to ignore them.

Why had her mother invited Dr. Leibowitz? It had been years since she'd last seen him, and the only times her mother dealt with him was when she needed him to write prescriptions for her patients. Combined with Judy Stein, who knew who else Marla invited? Perhaps the guy who fixed the roof last year would lead the wedding party down the aisle.

She looked to her nightstand and saw the pink velvet notebook that she originally got for vow writing. She couldn't think of anything that wasn't horribly generic. She would have to come up with something soon, but everything she considered seemed wrong. She couldn't talk about honesty when there was a secret fetus between them, and she couldn't say anything about "forever" because that would be presumptuous, and possibly a jinx. One time in seventh grade she wrote in her diary that she felt she was starting to become popular. Later that day, the popular girls she thought were hanging out with her because they liked her poured a bottle of Fruitopia on her head in the cafeteria. Never again.

She heard the front door open, and the sound of someone groaning. Downstairs she found David in the front hall, supported by Kevin and Mark. He looked pale and drained and had an inflatable doughnut-shaped pillow hanging from his neck by a string.

"Oh my God, what happened?"

"He injured his coccyx," Mark said like a doctor on television. "He's on three hundred milligrams of Vicodin. He's going to be fine."

"He injured his what?"

"Tailbone," David said weakly.

"What's the giant doughnut for?"

"It's a butt doughnut. He has to sit on it. His coccyx needs to heal and he can't put pressure on it."

"Are you—how did this happen?"

"Basketball," David said.

"Your fiancé here got a little aggressive and landed on his ass," Kevin said. "It happens to the best of us, man."

"Shut up," David snapped.

"Aw, sweetheart." Emily hugged him, trying to ignore the inflatable doughnut between them. She moved it to one side and he grunted. She helped him to the family room. He positioned the doughnut on the couch and sat on it.

"I've ruined the wedding." His words were slurred and his head bobbed to one side. "I love you." He closed his eyes and dozed off.

She looked at him. He was in pain and on drugs, sitting on an inflatable doughnut. There would have to be a time better than this to tell him he was about to become a father.

NIGHT 4

Emily

"STOP THAT," DAVID GRUNTED.

"Stop what? I'm not doing anything." She lay next to him in bed, wearing loose white pajama shorts and a tank top. It was so hot that she would have preferred to be naked, but she didn't want to risk running into Matt in the shared bathroom.

"You're putting too much weight on your side of the bed and it's hurting my tailbone. I can't be on an angle."

"Too much weight? Really?"

"I'm not calling you fat, if that's what you're insinuating. You're just moving around too much. I need to be completely still, and I can't have any friction on my tailbone."

She lay on her back and crossed her arms like a mummy. There was no way she would be able to fall asleep like this. Already he had nixed the idea of actually sleeping underneath the covers because apparently he needed all the sheets and blankets under him to cushion his tailbone as well as a pillow under his butt and two under his head. She had gladly sacrificed her pillow to make him comfortable, but his grumbling hadn't stopped.

"You know, you could just let me take more Vicodin," he said.

"I texted Mark and he told me you can take more tomorrow. You've had enough today, and people overdose on it by accident all the time. The last thing I need is for you to die on our wedding week. It's like a story right out of the *Daily Mail*."

"Fine. Well, if you're not going to let me take it, then don't roll around in bed."

"What about putting the doughnut underneath you?"

"It doesn't work so well when I'm lying down. It keeps sliding around."

"What if I…" She started sitting up. He winced as the weight on the bed shifted. "…made this…very special for you?" She began to trace her fingers along his inner thighs. "Nature's Vicodin."

"Unless you're offering me actual Vicodin, stop. I don't want a blow job."

"Get out. You've never turned me down before."

"Well, I didn't have a bruised ass before."

Emily's heart raced. She thought about all the articles she had read that cited "less sex" as the first sign of a failing relationship. What man turned down a blow job? Obviously one who was no longer in love. Or perhaps not even attracted! She grabbed his hand and squeezed. "Please tell me this isn't your way of getting out of the wedding. Oh my gosh, I should have seen this coming. If you're having second thoughts, just tell me."

David rolled his eyes. "I'm not having second thoughts. I'm just in a lot of pain. Stop making everything about you."

She wondered for a moment if he had not actually injured his tailbone. The only people who had corroborated his story were Mark and Kevin—his two best friends, who would gladly help him invent a ridiculous fiction to get out of something. Maybe it went beyond second thoughts. It was a full-on runaway groom ruse.

"I'm going to ask you something that may sound silly," she said. "Just bear with me."

"Seriously, not now."

"I can't even *ask* you something?"

"Usually I'm happy to reassure you and comfort you, but right now, I'm the one who needs to be comforted. I need to know that you can go thirty seconds without worrying about something because you're not making me feel any better."

"I tried comforting you and you got annoyed because I was moving too much!"

"I just need quiet right now. Don't take it personally."

"Would you feel better if I left you alone for a while?"

"Yeah, that would actually help. I just need to be able to fall asleep. Thanks, babe."

She hadn't anticipated him actually accepting her offer to leave him alone. Now she was stuck: she couldn't sleep in bed with him where she actually wanted to be, and she knew she wouldn't be able to fall asleep anywhere else. She heard the television buzzing from downstairs. She got out of bed and walked downstairs. She just prayed that whatever was on television wasn't an episode of *Two and a Half Men*.

Lauren

"How late are you going to be working?" Lauren had her *Cunt Magazine* blog open while Matt lay beside her in bed.

"I don't know. Late."

"I'm probably going to sleep pretty soon."

"Just let me just finish this post, and then I'll go to bed."

He perched his bony chin on her shoulder to read her blog. She shrugged him off. "That hurts."

"Yikes, sorry."

Lauren typed furiously, trying not to think about the fact that he was looking at every letter on her screen. His face wasn't pressed against her anymore, but she could still feel his limp yet overbearing presence behind her.

"How about we cuddle after you're done?" he asked.

She flinched. "Could you please? I'm trying to work."

"Fine, I just thought it would be nice to cuddle."

"We'll cuddle later. This article is really important."

"What's it about?"

"Misogyny in *SpongeBob Squarepants.*"

"Huh," he said, scratching his chin. "You mean the show about the yellow sponge with the annoying laugh?"

"Yes, the one I won't let Ariel watch."

"Oh, sorry, I didn't know you had a problem with it. I've let him watch it before."

"Every *time* with you, Matt," she sighed. "Anyway, if you must know, this article is going to examine how *SpongeBob Squarepants* features no good female role models for girls and nonbinary femme children, while it contributes to problematic stereotypes. Sandy the squirrel? Classism. Pearl the whale? Fatphobia, that one is obvious. Mrs. Puff? More fatphobia, plus she's a woman who teaches at a driving school and constantly gets into car accidents. There's the episode where Mr. Krabs practically offers her money for sex. And there are no characters of color, by the way."

"Aren't they just fish? Can they be of any race?"

"Okay, maybe I won't write that part, but the rest stands."

"Plus SpongeBob is yellow."

"Could you please?"

"I don't understand why you're so upset about it, is all. It's just a cartoon show."

"Everything is just something else. Marital rape used to be *just* sex."

"Sweetheart, you can't compare marital rape to *SpongeBob*."

"Oh, I don't have your permission? You're *telling* me what I can compare *SpongeBob* to? I'm on my last nerve, Matt, seriously." She was somehow yelling and whispering at the same time.

"Sorry. I'll leave you alone." He headed for the nursery. Moments later, Lauren heard Ariel squealing, Mia growling and Matt imitating a dinosaur.

She heard her phone's cat-meow ringtone. It was Kayla, the cofounder of *Cunt*.

"Hey," she said when Lauren answered. "How's the wedding week going?"

"My sister is a needy mess, my brother is a raving misogynist, my mother is a fatphobic piece of shit and weddings are obsolete structures of white colonization. But what else is new?" She waited for the inevitable laugh or some validation of her cutting wit, but Kayla's tone was cold.

"I was actually calling you about your blog."

"Sorry I'm late with the *SpongeBob* post. I'm totally ripping apart that show." Lauren fondly remembered the late nights in Kayla's Bushwick apartment when they were in their midtwenties, smoking pot and drinking cheap wine, coming up with the brilliant ideas that started *Cunt Magazine*, like their debut post "My Clitoris Is Better Than Your Penis, George Bush."

"You may want to put that on pause. We need to talk about that hashtag you created a couple weeks back."

"Which one?"

"#freeyourvaginasgirls."

"What about it?"

"Well, it looks like we've found ourselves in a bit of a PR debacle. A bunch of hebephile rights' activists have co-opted the hashtag to get thirteen-year-old girls to post vagina shots on Twitter. And now we're being blamed for it."

"Hebephiles?"

"They're pedophiles who prefer preteens and teenagers to children. They've been doing a lot of their so-called activism on Twitter, and now they're using your hashtag."

"Fuck that. Anyone in their right mind would know that I meant #freeyourvaginasgirls as a protest against feminine hygiene products that shame women for their natural aromas."

"I know what your intention was. But to make matters worse, there's a well-known transgender blogger who isn't particularly happy with your use of the word *feminine* hygiene or your association of vaginas with girls. You know better than anyone that not all women have vaginas, and not all vaginas belong to women."

"Kayla, are you mad at me?"

Kayla paused. "Mad? No, I'm—well, if anything, I'm a little disappointed. I mean, coming from you. Where is the nonbinary and trans representation?"

"I'm sorry, but... I wrote that article from the heart. It represented something that I've struggled with my entire life— being ostracized for how my vulva tastes, smells, looks..."

"Oh, please don't say *vulva*—it grosses me out."

"What I'm saying is that girls...or *anyone* who has a vagina... should free themselves from these oppressive and unsafe products. I mean, come on, you were the one who performed 'My Vagina Tastes Like Indignity, Bill Clinton' at the Vassar spoken word contest."

"Oh shit. Don't remind me."

"Remind you of what? The best damn poem you've ever written?"

"I think we're getting off track here. I know you want *Cunt* to change the world, and that's great, but in the meantime we need to make sure we stay afloat. I know you didn't mean to offend transgender people, but that's what's happening, and now we have to deal with the hebephiles. And this is happening only weeks after, well, you know—"

"Oh, that's completely unfair to—"

"It's pertinent, Lauren. It was another hashtag."

"I know it pissed people off, but I still don't see what was wrong with the hashtag #killwhitey."

Kayla sighed. "As a white person, it's cultural appropriation for you to try to kill whitey, even just in word form. That's not your struggle."

"Well, what am I supposed to do about the *SpongeBob* article?"

"Look. You know I love your writing. You're a rock star. But I'm going to have to put you on leave. I have to think about *Cunt*."

Emily

"This Janice chick is so fucking hot," Jason said. "Just look at her."

He and Emily were sitting at the kitchen counter, watching Home Shopping Network on the mini TV. Jason had a bottle of red wine open and was refilling his glass. On TV a middle-aged blonde woman was modeling a rainbow-colored poncho. "I'd really like to rip that cape thing right off her and—"

Emily turned off the TV.

"Hey!" he said. "What did you do that for?"

"It seemed like the right thing to do."

Lauren came in and plopped down on a stool. "I seriously need a drink."

"You got it." Jason pulled down a wineglass from the cabinet and filled it. Lauren knocked it back. "Damn, this is good. Where did you get it?"

"I found it in the back of Mom and Dad's liquor cabinet. They've been holding out on us. Want some, Em?"

"Oh, no thanks." She instinctively put her hand over her belly, then slipped it away behind her back. Hopefully Jason was too drunk to notice.

"Why not?"

"I'm on a diet."

"You were drinking two days ago. Now you're on a diet?" He pointed at her with his glass.

"I gained weight since then."

"Since two days ago?"

"Yeah."

He turned to Lauren. "No eating disorder comments from you? That's weird."

"I'm tired." She shrugged.

Jason refilled Lauren's wine. "What's wrong?"

"I'm in trouble with *Cunt*."

"Story of my life," he said, a giddy glint in his eye. She didn't look amused. "In all seriousness, what could you have possibly done? As much as I find you annoying as shit sometimes, I can at least credit you with being the least racist, most feminist person I know."

Lauren exhaled deeply and took a sip of wine. "Basically, Kayla doesn't care if we change the world. She just wants to make sure we stay in business. Who cares about business? Who cares about reputation? I shouldn't have to apologize for something just because other people took it the wrong way."

"Didn't you force your professor at Vassar to publicly apologize for his use of the word *overweight*?" Emily asked.

"Yes, because the correct term is *people of size* if said by someone who isn't a person of size themselves. I can say *fat* because I am fat. This particular professor was thin, so he had to use the correct term."

"I don't see why it mattered since he was just describing Henry VIII," Emily said.

Jason turned to Emily. "Why are you in such a shitty mood?"

"I know you guys are both going to laugh at me for this, but I can't help feeling like David's faking a bruised tailbone to shut down the wedding."

"Has he said anything to make you believe that?" Lauren asked.

"No, but… I don't know, it's just the kind of thing that would happen to me."

"Nothing like that ever happens to you."

Steven and Marla came in, back from their dinner and late-night movie date. Steven was wearing pressed khakis and a powder-blue Oxford shirt. Marla was swathed in an elaborate arrangement of paisley scarves and beaded necklaces that obscured whatever outfit she was wearing underneath.

"Hello, hello," she said, ever-so-slightly tipsy.

"We just went to a new Malaysian restaurant, which was about as Malaysian as I am," Steven said, shaking his head. "What a joke. And as for the movie, I maintain that nothing decent has been made in this country past 1977. Have you ever heard of this woman, Melissa McCarthy? Why is she famous?"

"Join the party," Jason said, raising the bottle.

"What are you drinking?" Marla said.

"Some wine I found. Hope you don't mind."

She examined the bottle, then threw back her head in horror. "Oh my *God*!"

"What's wrong?"

"This is the Château Lafite Rothschild!"

"Look, Mom, I'll buy you another bottle if it's a big deal."

"You could never afford this, Jason. It was a gift from my father for our twentieth wedding anniversary."

"I wonder what wine Aunt Lisa got," Jason snickered.

"Aunt Lisa and Uncle Larry never made it to twenty years because she's a clinical narcissist." Marla put her hands on her hips.

"I was fucking with you, Mom."

"You really need to cut down your drinking, Jason," Steven said, releasing his wallet and multiple key rings from his baggy pants pockets, then placing them in a dish on the counter. "You've been drunk every single night since you arrived. Do you think WalkShare is ever going to get off the ground if the founder is drinking nonstop?"

"That's not why it isn't getting off the ground," Emily said.

"All the greatest start-up founders drink during the workday," Jason said. "If I want to have a drink when I'm not even working, I don't see why you should care."

"That's easy for you to say, Jason," Steven said. "You're never working!"

"I can't believe you would fucking go there, Dad. Just because I didn't wind up becoming a lawyer or a doctor or whatever other bullshit career path you would have preferred doesn't mean I don't work. I'm sure everyone said the same thing about Bill Gates."

"At least Bill Gates got into Harvard," Marla said, mostly to Steven.

"The only reason anyone goes to Harvard is to be able to

tell people they went to Harvard," Jason said. "Exhibit A—Mom."

"All right, that's enough," Marla said.

"I can't believe you're getting so pissed off about a bottle of wine." Jason got up as if he were going to storm out, but instead lingered by the door leading to the stairs.

"The wine is not the issue. The issue is the three of you." Marla pointed at each of the three siblings. "Your constant lack of gratitude and pervasive sense of entitlement. Before you opened that bottle, at the very least you could have asked me if it was okay."

"You're right, Mom," Emily said, her voice rising in anger. "You should always ask someone first before doing something that affects them. Like maybe you could have asked me before you invited my childhood psychiatrist to my wedding."

"What?" Marla said, taken aback. "What are you talking about?"

"Why did you invite him, Mom?"

"That—that has nothing to do with this."

Steven abruptly turned to Marla. "You fucking invited him?"

"We can talk about this later."

"Seriously, Mom," Emily said. "Why would you do that? I haven't seen the guy in years, first of all, and second of all, he knows some extremely personal things that I told him when I was in therapy with him."

Marla waved her hand around. "Oh, come on, I don't think Dr. Leibowitz is going to go around at your wedding telling everyone about how you used to only be able to climax if you rubbed yourself through your clothes and thought about Jimmy from *Degrassi*."

"Mom, what the fuck? How did *you* know that?" Her stomach flipped and she thought she might throw up again.

What else had Dr. Leibowitz told Marla? It had all been so long ago. By the time she was in high school, she had developed more discretion about her masturbatory habits, but there were all the times she had said things along the lines of "I hate my parents" in fits of teenage rage. How much of this did he dutifully disclose to his BFF Marla?

Marla paused. "You told me that, sweetheart."

"I really didn't."

Steven was still glaring at Marla. "Why would you invite him?"

"He's a friend." Her voice went high at the end of her sentence.

"He's *your* friend. Not mine."

"When will you just let that go, Steven?"

"Why the hell should I?"

"Because it happened years ago!"

The room was silent. Marla felt the eyes of all three kids on her.

"This is idiotic," she said. "I'm going to bed."

Steven did not follow her. He headed for the front door. The wine in the glasses shook as the door slammed.

DAY 5

David

EMILY HAD INSISTED that David not take any more Vicodin until she got back from her dress fitting, but once she was gone and the coast was clear he took one anyway. It wasn't too hard to find the bottle. He had seen her hide it inside her old American Girl prairie wagon while he pretended to be asleep. He would have felt guilty about this betrayal if Emily's fears of an overdose were justified. He hadn't taken enough to do that—just enough to stumble around the bedroom for a while trying to find his pants.

The kitchen was empty. Starving, he opened the fridge. When he had first arrived at the house, there had been nothing substantial in there, but at some point over the past week, Emily's parents appeared to have filled it to the gills with gourmet food from the hot section of Whole Foods. His mouth watered at a half-eaten container of buffalo chicken salad. It would be high in protein, but unfortunately the mayo in it was most likely made from canola oil or soybean oil, both strictly forbidden by LifeSpin. He considered this quandary. It was only chicken salad. What percentage of it was mayo—two? Five at the most? There were much worse

things he could eat. He would need the protein for his recovery anyway, and the mayo was merely collateral damage.

He took the container out of the fridge and used his bare hand
to scoop chicken salad into his mouth. *This is fucking amazing.* So
salty, so creamy, so tangy—he would have to find out how to
recreate this at home. With the correct oils, of course—avocado,
coconut and olive were the only truly nontoxic ones. He shov-
eled more and more of it into his mouth until it was all gone.

He was still starving. He was too hungry to ask himself if
it was rude to raid his future in-laws' fridge. He felt his phone
vibrate, but he didn't pick up. He was too focused on a container of shrimp scampi. It was untouched, pristine. Perhaps if
he ate the entire thing, Marla would forget she ever bought it.
And there was pasta in it, but so what? He had already eaten
the mayo. Maybe he was due for a cheat day.

He scarfed down the shrimp scampi and burped a long,
decadent burp that tasted like roasted garlic. Now he needed
something sweet. For the past two years, he hadn't eaten
any desserts other than one extremely disappointing coconut milk–based gelato. He went to the pantry. One piece of
candy would do, if they had any.

In their pantry, Marla and Steven had stocked at least
twenty boxes of Pop-Tarts of varying flavors, none of which
seemed to be expired. Was this a treat intended for their visiting kids, who presumably liked Pop-Tarts when they were
little? Or was this Steven's plebeian guilty pleasure, which
he ate while allowing himself one episode of *Hardcore Pawn*?
David had no idea, and it wasn't long before his mind was
flooded with his own Pop-Tarts–based childhood memories.
His mother used to buy them in bulk, and yet he and Nathan would always argue over which one of them was eating
an unfair amount.

Wildberry was always David's favorite, and there it was,

with an expiration date still two years away. He tore open the package. Fuck LifeSpin.

As he stared trancelike into the glowing slots of the toaster, he heard footsteps. He quickly tossed the empty food containers into the trash before Jason appeared. He was freshly showered and wearing a T-shirt that said Me Love You Long Time next to a cartoon geisha. "Morning," he said. "How's your ass?"

"Hurts. What the fuck is your shirt?"

Jason looked down. "Funny, huh?"

"Did you buy it in the fifties?"

"That's a lot for a T-shirt. It was just twenty-five bucks, actually."

David was too tired to say anything else. For a moment, he felt fleeting respect for Lauren. How did she maintain the energy to call Jason out when he did something offensive every five seconds?

Jason opened the fridge and surveyed its contents. "Huh. I thought there was some shrimp scampi in here."

"Maybe Matt ate it."

"Where is everyone?"

"The fit. Getting fit." The Vicodin had kicked in and was making him foggy.

"Huh?"

"Fitting." David burped.

"You mean the dress fitting? Avec les bridesmaids?" He mixed up French and Italian stereotypes and began wiggling his hands around with his fingers pinched together like Tony Soprano.

"I think."

"Then I'll be on my way." He closed the fridge, grabbed his car keys, and was out the door. David retrieved the Pop-Tarts from the toaster and started lustily eating one. His phone buzzed again. He took it out and squinted at the screen. It wasn't Emily calling—it was Zach.

"Hey, Zach, what's up?" David held the phone with his greasy Pop-Tart fingers.

"Thank fucking goodness I was able to get ahold of you. This is nuts."

"What happened?"

Zach sighed. "Well, for one, we both officially don't have jobs anymore."

David felt his legs go weak. He dropped to the floor and sat in front of the fridge, his brain still not entirely sure how to make sense of what he just heard. "What? How is that possible with the funding from BluCapital?"

This was a joke. Robert must be hiding behind Zach's desk as Zach muffled the receiver so they could giggle together. For sure, that was what was happening.

"It's worse," Zach said.

"Worse than Zoogli going under? How is that possible?" His hands had started trembling involuntarily and his stomach felt like it was about to expel all the contents of his binge onto the floor.

"Robert took off with the BluCapital money. Deposited it to his personal account in the Cayman Islands, and he's left the country. The SEC is investigating."

His mind immediately went to Robert, surfing in an ocean of money. "What the hell am I going to do now?"

"I don't know, man, I'm worried about myself too! I may have to move back in with my parents."

David took a small moment to revel in the fact that "rock star" Zach, at twenty-nine, might have to move back home. At least Emily's job at ClearDrop could buy them a few months while David looked for another position.

Then his vision went slightly blurry as it dawned on him that all the glory and comfort he had imagined he and Emily would soon step into was gone. There would be no house, no new car, no retiring young. They might need to move out of their already-overpriced one bedroom and start subletting a spare bedroom in the Tenderloin. Maybe they'd even have to move to Idaho or something, and all of his old friends from high school would laugh about how he effectively flunked out of San Francisco. And Zach was no longer his competition. They were just two sad men on the phone with nowhere to go and nothing to do.

"Are you still there, man?"

"Yeah. I've got to go. Thanks for telling me, Zach. Good luck." He hung up and reached for another Pop-Tart. Fuck it.

Kevin

Kevin had texted with Jennifer all night, finally jerking off to one of her bikini photos she tweeted from 2012. He wasn't as interested in porn as some other men were. He vastly preferred women he knew wanted to sleep with him. He woke up the next morning fully recharged and went to the hotel gym for a quick cardio session. On his way from the gym back to his room, he heard a man arguing with the woman at the front desk. It took Kevin a moment to recognize him. It was Emily's dad.

"All I'm saying," Steven said, "is that just because I *touch* one of the bottles in the minibar doesn't mean I should be charged for it. I had a change of heart and I didn't drink anything, so why am I being charged thirty dollars?" This was the loudest Kevin had ever seen him talk. Normally, he was so quiet it was hard to hear him at all.

The young woman behind the front desk tried to keep her composure. She spoke calmly and politely. "The sensors charge you every time you touch a bottle, which means you shouldn't pick up anything you don't plan to drink. Our records show that you touched bottles of Bombay Sapphire, Jack Daniel's and Grey Goose."

"Yes, but I didn't drink them. This is Kafkaesque!"

"This is just our hotel policy. Can I ask why you picked up all of those bottles and drank none of them?"

"Why does it matter why I picked them up? This isn't psychoanalysis." Steven turned away from the front desk in a huff and found himself face-to-face with Kevin.

"Dr. Glass?"

"Yes?" It was clear from Steven's blank expression that he didn't recognize him.

"Kevin. David's best man."

"Oh! Yes, of course."

"So, um, you're staying here?"

"Ah. Yes. Well, you know, with the full house and everything, it seemed like a good idea."

"Okay. Well, see you at the rehearsal dinner?"

"Yes."

Once Steven was out of sight, Kevin took his phone out and texted Jennifer: Guess who I just saw at the Ritz? You can't tell anyone.

Emily

"It's not that I think Joyce's daughter is stupid," Marla said. "She just isn't as smart as my kids, and if *they* didn't get into Yale, I don't think she has a chance in hell."

Emily and Lauren arrived at the fitting to find Marla deep in conversation with Diana, the sixtyish owner of the wedding dress boutique. Gabrielle, Jennifer and Maddyson were waiting on the blush velvet love seats, staring at their phones.

"Hello, Emily!" Diana said, turning around. "And… Lauren? It's been forever!"

"Yes, it has," Marla said. "I'm just going to get this out of the way to avoid any awkwardness because I know you're too polite to say anything—I apologize ahead of time for—"

"Mom, it's fine," Emily said. "Diana isn't offended." Perhaps she should have let her finish. There was a hell of a lot for which Marla needed to apologize.

"I'm not offended by what?" Diana asked.

Marla struggled to get all the words out. "I just think it's a bit…millennial…for Emily to have bought a dress from some megastore in San Francisco instead of your boutique. But I suppose I can't blame her for that."

"Millennials actually avoid brand names and big chains," Maddyson said. "That's a Gen X thing."

"Why would I mind that?" Diana said. "Emily lives in San Francisco. Of course she would prefer to buy a dress from someplace close to her. If she bought a dress from my shop, she'd be flying back and forth across the country just for dress fittings! Either that, or FedExing a two-thousand-dollar dress across the country!"

Diana said these things as if they were clearly ridiculous options, unaware that Marla had once suggested both of them to Emily in earnest. Diana turned to Emily. "I hope you don't mind me embarrassing you for a moment, but you have really turned into a beautiful woman. I can't wait to see this dress on you."

Although a small part of Emily worried that this was a subtle reference to her looking old—nobody called anyone a woman anymore, you were a girl until you were fifty—she was mostly thrilled that anyone could find her beautiful that morning. She hadn't slept well, and her eyes looked sunken and purple.

She had seen Diana a few times during her childhood when she went with Marla to her shop. Diana would tailor Marla's dresses at a discount, in exchange for Marla listening to the depressing details of Diana's marriage. "You're not really her friend," a nine-year-old Emily had said to Marla on one drive home. "You just use her to get discounts." Marla had responded, "All friendships require give-and-take, Emily.

Besides, she's basically getting free therapy, and trust me, if there were more people doing what I do with Diana, the world would be a mentally healthier place."

"By the way, Emily," Marla said, procuring a tissue from her bag and blowing her nose. "I want you to know that I am missing Aunt Ellen's funeral. I knew you needed me here, so, once again, I put your needs above my own." She sighed dramatically.

"I thought you said it was just a shindig at cousin Hannah's house," Emily said. She then wondered why that was the detail about which she chose to argue.

Marla crumpled up the tissue and tossed it into a fancy garbage can in the corner that looked like a hatbox. "Funeral, celebration of life, whatever you want to call it. The point is, I'm missing it because of you. I just want you to think about that for a second. I'm not saying I need you to apologize, just think about it."

"The alternative would be missing my wedding, or at least missing the rehearsal dinner, to attend the funeral of a woman who you purposely didn't invite to the wedding." Emily considered that Marla was actually only staying because of her argument with Steven, but she didn't say anything about that.

Marla sighed. "Well, Emily, that's an entirely different topic. I wanted to invite Aunt Ellen, but if I invited her, I'd be very concerned about her taking advantage of the open bar, plus, suddenly Hannah would start to wonder why *she* wasn't invited and I refuse to have Hannah anywhere near children. She has some very problematic issues around her sexuality. Way too obsessed with horses as a girl. It was creepy."

"Okay, Mom." Her mind went to her art show, her senior year of high school. Marla had every intention of coming, but routinely threatened that she might "have to miss it" because her friend Karen's fifty-fourth birthday party was that night. Apparently Karen's husband recently left her for the family veterinarian, and it meant a lot to her that all her friends be there for her first birthday as a divorcee. When Emily insisted that her art show should come first, Marla cocked her head and said, "You're a profoundly gifted artist, I'm sure you'll have more opportunities to show your work. But Karen will only turn fifty-four once, and to be honest, the poor woman looks about sixty-eight. Is your high school show really worth more than the complete dissolution of my best friend's life?" Emily was too young to realize that Marla was merely testing her, or that Marla actually hated Karen, for that matter. She had cried to her father, who explained to her that he would still be at the show, and many kids at the art show weren't going to have either parent there, and many people's parents are dead anyway, so what was the big deal? Picasso's parents never showed up to cheer him on, and he did just fine. Sure enough, once Emily had accepted that her mother wasn't coming, Marla graciously announced the night before the show, that after a great deal of reflection, she was putting Emily's needs before Karen's and would be attending the art show, because if she didn't, God knows what kind of resentment Emily might hold for years to come. Emily was embarrassed that it took her ten years to discover that this was her mother's go-to move to get attention when someone else was in the spotlight.

Diana called Maddyson to try on her bridesmaid dress, and Emily sat next to Lauren on one of the love seats, laying her dress over the arm and smoothing it out. She whispered to Lauren, "Have you heard from Dad?"

"He accidentally dropped a location pin at the Ritz Carlton. I was going to tell him, but then I thought, fuck Dad."

"Fuck *Dad*? Mom cheated on him." She hated that she had to say these words. *Cheating* didn't even seem like it did the affair justice. Cheating was a one-night stand, something people did in college. This was something else, and it had presumably gone on for years.

"That's not necessarily true. We still have no idea what she was referring to. They're friends, anything else is speculation. For all we know, Dr. Leibowitz might not be attracted to Mom. He might not be straight. He may not even identify as male."

"I think the beard kind of gives the 'male' part away."

"Still, society is way too harsh on adulterous women. I'm not saying it's okay for her to cheat on Dad, but there are two sides to every story. Maybe Mom fell in love with someone else because Dad was a shitty husband. Maybe Dad is just possessive and jealous, and Mom didn't even cheat. You know, so many men just want to control 'their women' because they fear that if they allowed them to do what they wanted, they'd finally realize their true power."

"Okay, well, I don't think Mom screwing our old shrink is particularly empowering of her, but agree to disagree." She barely wanted to look at her mother, and now that extended to Lauren. How could anyone be so cavalier?

Diana was pinching loose fabric around Maddyson's bust and chatting with Marla. "I told Jerry, yes, I'm happy he's made a friend, but it really is inconsiderate of him to rush off with Michael to East Hampton every other weekend while I'm stuck taking the dog to the vet and dealing with the plumbers. Trust me, I like my alone time too, but it seems like he's just trying to get out of—"

"Having sex with you?"

"What? No, he's just trying to run away from adult responsibilities. Guess who had to get the dog's anal glands expressed *and* weed the garden all by herself? Meanwhile he's at some tiki bar with Michael sharing a scorpion bowl."

The door swung open and Jason appeared, wide smile on his face. "Ladies..."

Marla frowned. "What are you doing here?"

"Wanted to show my support."

Diana smiled at Jason. "I don't think we've met."

"This is Jason," Emily said. "He's my brother."

"Ah! Little brother?"

"Actually, he's seven years older."

"I'm terrible at guessing ages. Okay, we're ready to take a look at your dress."

Alone in the fitting room, Emily took off her shorts and tank top, kicked off her shoes, and looked at herself in the three mirrors. Under the harsh lights, she could see herself from the front and both sides. She didn't look as bad as she had expected. She had a dimple here, a lump there, and two heaving boobs that made her feel like a cow, but she looked nice. She had to think about the attributes of her body that had nothing to do with attracting men. At the very least, she had successfully *conceived* a child. That had to count for something. Unfortunately, having children was something a lot of people could do, including idiots and assholes, so her sense of pride in having gotten knocked up quickly dissipated.

"Emily, hurry up in there!" she heard Marla shout. "Are you staring at your nose in the mirror again? I've told you a million times, big noses add character."

"Stop it, Mom. I'm just getting my dress on."

She pulled the dress off the hanger and stepped into it, careful not to rip the delicate white silk. She tried to zip up the back, but the zipper wouldn't budge.

"Um… Diana?" she called out. "Can you help zip me up?"

Diana parted the curtains and tugged at Emily's zipper. The dress stopped zipping right at her bust. "Ah, did you gain a little weight?" Diana asked.

"Maybe… Is there anything we can do?"

"I can take it out in the bust a little. A lot of women would dream of gaining weight in the bust. Your hips seem to fit fine!"

Emily gulped. The last thing she needed was to draw attention to her growing boobs. After all those years of wanting them to get attention, now she dreaded it. If Marla found out she was pregnant before David did, it would be a guaranteed shit storm.

"Voilà!" Diana said, opening the curtains. Emily faced the others in her dress for the first time. Gabrielle began to tear up, raising her hands to her mouth.

"You...look...stunning! Doesn't she, Jennifer?"

"She looks *amazing*," said Jennifer, eyes on her phone. She looked up. "Oh yeah," she added. "You really do. Sorry, I'm texting Kevin."

"Mom?" Emily asked, turning to Marla. All she wanted was a sign of approval. Even a nod would do.

"Well," said Marla. "You look a bit like you came out of a porno, but otherwise, fine."

"Mom, no porno features a woman in a floor-length wedding dress."

"The boobs," Marla said. "They're just too much. You looked so much classier in the pictures you sent me from San Francisco. Why is it so tight all of a sudden?"

"It looks like she gained some weight," Diana said. "Nothing to worry about, I can take out the bust a little."

"I'm not paying for that," Marla said frostily. "Emily chose to gain weight."

"Mom, you said you weren't paying for alterations if I lost weight."

"Implicit in that statement was that I would not pay for alterations resulting from a weight change in either direction."

Gabrielle stood up. "I'll pay. Emily, consider it part of my wedding gift to you."

"Thanks, Gabrielle."

"Let's not paper over this," Marla said. "I think there's a bit of an elephant in the room."

"And which elephant would that be, Mom?" Emily said.

"I think everyone here is very worried about your unhealthy relationship with food."

"What?"

"I don't mean to speak for your friends, but I think it's clear to all of us that you have an eating disorder."

Gabrielle opened her mouth to say something but thought better of it.

"Mom, you haven't eaten anything other than yogurt in twenty years," Emily said.

"That's not true, I ate buffalo chicken salad yesterday. I'm saving the rest for lunch today."

"This is so stupid. I don't have an eating disorder."

"Well, what am I supposed to think? You're part of this LifeSpin thing, with the wheat restriction and the sugar restriction, and now I see you've gained all this weight. You're binging."

"Mom, I'm not binging. I didn't even gain that much. And I don't know why you think it's appropriate to bring this up in front of my friends, in public no less."

"I don't mind," Maddyson said. "I find it interesting. I'm live-tweeting it right now."

"Can you stop that?" Emily asked. Maddyson shrugged and put her phone down.

"I think this binge eating is something you need to work on in therapy," Marla said. "Don't you see what happens when I'm not permitted to be in contact with your therapist? It's ridiculous to expect a person suffering from anxiety to have the self-awareness necessary to raise the important topics."

"Oh, so you want to have sex with my current therapist too?"

"Emily!"

"Well, you obviously needed to sleep with Dr. Leibowitz to get the *important* information about me."

"Emily, you need to stop this right now. This is extraordinarily embarrassing for Diana."

"No, Mom. We're talking about it. How could you do this to Dad? I don't care how long ago it was, it's so fucked up. And you wonder why I have all these so-called trust issues." Between Jason and her mother, Emily was certain that she could never, for even a moment, relax in her marriage. Monogamy wasn't really a vow, it was just a suggestion. Her mind went to her wedding vows. *Well, at least I can write a compelling paragraph on how I'll never cheat with our kid's psychologist. That'll be touching.*

Gabrielle looked mortified. "Um, do you want us to—"

Marla wheeled to face her. "No. I don't care who hears this. Stay where you are." Gabrielle froze. Marla turned back to Emily. "As a person who has never been married a day in her life, you have no right to judge my actions. Abe is a wonderful, intriguing soul, and for years we *were* just friends. But then your anxiety began to crop up and he was there to help. You have no idea how hard your anxiety was on me. And when one is under such severe emotional stress, it makes sense that one might attach oneself to the person who is the most supportive. Abe Leibowitz was a saint. He saw you at a discounted rate. He prescribed you all those meds. And when it was time for you to take your SATs, he wrote you the note that got you extra time."

"Got it. So you fucked Dr. Leibowitz so I could get extra time on my SATs?"

"This is ancient history."

"How ancient, Mom? When did it start? Wait, is Dad even my real father?"

"Of course he is. You inherited his inability to read social cues." She turned back to the bridesmaids. "Well! Shall we try on our dresses?"

Emily slumped into an ivory armchair and looked at her mother, a slideshow of disgusting images of her and Dr. Leibowitz running through her mind. A drunken kiss or a flirty text was one thing, but she couldn't wrap her mind around how her mother could have kept an affair going for years without remorse. Or for that matter, how her father could have forgiven her whenever he first discovered it. What did she even see in Abe? Granted, Emily couldn't figure out what she saw in her father either. Or what either of them saw in her mother.

Despite all of Marla's shortcomings, Emily never would have expected this. She knew her parents' marriage was littered with cutting intellectual putdowns and snide remarks, but an affair almost seemed too trashy, too plebeian for Marla. If Marla couldn't be trusted to stay faithful in a marriage—even an admittedly dull one—who could? At the very least, Marla's desire to be right all the time should have prevented her from making such a huge mistake. A whole new wave of terror washed over Emily as it occurred to her that David might be no better. He might frame his affair differently, perhaps he would just "fall in love" with a cute new sales rep at Zoogli and tell Emily he still loved her but wasn't in love with her. People would do anything to justify their own terrible actions, and the worst part was that anyone was susceptible.

Jason

While Gabrielle tried on her dress, Jason took Gabrielle's empty seat to get closer to Jennifer. She looked like a real ice queen, but Jason chalked that up to the shameless display of dirty laundry she had just witnessed being aired.

"Hey, Jason," she said. She was texting, her eyes glued to her phone. The one thing Jason liked about women over twenty-five was that they were less likely to be obsessed with their phones. He already had to compete with an iPad when it came to getting Mia's attention, now he had to try to conquer technology with twenty-nine-year-old women too? He glanced over at her phone to see she was texting Kevin, that pretty boy.

"Texting Kevin, huh?" Jason asked. "He's a little young for you, don't you think?"

Jennifer's lips thinned. "Only one year."

"How many kids do you have?"

"Uh, I'm single. I don't have any kids." She turned away slightly.

"Sorry about that. You just have that mom look."

"What the fuck? That's incredibly mean."

"I'm just playing. How else would I get the attention of a woman who looks like you? Come on, give me credit for trying."

Jennifer flipped her hair over her shoulder. "You're my friend's brother, and we're at a bridal boutique. Also, I'm pretty sure you have a front row seat to your parents' marriage falling apart. Is this really the time?"

"When *would* be the time? The wedding? Come on, give me a chance! Give me just five minutes of conversation and I promise I'll be way more interesting than that penisless Ken doll you're texting." He wondered if this was getting dangerously close to begging, which would be the exact opposite of demonstrating high sexual-market value. Oh well, the words had already come out of his mouth.

She put down her phone. "Okay. Go. What's your story?"

"I'm an amazing dad, I lift weights three times a week and I'm an extremely generous lover." He had to be careful not to make himself seem too generous. There was a difference between men who loved giving oral sex because they loved controlling a woman's pleasure, and men who did it to make up for a tiny dick or otherwise lackluster ability in bed. It was a bit too early in the conversation to discuss dick size, but hopefully she'd figure it out eventually.

"What do you do for a living?"

His favorite question, other than "My place or yours?" What a lucky moment! "I'm the CEO of a technology start-up. I know, I know. I'd be better suited for San Francisco than New York. But look, once *we* get married I can move out there!" He grinned.

She smiled back. "So you're wooing me with marriage talk?"

"You're nearing thirty and single. It usually works on chicks like you. Let me guess—you were fat as a kid."

Her brow flattened. "How did you know?"

"You take way too good care of yourself not to be compensating for something. I feel you. I'm divorced, and that's what fuels my desire to lift at the gym—stronger and harder each time." Luckily Lauren was trying on her dress and not close enough to start scolding him for being "creepy."

"I got off a relationship fairly recently too." Her voice finally softened. She might as well have taken her dress off, he was so in. He was practically balls-deep in her brain.

"What happened?"

"Well, we had been together for a while. I was at the point of wanting marriage, or even just a guarantee that it was going in that direction. He told me that he wouldn't be making enough money to afford the kind of ring he knew I wanted. He did pro bono work as a pediatrician for a free clinic—it sounds great, but I had to pay for everything. And I don't mind paying for some things, but sometimes I want to be taken care of, you know? And I just knew, right then and there, he wouldn't be able to support my lifestyle the way I wanted. I'm not a gold digger or anything, it's just…if I am going to have a date night with my boyfriend, I don't want it to be at Chipotle."

"You have expensive taste. I get that. Luckily, you're hot enough to be that much of a bitch and get away with it." He winked.

She gave him a half smile. "Heh. I guess!"

"Jennifer," Diana called over from the fitting area. "You're up."

Jason watched as Jennifer went behind the curtains and began changing. With Diana and Marla deep in conversation, and Emily, Gabrielle and Maddyson stuck on their phones and looking bored, Jason knew he could pull his greatest move yet without immediate detection. He crept behind the dressing area and whipped open the curtains from the other side, so none of his family members would see him coming in. "Hey there," he said. "So are we doing some oral, or what?"

"What the fuck?" Jennifer looked like she had just opened a Tupperware full of mold.

"What's going on in there?" Marla asked.

"Jason just asked me for a blow job," Jennifer said, opening the curtain. Everyone looked aghast.

"Whoa, whoa," Jason said, stepping backward. "I wasn't asking for head. I was going to eat her pussy out."

"Ugh," Jennifer groaned in conjunction with the other women. "Could you have phrased it in a more disgusting way? Besides, I don't let guys do that."

"Jennifer," Lauren said, "while I agree Jason is being a complete piece of assgarbage, you need to examine your internalized misogyny. What's so bad about receiving oral sex?"

"I wouldn't worry about that," Marla said, putting her hand

on Jennifer's shoulder. "I actually hated cunnilingus until I was well into my thirties."

"Ugh, Mom," Emily said. "You're clearly talking about Dr. Leibowitz."

"Well, this entire dress fitting has become somewhat of an airclear, so I'll just say it: your father could label every city on a map of China, blindfolded, but couldn't be bothered to locate my clitoris."

"Mom, that's so disgusting," Jason said.

"You're such a fucking dickpipe, you know that?" Lauren said, stepping closer to Jason. "You think words like *clitoris* are so gross, but you completely fail to see how gross your own behavior is, literally every second of the day. No wonder Christina left you."

"Oh yeah, Lauren? Well, at least I'm not a wannabe activist who conveniently hides all the things that make me just as privileged as the people I claim to hate. Question, do Mom and Dad mail you your rent checks, or do you have some sort of direct deposit thing going on?"

In a move that seemed almost instinctual and out of her control, Lauren charged at Jason and pushed him over. He fell on his ass, knocking a bunch of safety pins off a wooden stool.

Marla gasped. "Jason!"

"I...I...think I broke my coccyx."

"How is your posterior, brother?" Nathan asked.

"The Vicodin David slipped me is helping. It really is the wonder drug."

Nathan's bedroom had the unmistakable smell of Cheetos. A large bookcase stood against one wall, cluttered with thick paperback fantasy books and action figures still in their boxes. His bed was unmade, with an empty bottle of Mountain Dew peeking out coyly from the sheets.

"You seem glum, milad," Nathan said.

"You don't even want to know. I just had one of the most humiliating experiences of my life."

"It couldn't be more humiliating than getting banned from a LARPing convention—only because you were being historically accurate!"

"I don't even want to know what that means. Okay, let's get started. Before we figure out what you'll wear to the bachelor party, I feel the need to address…this whole thing." Jason gestured in Nathan's general direction. "You need to fix it."

"What's to fix?" Nathan sat at his computer chair, arms folded in his lap. He was wearing a ponytail again, which masked his greasy scalp slightly, but made his face look wider and exposed the acne by his sideburns. He wore a gray T-shirt that read Religion: the Opiate of the Masses.

"Your whole thing. This whole look, this whole strategy, whatever you want to call it. Girls don't like this. They like Ryan Gosling, not Comic Book Guy. Do you shower?"

"I do shower, verily."

"More than a few times a week. Every day. You need to actually wash your hair too. It's not like you have a regular job that takes up all your time, so this should be pretty easy."

Nathan scowled, but nodded.

"You also need to get into shape. Obviously you can't lose weight before the wedding, but if you want to attract the ladies, at least get to an average BMI. You don't need to be a bodybuilder or male model, and frankly I don't even think that's possible, but if you get all *this*—" he indicated Nathan's body, making a giant blob shape "—under control, then you might have a fighting chance with the girls."

"My good sir, we only have a few hours before the bachelor party. I cannot alter so much about myself. I only summoned you here to help me decide which cape I should wear."

"No capes. And another thing—this weird medieval dialect just freaks women out. Stop it."

"With all due respect, good sir, I only wish to attract the type of lady who enjoys such courteous talk."

"What is your type?" Jason sat on Nathan's bed. "Paint me a picture."

"I like petite women: delicate, slender and feminine. Preferably eighteen to twenty. Once they get older than twenty-one, they become entitled and hardened, demanding a man be employed, live on his own, have his own car. Their looks decline and their standards rise to the point that no normal man could fulfill them! It's laughable."

"You're really making me not want to help you," Jason said.

"Oh? And why did you agree to help me in the first place, if you could not handle the truth about decaying Western society?"

"Because you—well, first of all, you asked for my help, and second of all, I just..." He paused. Why *was* he helping Nathan? He doubted there was any chance for him, and yet, despite all the things that made Nathan unappealing, Jason had a small glimmer of hope that perhaps Nathan would find his own girl, a nerdy redhead who wore retro clothing and studied fictional languages. Maybe Jason was an asshole, but at least he would have done one good thing. "Fine, Nathan. I don't want to see you wind up like me. Although actually, given your current trajectory, winding up like me would be a gift from God."

"Ah, you're a fundamentalist," Nathan said. "No wonder you have such inane ideas about relationships. I suggest you read this atheist blog I found called *The True Enlightenment*."

"Isn't that your blog?"

"Yes, but I found it."

Jason pursed his lips together in frustration. "Look, what I meant to say was…you only get one life. And I fucked mine up. I married the wrong person, I treated her like shit, my daughter probably wishes I was a giant blow-up doll of Olaf from *Frozen*. And if you keep going the way you're going, you'll be a hell of a lot worse off than me. Because it's not just about your weight or your hygiene. At the end of the day, you're afraid of women. That's even more of a death sentence than being an asshole like me. You could be the most attractive guy in the world, but with your attitude, you won't get anywhere."

"I don't have time for this feminist nonsense," Nathan said. "Next thing you know, you'll call me a 'misogynist' just because I think women hit their peak at eighteen, which for the record is reproductive age and perfectly legal."

Jason put his hand on Nathan's sweaty, T-shirt covered shoulder. "Look, I'm the furthest thing from a feminist. I have a Reddit username called FuckBitchesChuckBitches. But the point is, you need to change. You can't stay fourteen forever."

Nathan looked down at the floor in between his feet. "You say this like I can be turned around. Like I'm the girl in the romantic comedy who's only ugly because she's wearing glasses."

"No, I think you're pretty ugly all around. I'm just saying some minor improvements could take you from being a two to a four. And—voilà—if you finally have the confidence to speak to women and treat them like humans, maybe you'll bag yourself an average-looking girlfriend."

"I shall consider it. Now enough with this emotional dribble."

"It's *drivel*."

"I'm speaking in Middle English. Anyway, let's focus on the basics. Is this ensemble acceptable for tonight?" He motioned to his T-shirt.

Jason grimaced. "Of course not. It's so far from acceptable, it's an abomination. Do you have a decent blazer?"

"I wore one for my college graduation. It's in my closet somewhere."

"Cool. Wear that. Wash it first, if you have time, because I imagine it doesn't smell great. Just a feeling I'm getting. Maybe pair it with a collared shirt, no tie—or a T-shirt. But not these argumentative, weird T-shirts with quotes on them. Just a normal T-shirt. And no stains or holes. Actually, just go with the collared shirt. I'm afraid of what might happen with a T-shirt."

"I suppose I could do that."

"As for pants, no cargo shorts. This is not a Blink-182 concert. And please, no dirty white sneakers. Do you have a good pair of dark-wash jeans and some dress shoes?" He was trying to imagine a well-groomed Nathan, but was having quite a bit of trouble. He hoped this advice would help him, as opposed to somehow making him look worse the way makeovers tended to make women look more masculine if they went too heavy on the eye makeup and contouring.

"My stepmom got me jeans for Christmas. And I have a pair of shoes from my dad's wedding."

"Wear those tonight. Oh, and shave the beard. Or at least trim it, especially all the hair on the neck. And promise me, whatever you do, no weird hat or trench coat. It makes you look like Jack the Ripper."

"But women like mystery."

"Not that kind of mystery. Women don't want to feel like they're being followed by a flasher."

"I would never sully the delicate eyes of ladies with such lewd and indecorous behavior! Is that really what you think of me?"

"No, I think you're an awkward kid who needs some help with girls, and unfortunately, the way you behave sometimes makes you seem like a sexual predator. I know it sounds harsh, but I'm only saying this because I'm your friend." He got off the bed and put his hands on Nathan's shoulders. "You're an awesome guy waiting to happen. Tonight, you are going to make it happen."

Emily

The kitchen looked like it had been ransacked. Dirty plastic food containers and silver Pop-Tart wrappers littered the counter. A half-eaten Twix bar and several Chinese food delivery menus sat next to the landline telephone.

Upstairs, Emily found David in bed, chomping on a raspberry Pop-Tart.

"Sweetie, are you okay?" she asked.

"Under the circumstances." He let out a little weird laugh. "Ready to hear something fucked up?"

"What? What the hell is going on?"

"I heard from Zach. I can't reach Robert. All the money from the second round—all the BluCapital funding—Robert transferred it to his personal account in the Caymans. He's left the country."

Blood drained from Emily's face. "What?"

"You can read it for yourself—it's all over the internet. Zoogli was a Ponzi scheme. The SEC is investigating. They've padlocked the offices."

She sat down on the side of the bed and tried to breathe deeply. On some level, she hoped that asking enough questions would change the narrative—that this would all turn out to be not nearly as bad as it originally sounded. But her gut knew better. Something was wrong. She should remember this feeling and compare it against all the other times she felt something was "definitely" wrong, like the month she suspected her landlord was a serial rapist because he drove a white van. This went beyond anxiety. Her whole body felt like it was prepared to literally fight an incoming enemy. But what enemy? Financial ruin? Great instincts her caveman ancestors gave her—if only they could be used for modern predicaments. "So you...you don't have a job?"

"Nope," David said, finishing off his Pop-Tart and licking crumbs off his fingers.

Emily's vision blurred and she felt like she was going to faint, just like how she felt right before her first pelvic exam. If only seventeen-year-old Emily knew how much worse it was going to get. And the doctor didn't even put a finger up her butt like she had feared. "What are we going to do?"

"Don't you realize?" He sat up in bed. "We can do anything. That's what's so amazing about this."

"Amazing?"

"Look, you hate working for Linda. So quit. Let's travel for a few months. We have enough money saved up. So many of our friends are still in student loan debt, we're better off than you think. We can stay at hostels—it won't even cost that much. You've always wanted to go to Italy!"

"Italy?"

"Totally! I mean, when else are we going to get to do this? This is the kind of thing we should be doing while we're still young and don't have kids."

Emily put her head in her hands and began to quietly weep.

"What? What's wrong?"

"You're just so sweet." She hugged him and tried to disguise her tears by letting them soak into her hair. Between them there was the baby, still blissfully unaware of how shitty his life was going to be.

NIGHT 5. PART 1: THE BOYS

Jason

"NOW THIS IS what I'm talking about," Jason said. Nathan had showered. His hair was washed and combed. He wore a crisp, white collared shirt and a navy blazer.

"You're not quite a five yet," Jason said, standing behind him and inspecting him in the mirror. "But you're at least a four. Maybe even a four and a half."

"Gadzooks."

"Every time you say that shit you're back to a three."

David

"You boys are just precious!" Susan admired the groomsmen as they gathered in the kitchen for a round of Chivas before heading out. They were all dressed in a uniform of slim-fit jeans and collared shirts, except Matt, who wore a retro color-block polo shirt and a pair of awkwardly cropped chinos that revealed his skinny ankles.

"Let me just get one picture of you boys to put on social

media." She held up her iPhone. "One, two…three! Oh, wait. Sorry. I just took a picture of myself by accident. Selfie! Let's try this again."

"I've walked past those chicks four times now, and they were taking group selfies every single time," Jason said. "That's the problem with young women. They're hot, but they're idiots."

"You know," Mark said, taking a sip of his drink. "I'm sure one of those women has walked by us four times, and she's going back to her group of friends saying, 'What is it with thirty-year-old men? Every time I walk by them they're ordering more drinks.'"

"Fair point, but tonight is the night to drink. It's David's last night as a free man!"

"I'm wondering if this isn't the best place," David said, looking around. Glo-Fi had been Kevin's choice. He insisted it was one of his DC friends' "favorite New York hotspots." Nobody thought to question why an unnamed person from Washington, DC, had become the authority on New York City bars. The Glo-Fi crowd was mostly under twenty-five, and in the past hour the DJ had played six Selena Gomez songs. David cringed when he saw a few twenty-three-year-old frat boys ordering Fireball shots and chanting, "What happens in Glo-Fi stays in Glo-Fi."

"I get what you're saying," Jason said. "It's not wild enough."

"It's not that," David said. "I feel like Chris Hansen is going to show up and ask me to have some lemonade."

"It's your last night out as a single man and you're complaining that the women around you are too young? What's wrong with you?"

"That's what's wrong," David said, pointing to a possibly underage girl crying hysterically on the floor of the bar, mascara dripping down her face, while her five best friends stroked her hair in unison.

"It's not so bad," Kevin said. "Trust me, my buddy Conner knows New York. Have you guys heard of this place called Magnolia Bakery?"

"I agree with Kevin," Jason said. "Just wait for this place to heat up. Minus that one crazy chick, most of the people here are still just on their fourth drink of the night. They're practically sober."

David, woozy from Chivas and Vicodin, looked around the bar. The women looked as if they had agreed on a uniform before going out: black leggings, loose tank tops, weather-inappropriate paisley scarves and no makeup. They looked like tired art students picking up tofu burgers at Trader Joe's.

"I'm surprised you're defending this place," he said. "The girls here aren't even that sexy."

"I get it, the girls are a little Oberlin-y." Jason took a sip of beer. "But it's still early. The girls in short skirts will show up later." He turned to Nathan. "So you going to try your moves on some girls in this bar? No time like the present."

Nathan frowned. "This one looks fairly decent, I suppose." He motioned toward a freckled girl in her early twenties with a red floppy bun. She wore a khaki green utility jacket and ripped jeans. Despite her aggressively low-effort styling, she was cute. Nathan straightened his blazer and walked over.

"Greetings, milady," he said, jumping in front of her. "You look…dare I say…quite stunning tonight."

David cringed as he watched Nathan bow his head, take her hand in his, and plant a long, slow kiss on it.

"What is thy name, milady?"

"I'm…Erin."

"Erin, what a lovely name. Care for a potable—"

"Hey there, Erin," Jason said, squeezing in between her and Nathan.

"Hi." She crossed her arms.

"You've got nice fair skin," Jason said. "Too bad that means you'll age like milk. Gotta keep up on the Botox. I'm just kidding."

"Fuckwad." Erin walked away.

Nathan turned to him. "Jason, I trusted you! Why did you scare off that fine maiden with your words of discouragement? Such an indecent thing to—"

"Stop it. That's how you talk to women. It makes you seem higher value."

"Let's forget about girls for once," David groaned. "Who wants to get pizza?"

"Pizza?" Jason raised an eyebrow.

"Yeah—I haven't eaten pizza in years. And Mark agrees this bar sucks."

"It does suck," Mark said. "And if the bachelor wants pizza, give the man pizza!"

"Okay, buddy," Jason said, "we'll get some pizza, but I think it's more important that we drink our nuts off and find some strippers."

"No strippers," David said. "Who wants doughnuts? Anyone?"

"Are you okay?" Kevin asked.

"He probably still has some Vicodin in his system," Mark said, sipping his beer while he browsed Amazon for strollers on his phone. "I prescribed 300 milligrams, but maybe he should taper."

"I'm just trying to enjoy the night," David said. "I was on Vicodin in high school when I sprained my ankle and I drank and I was fine. It's not like I'm driving. Jason, do you know any good clubs? But not strip clubs, just fun clubs with good music. I want to let loose tonight."

"You certainly are making a fast recovery," Kevin said, amused.

"Like I said, it's the Vicodin," Mark said. "He'll feel like shit tomorrow. Make sure he doesn't have another drink."

"Stop talking about me when I'm right here," David said. "Who's down for a club?" As much as he knew it was against the official code of bachelor parties, he wished Emily was there. Emily still loved going to clubs with him as much as she did when they first met. She had resisted the late-twenties urge to brag about how tired, busy and bored she always was, and how the only thing she enjoyed was watching Netflix. They had their nights in, of course, but Emily often said she liked to treat every date as though it was a first date, complete with spending two hours to get ready.

Jason sighed. "We're a group of six dudes. The only way we're getting into a club is if pretty boy Kevin blows the bouncer."

"Oh, fuck off," Kevin said, laughing.

"The truth is," Jason said, "the only place we can go where we'll actually get in, and get bang for our buck, is a strip club."

"No way in hell," Mark said. "Strip clubs are the exact opposite of 'bang for buck.' Men shell out huge sums of money just to pretend that women like them, and then they don't even get anything out of it."

"Not if you know my tricks," Jason said. "Come on, guys. David—you said you wanted to let loose. Let's do it."

A wiry little stripper with fried-off hair slid down the pole in her finale and collected the tips on the stage floor that weren't already stuffed in the back of her lime-green G-string.

David looked to his left and saw that Jason was mesmerized, like a child staring at a Christmas tree for the first time.

"Can I get you boys anything?" The cocktail waitress wore thick eyeliner and a tight black dress that barely covered her butt.

"I care not for a lap dance, my fair lass," Nathan said, waving her off. "For I am a man of higher station than any of the brazen wenches in this establishment. Sully me not with your debauchery!"

"Sir, I'm asking you if you want a drink. I'm not a dancer."

"Oh. In that case, I shall take a glass of red wine. Your finest."

"And the rest of you?"

"Four Sam Adams," David said, clearly throwing Mark's caution to the wind.

"Anything else?" the waitress asked.

"*And* five—no, make it seven—shots," Jason added. "Jäger."

"Seriously?" Mark laughed. "Seven? There are only six of us, and only five of us are drinking."

"I know, genius. One for each of you betas, and three for me." He leaned in to the others, speaking confidentially. "Gotta pregame for the champagne room. That's where they take you for the threesomes."

"You've had threesomes with strippers?" Mark asked.

"No. But my buddy Chris did, back in college."

"The only thing less believable than a guy telling you he had a threesome with strippers is a guy telling you that his friend you'll never meet had a threesome with strippers."

"Go back to shopping for diapers on your phone, dude. Leave the strippers to the single men."

"Fine by me." He took his phone out again. David looked over and saw that Mark was texting Gabrielle. That reminded him, he should text Emily. He didn't want her to worry, which she often did when it had been a few hours with-out contact. When he opened his phone, there were already two texts from her. The first said: Love you, baby. Thinking of you! The second was an inexplicable picture of her boobs, sent two hours later.

Kevin leaned over. "Are those Emily's boobs?"

"Uh…no," he said, quickly putting his phone away.

"So you were looking at porn…at a strip club? Man. That's sad."

"Shut up," David said. "It just popped up."

"Sure, I'm sure it was random. You were holding it for a friend, right? Classic."

When Kevin wasn't looking, David pulled out his phone again and wrote back to Emily. Wow, very nice. Love you, sweetie. He considered adding that her boobs were nicer than any of the strippers' boobs but then remembered she might not like him being at a strip club at all. He sent a second text. I wish you were here.

"So you must do a ton of crunches, right?"

David was on his third beer, which Mark strongly advised against, sitting at a table with a stripper named Cynthia. She was pushing forty but had an impressive six-pack.

"I guess so."

"I haven't been able to work out since I hurt myself. But you know what I learned? I don't have to go to the gym every day. I'll survive, you know? It's incredible to know that. That injury was the best thing that could have happened to me."

"I thought you said losing your job was the best thing that could have happened to you."

"That too. I mean, we're free now, you know? Really free. After the wedding, we can do whatever we want. We can take our savings and move to Bali."

"Bali?"

"Fuck yeah! We'll live off the land! We'll dance on the beaches and shit!"

The stripper took this in. "I don't know. Bali? I mean, I like where you're going with this, but Bali seems like a predictable choice."

"Eh, good point."

"I wish I had your attitude. Hell, every day I worry this place is going to kick me out for getting too old. The funny thing is, I still do really well with the college-aged boys. They all have these MILF fantasies. Blame porn, I don't care. It's the guys my own age who aren't interested. I guess I remind them of their impending mortality."

"You have a point about Bali. Maybe I'll open a restaurant. Or become a basketball coach. I don't have to be over six feet to be a coach, right? Or maybe I could start my own company. What if I became a farmer?"

"Everybody wants to be a farmer. It's all that farm-to-table crap. It's kind of a saturated market."

"Maybe."

She smiled at him. "You'll figure something out."

"Thanks," he said. "I don't mean to sound creepy, but you remind me of my mom. She's dead."

Jason

"I'm Judi and this is Diamond."

The two strippers led Jason into the Champagne Room. Other than the champagne itself, there was little to suggest that the room deserved its designation. The lights were dimmed to hide the scuffs on the walls, and the red shag carpet resembled a skinned Muppet.

"Is this where the…magic happens?" Jason asked. The moment he said it he realized these women might not have been old enough to get a reference from *Celebrity Cribs*.

"One hour in the champagne room is $500," Judi said. "If you actually want to drink the champagne, that's another $100."

Jason pulled the champagne out of the ice bucket. It wasn't a brand he recognized. Its metallic, hot pink label read Classique Strawberry Champagne and in small print below that, Champagne Beverage.

"Okay." He had blown through his cash and was now using his credit card.

"And there's a ten percent service charge," Judi said, brandishing an iPad with a Square device attached to it. Jason felt as if he were at the AT&T store, setting up his new phone plan.

Diamond popped the champagne and poured him a glass, then poured glasses for herself and Judi.

"So let's begin," Judi said. "You mind if I make out with Diamond?"

"Mind?" Jason laughed. "Get your freak on, ladies!"

"Okay then." She put her hand behind Diamond's blond hair extensions and opened her mouth wide, the way people do when they are putting their fists in their mouths on a dare. The two women lunged at each other's faces for a while, sticking their tongues out strenuously.

Jason reached out to touch Judi's thigh. "Mind if I…"

"Oh, you paid just to watch us," said Judi. "If you want to touch, that's another $200."

David

"Milady, your creamy skin glows in the darkness like a beacon of light. You are but a vision of purity in this otherwise tawdry establishment."

Nathan was getting his fifth lap dance of the night. The stripper looked bored. "Don't Tell 'Em" by Jeremih ended and she hopped off his lap.

"Come on, Nathan, we're getting out of here," David said.

Nathan looked outraged. "But you don't know how far I was getting with her!"

"How far you were— She's a stripper."

"You don't understand, dear brother. She isn't like the others. We have a connection. I must find her. I must make her mine."

"We're leaving. Now. I want some fried chicken."

They drove home in silence at two in the morning. Mark was at the wheel. Matt was in the back seat, his head drowsily bobbing forward. Drool was making the journey from his mouth to his beard to his polo shirt collar. At some point in the night, his refusal to drink anything other than artisanal absinthe had faded.

"You okay?" David asked.

"Lauren's a *bitch*," he said, stretching the word *bitch* so that it seemed to last ten seconds.

"Hey, that's my sister," Jason said. David couldn't tell if Jason was actually offended or just meaninglessly spouting words. He had been doing a lot of that since they left the strip club.

"That lap dance I got tonight was more action than I've gotten in the last three months," Matt grumbled. "She hates me. What's her problem? Why doesn't she want to fuck me and strippers do?"

"News to Matt," Jason said. "Strippers don't want to fuck you either. I learned that the hard way tonight."

"So there was no threesome?" Mark asked, amused.

"I paid more than $1,000 to get in the room, get 1.5 lap

dances, drink the champagne and touch them—only their legs, by the way—and then they kicked me out for being belligerent and disrespecting the club rules."

Nathan let a worldly laugh escape. "While you gentlemen bemoan the harpies besetting you, I sing the sweet melody of true love. I met my soul mate tonight!"

"Don't mind him," David said. "He doesn't understand strippers."

"There's always that one guy," Kevin said. "Same thing happened at the last bachelor party I went to."

"I should have quit while I was ahead today," Jason said. "Jennifer is way hotter than those two strippers I was with, and I got head from her for free."

David looked up, surprised. Kevin, who had been staring out the window on the turnpike, whipped his head around.

"Wait, what?" Kevin said. "When was this?"

"Earlier today."

"Gabrielle told me you just asked her for head, and she said no," Mark said.

"Women lie to save face," Jason said.

Mark narrowed his eyes. "Right."

"She's never gonna marry me," Matt said, mooning, seemingly ignoring their conversation. "She says it's for gay rights but that's not true. She just doesn't want me. It's all about Ariel. David, here's my advice to you: never have kids."

NIGHT 5. PART 2: THE GIRLS

Emily

EMILY COULDN'T BELIEVE how many penises Gabrielle had incorporated into the bachelorette party decor. Mark and Gabrielle's hotel room at the Ritz Carlton had been transformed into a penis wonderland, glowing pink like the Barbie aisle of a toy store.

Emily wore a sexy white bandage dress, but she couldn't help worrying about the dress's thick bands, which bisected her belly, giving her baby some weird dent in its head. She had been so excited to wear it when she was planning her bachelorette party, but now all she wanted to do was go home and put on pajamas.

As planned, the rest of the women wore black dresses to help Emily stand out. Lauren was the one exception. She wore ripped jeans and a black T-shirt that said I Breastfeed in Public. A few months ago, Emily might have admonished her for wearing something that would ruin all the group photos, but now she barely cared.

"Are you okay?" Gabrielle asked Emily. "This is supposed to be the second most fun night of your life!"

"I'm fine. Just tired."

"No worries. It's your night! I thought that to warm up a bit, we could pregame here and hang out. First thing on the schedule…games!"

She went into her minifridge and got a bottle of cupcake-flavored vodka, placing it on the coffee table. "Here we go, ladies. I also bought some chardonnay, so if you're feeling like taking it easy tonight, you can take shots of wine. Our first game is…never have I ever."

"I'm actually not drinking," Emily said.

"What? No, you're crazy!" Gabrielle put her hands on Emily's shoulders. "You can't not drink! You're the *bride*!"

"I'm detoxing. I want to be healthy before the wedding."

"No fun!" Gabrielle said. "Please tell me the rest of you ladies will be drinking. Except you, Maddyson." She wagged her finger at Maddyson jokingly.

"What the fuck?" Maddyson shouted, slamming her phone down on the table. "This isn't fucking North Korea."

"I can't let an underage person get drunk on my watch. It would be irresponsible of me."

"Why am I even *invited* then? If we go to a bar after this I'll just drink there."

"It's true," Emily said. "She got drunk earlier this week."

"Okay, fine," Gabrielle sighed. "But you can't brag about this on social media."

Maddyson rolled her eyes. "Nobody calls it that anymore."

Gabrielle knelt down in front of the coffee table. "Okay! Each of you ladies can grab a penis shot glass from the table. So the way this works is, each person says something they've never done. Then, if you *have* done that thing, you have to put a finger down, and take a shot. I'll go first. Never have I ever done it in the butt!"

"Really?" Maddyson said. "But you're, like, older. And you're married."

"Not all married people do it in the butt." Gabrielle didn't seem offended by the "older" remark. Emily supposed that was a privilege of people who were otherwise told they looked young. Such a remark, aimed at Emily, would have ruined her entire day.

"I feel like they all go for it eventually. Wouldn't it get boring otherwise?"

Emily gulped. She had never wanted to do that with David. Did any woman actually *want* to do that? She was suspicious of women who claimed they loved it. They were like women who claimed they loved football. Sure, they'd watch it, tolerate it and maybe even enjoy it, but it wasn't like they'd independently suggest it.

The only woman who put her finger down for the anal sex question was Jennifer, who coyly looked around before taking a shot.

"So…" Gabrielle said, finger-tenting wickedly. "How was it?"

"It was with Carl, you remember him. It was our anniversary!"

"And did you like it?" Gabrielle asked.

"Ew, no," said Jennifer, wincing as the shot made its way down her throat. "He just really wanted to do it, so I gave in. Then the condom got poop on it and he freaked out and never wanted to do it again."

It was Maddyson's turn. Emily wasn't sure if Maddyson was a virgin or not. What was the average age for virginity loss—eighteen? Seventeen? Fifteen? The only things she heard about teenagers came from fear-mongering news specials about dangerous teen trends that sounded made up, like rainbow bracelet sex parties.

"Never have I ever…" Maddyson paused, looking around the room, "…done Molly while in a hot tub with an aspiring DJ who I gave a blow job to while his friend watched."

"What the heck?" Jennifer asked, choking on her penis-shaped glass of chardonnay, which she was drinking on the side, irrelevant to the game. "Is this just something you did, that you wanted to tell everyone about?"

"I thought that was the point. I can't think of anything else I haven't done. Other than butt sex."

"I'm sure there's something," Emily said.

"I guess I've never drunk pee."

"Is that what we're stooping to?" Lauren asked.

"Well, sorr-*y*. I've already done loads of sexual stuff, and I do lots of drugs, so whatever."

"Ears, ears!" Gabrielle said, covering her ears with her hands. "Not in front of me! I'll feel the need to tell your mother!"

"You won't say shit," Maddyson said. She reclined in her chair as she delicately twirled the plastic penis shot glass between two fingers like a baton.

"I'll go next," Jennifer said. "Never have I ever had a threesome."

Maddyson and Lauren both took a shot.

"What?" Emily laughed as Lauren downed the shot. "*You* had a threesome?"

"Why is that surprising?"

"Well, it just seems like the kind of thing you'd hate, because it's all about the man, pleasing him—it's like a porn fantasy."

"Who's to say it was with a girl and a guy? For your information, it was with two guys I knew in college."

"What? Seriously? You got Eiffel Towered? You didn't find it degrading or whatever?"

"Nope. In fact, they didn't do much to me. I pegged one of them while he sucked the other guy's dick. That was pretty much the end of it." She said this as if she were recounting what she had that day for breakfast.

"Oh…my…gosh," Gabrielle gasped, her hands over her mouth.

Emily couldn't help but picture it: Lauren, wearing her beige sports bra and retro makeup, her short black bangs harsh against her moon face, thrusting a giant strap-on into the little pink butt of a college guy. Suddenly, she heard Lauren's voice in her head saying, *Why did you assume he was white?*

"They wound up being gay," Lauren said nonchalantly. "They're married now and they breed salamanders in Arizona."

"What about you, Maddyson?" Emily asked. "What's your story?"

Maddyson put down her shot glass and sighed deeply, as if she were a grizzled pirate about to tell his many tales of looting and plundering. "My friend Belinda and I three-way kissed with this guy Edmund at camp," she finally said.

"That's not a threesome," Jennifer said.

"You didn't specify sex! How was I supposed to know?"

"Let me just add," Lauren said, "that sex doesn't have to be P in V."

"What's P in V?" Jennifer asked.

"Penis in vagina."

"You mean…sex?"

"No. I mean P in V."

"Let's move on," Gabrielle said. "Lauren, what have you never done?"

"Hmm," she said, tapping her chin with her index finger. "Let me see…never have I ever…fully come to terms with my white privilege."

"Huh?" Jennifer said.

"You heard me. I mean, obviously this question doesn't apply to Gabrielle, but for the rest of you. I have never fully understood the scope of my white privilege. The other day a policeman walked by me and didn't stop me for anything, and it took me a few minutes to realize that was my white privilege."

"You sure know how to ruin a buzz," Jennifer said. "And besides, I'm half Japanese."

"Just because you're a person of color doesn't mean you don't have white privilege. I thought you were white when I first saw you."

"Okay, well, I guess I take a shot then," Jennifer said, "because I've never even heard of this stuff."

"I guess I'm exempt from taking a shot," Gabrielle teased. "How racist, Lauren. Your question only applies to white people."

Lauren's jaw dropped. "I am *so sooooo* sorry," she stammered. "I hadn't even *thought* of that, but that is no excuse. I totally fucked up. I'm horrible."

Gabrielle smiled nervously and blushed. "Um… I'm totally joking. It's fine. I guess I was just expecting something along the lines of, 'never have I ever skinny-dipped.'"

Lauren shrugged. "I skinny-dipped during my period for a protest against the Peninsula in Midtown," she said. "So that wouldn't work."

Emily sat blindfolded in the dark in the center of the room. She assumed that whatever was about to be unveiled for her had sparkly penises on it. "Time for your surprise!" Gabrielle said.

"It's not a stripper, is it?"

"No, of course not. Just stay still." Through the candy-pink polyester of the blindfold, Emily could see the lights being turned on. She heard whispers, little giggles and hushing.

"Guys, what *is* it?"

She heard EDM. Someone's hands were behind her head, untying her blindfold, which fell to her lap.

She saw a tall bronzed man wearing nothing but a thong depicting a cartoon pink elephant face. His flaccid penis flopped around inside the sheer pink elephant trunk. His bulging muscles were oiled up and his short black hair was gelled, spiked and shaved on the sides. He appeared to be wearing clear lip gloss and shimmer bronzer on his cheekbones.

"It's the bride to be!" He jiggled toward her in a splayed-leg hop. "Time to get *down*!" He spread her legs with his disturbingly slippery fingers. She clamped them shut.

"No, no, no," she said. Her heart was racing.

"Aw, don't be a party pooper!" Gabrielle said. "I was taking pictures!"

"Delete those," Emily said. "Get rid of all this."

"Uh…" The stripper put his hands on his hips and looked down sadly at his penis-filled elephant trunk. "I was booked for two hours. I still need to be paid."

"Who's paying for this?" Emily turned to Gabrielle. "You told me it *wasn't* a stripper."

"I couldn't say that it was—then it wouldn't be a surprise." She turned on the lights, further illuminating the glitter on the stripper's face.

"Well, shut this down," Emily said.

Gabrielle turned to the stripper. "Don't worry, I'll still pay you. That's three hundred for the two hours?"

"Not including tip," he said, arms crossed, trying his hardest to look serious while wearing the elephant thong.

"I feel sick, guys," Emily said. She didn't feel nauseous as she had the past few days, but her stomach was flipping, twisting, contracting. "I basically just cheated on David."

"Oh, come on," Maddyson said.

"Seriously, you guys. He touched me. David would be so pissed off. We had a no-touching policy tonight. I said strippers were okay, but no touching. Should I tell him?"

"Why would you tell him?" Jennifer asked. "It's not even a big deal."

"Yes, it is!"

"Ma'am, calm down, I only touched your knees," the elephant stripper said. Suddenly he was all professional, like a United Airlines customer service agent calming down an irrational person trying to claim expired miles.

"Ugh, I need to text David." She reached for her phone.

Gabrielle lunged at her. "Don't! Why tell him? I guarantee you he's at a strip club now. You have nothing to feel bad about!"

"Fine. I'm not going to tell him what happened but I am going to text him." She typed, Love you, baby. Thinking of you!

"I'm sorry if I made you uncomfortable, ma'am," the stripper said.

"Okay, stop calling me *ma'am*, I'm twenty-eight."

"You're only twenty-eight?"

Something in his voice sounded familiar. She took a closer look at him.

"Wait, are you… John Russo?" She squinted.

"Fuck yeah!" he said, smiling and putting his hands on his hips.

"I'm Emily Glass."

He looked perplexed. "Do I know you?"

"We went to high school together."

"Oh, fuck, wait! Are you the girl who got her period in chemistry class and the guy next to you kept asking who packed tuna salad for lunch?" He pointed at her and smiled at the other women in the room as though they would know what he was talking about.

"I mean, yeah. I did other things too, obviously."

"Yeah, sure, sure. Shit, Emily Glass! We used to call you Emily No-Ass! I remember my girlfriend totally *hated* you."

"Wait, which one?"

"Larissa Shapiro. You guys had a weird frenemy thing going on, right?"

"No. I didn't even really know her. She just told everyone I was a lesbian freshman year for no reason."

"Shit, man. That is so Larissa. Fucking crazy. So what are you up to now?" He crossed his arms, as if to cover up his nipples out of modesty.

"You don't really remember me that well. You and Larissa made my life a *living hell*. And her friend Sabrina, or whoever."

"Oh *yeah!*" he said, as if recalling a character from his favorite childhood cartoon show. "Sabrina was awesome."

"I cried every day after school because of you assholes!" she shouted. "Fucking douchebag!"

"What?" He furrowed his plucked brow. "What? How?"

"Um, I don't know—making up rumors about me so no boys would date me? Calling me Emily No-Ass? Telling everyone I had a hairy back? Writing *Dickslut* on my locker?"

John laughed nostalgically at *Dickslut*. Emily slapped him across his glittered face. At first she almost couldn't believe she did that—she had never physically fought someone in her life, minus that one time that she bit Jason's nipple in the pool when he had her in a headlock, but that was the nineties.

"What the fuck?" he said.

"That's enough, asshole," Lauren said, approaching him. "It's time to go. Take your money and leave, whore."

"Whatever," he said. "You're fat."

"Shit, nobody's carding!" Maddyson said. "This place could be okay."

"One day you'll be *happy* to get carded," Emily said.

"I get carded all the time," Jennifer said. "It's so embarrassing."

Emily looked at her. "Why is that embarrassing?"

"It's just… I'm a doctor, I don't want everyone thinking I'm eighteen."

Maddyson turned to her. "Don't worry. I'm eighteen, and you definitely don't look like anyone my age."

Jennifer smiled weakly. "Good to know."

They were in front of a Lower East Side bar called Establishment, its name engraved on a black sign above the front door, adorned with white engravings of a goat's head and a hammer. The women walked inside. It was dark, narrow and cramped, despite the absence of many customers. The wallpaper had been intentionally printed to create the appearance of moldy, chipped paint. There was a small loft above the bar with an old-fashioned wooden railing. Behind the railing was a random collection of antique spinning wheels.

"This place is weird," Jennifer said.

"A jar of mayo exploded in here," Lauren said.

"Ew, where?" Jennifer said.

"I mean all the white people. Fucking white people."

"Look at all the drinks!" Gabrielle pointed to the blackboard behind the bar. The names and ingredients of the drinks had been written in what looked like Victorian cursive.

Maddyson walked up to the bar. "I'll have a Rutherford Wisp."

"That'll be eighteen dollars," the bartender said. He was a husky man in his early thirties, wearing a gray tweed newsboy cap. He had a brown handlebar mustache and a saggy hole in his left ear where an earring used to be.

"Eighteen dollars? Is that a joke?"

"Our drinks are artisanal, miss," he said flatly. "If you want a Bud, you can go to O'Flannigan's."

"What's in a Rutherford Wisp anyway?" she asked, pulling cash from her cross-body bag.

"Chartreuse, lemon rind, bay leaf, lavender honey, grapefruit bitters, gin, elderberry liqueur, vermouth and egg white froth," he said, filling a shaker with ice.

Maddyson watched him make the drink. "Uh, can you add extra alcohol?"

"I can't alter the recipe. It's one of our rules." He pointed to a brass sign behind the bar that read No Drinks Will Be Altered, next to a little engraving of a top hat.

Gabrielle joined Maddyson at the bar. "I'll just have a glass of water."

"That'll be seven dollars, ma'am."

"For water?"

"Our water is pumped from an artesian well, then home infused. We steep it in lavender and cucumber peel before cooling it."

"You don't have just...regular tap water?"

"No." The bartender was starting to look irritated.

"I see a sink right behind you."

"That's not for drinking."

The other women sat down at the bar. Jennifer ordered a Foxtrot Julep, a greenish-white drink with a mandarin orange rind floating on the surface, and Lauren ordered Priestly Savage, the home-brewed beer.

"I made that beer," the bartender said. "Let me know what you think."

"It's delicious. Is this your place?"

"Hah. That's funny. If I had a bar, it would never be like this place. It's way too commercial. Not curated enough. I'm actually trying to start my own food truck, but with all craft beers, no food. What's your name?"

"Lauren."

"Will. You from around here?"

"I live in Greenpoint."

"Cool. I buy my spurs there. Hey, while you're finishing that up, I'll make you a Wilford-Humphrey on the house. How could I resist a woman who looks like Bettie Page meets awesome meets wow?" Lauren blushed.

"What world do we live in," Jennifer whispered to Emily, while staring at Lauren, "where we go to a bar and Lauren is the one getting hit on?"

"He's a hipster," she whispered back. "I can't explain hipsters. Maybe he's hitting on her ironically?"

Jennifer leaned over the bar and put her arms close to her breasts to push them together. "That drink sounds literally amazing," she said. "Perfect for the bachelorette party." While Jennifer complained to no end about "not being taken seriously" in her line of work, she was more than happy to use her sexuality to get anything, even just attention.

"This is a bachelorette party? Who's the bride?" The bartender turned to Lauren. "Not you, I hope."

"My sister," she said, indicating Emily.

"Forget this," Jennifer said, returning her breasts to their normal position. "Let's dance." She pulled Emily off her chair and brought her to the middle of the floor. Jennifer started rocking her hips back and forth to a Kanye West song. Emily was surprised that the bar even played rap, let alone mainstream rap. Was Kanye already ironic? She had expected 1920s music to start playing and for some man in a bowler hat and monocle to emerge from the janitorial closet and instruct everyone to do the Charleston.

Lauren

Will handed Lauren her drink. "The Wilford-Humphrey. Mint, seltzer, gin, crushed rosemary ice, lemon bitters and maple syrup with a dollop of extra virgin olive oil."

She took a sip. "This is amazing."

"So what's your story?"

"I'm a blogger for *Cunt*."

"I think my sister reads that," he said, totally unfazed. "It's a feminist magazine, right?"

"I'm one of their head bloggers. Ask her if she's heard of Lauren Glass."

"Are you married?"

"Oh, no." Technically it was true.

"Didn't think so. Personally, I don't even believe in marriage." He stared directly into her eyes. Eye contact was so terrifying and arousing at the same time, when it lasted more than a second.

"Why not? I mean, neither do I, but I'm curious." She took another swig of beer.

"I don't think a person's body can belong to another person."

"I agree," she said, sipping her drink. "I mean, my vagina is my vagina and I can put it on whatever penis, vagina or ambiguous genitalia I want."

"So well said," he said, nodding. "I can see why you became a writer."

Emily

Emily looked at her phone. It was past midnight and still no response from David. Maybe he had seen her text but didn't think it warranted a response. She was starting to worry that something had happened to him. Surely the other men in the group would have told her, but what if something happened to all of them? What if they got into the middle of some Sharks vs. Jets–style dance war?

"I need to text David something better," she told Jennifer.

"Do not tell him about the stripper. I guarantee you he's doing something worse. He's probably getting a lap dance right now. Men are pigs sometimes. Ugh, I hope Kevin isn't getting one. Would he get one?"

"I don't know. I barely know him and neither do you. Hey, can you help me out?"

"With what?"

"I need to send David a sexy picture. Come to the bathroom with me and take it so the angle looks good? Every time I try to take a sexy one of myself, it's either in the mirror so it's all fuzzy, or it's at a weird angle and it makes me look lopsided."

"You are crazy."

"I know, I know. But if he's at a strip club I need him to be thinking of me, not those girls with the fake boobs. I hear they're all prostitutes too."

"Ugh, now you're making me worry about Kevin."

"Come on."

Emily took her into the bathroom and locked the door.

"I'm just going to take off the top part of my dress," she said. "Can you snap a good picture of my boobs? Don't include my face, just in case he gets hacked."

Jennifer laughed. Emily rolled down the top of her dress

and unsnapped her bra, letting her bloated pregnancy boobs tumble out.

"Your boobs are *huge*," Jennifer marveled. "I am so jealous."

Emily knew this was the point where she was supposed to compliment Jennifer on something, or tell her that her boobs were just as nice, but she didn't have the energy for that. "What? They're the same as they've always been."

"I'm still jealous. I have no boobs, but I have this giant Nicki Minaj booty I'm trying to get rid of." She pointed to her butt, which was as small as a runway model's. Emily wasn't sure if that was a humblebrag or a "Please tell me I have a small butt" plea, since she wasn't sure if Jennifer was aware that big butts were now the societal ideal, so she didn't say anything.

Jennifer snapped a photo of Emily. Jennifer inspected it and started swiping.

"What are you doing?" Emily asked.

"Adding filters. Don't you want to look tanner?"

"Give me that. Thanks." Emily took the phone and texted the photo to David before deleting it. She didn't want drunk Jennifer accidentally texting it to a coworker.

They heard a noise coming from the other side of the wall. It sounded mechanical at first, but it was followed by a rhythmic pushing sound, grunts at two-second intervals and then moaning, screaming. Emily hadn't heard anyone having sex since college. She turned to Jennifer and put her hand over her mouth in a schoolgirl giggle.

"Someone is literally having sex in a bar," Jennifer said.

"Weirdos," Emily said, laughing and putting her phone away.

They left the bathroom, past a line of irritated women waiting to use it. "Oh my gosh," Jennifer said. She pointed to the men's bathroom, where Will, the bartender, was staggering out. His denim vest was draped over his hairy forearm and his newsboy cap was askew. Behind him, her mascara melting and her lipstick smeared, was Lauren.

"Lauren?" Emily shouted her name, hoping on some level that it wasn't Lauren after all, just some woman who looked exactly like her.

Lauren looked mortified. She stumbled forward, wrapping her arms around Emily's neck.

"I did a horrible thing," she moaned into Emily's hair.

DAY 6

Emily

THE NEXT MORNING, Emily stripped in front of her bathroom mirror to see if she was showing. Her boobs were ridiculous, that was for sure, but she couldn't tell if her stomach was big because of the baby or because she hadn't been able to take a dump since she arrived at her parents' house. She had gotten into quite a routine for this: 10:00 a.m. like clockwork in her office bathroom after eating a banana and drinking a cup of hot black tea. It was so predictable, she was fairly certain even Linda knew about it. Outside of those precise conditions, there was no way she'd be able to go. She couldn't shit on weekends unless she made herself a particular smoothie of pineapple, mint and parsley. David thought this was for her skin, and she didn't correct him.

She turned around to check out her stomach from the other side, and she heard a splash. Her elbow had tipped her makeup bag off the sink and into the toilet. She screamed as she saw her precious Tom Ford lipstick sinking to the bottom of the toilet bowl.

"What the hell?" Lauren was outside the bathroom door. "Emily, are you okay?"

"All my makeup is ruined!"

Lauren opened the door. She saw the makeup in the toilet and shrugged. "Just rinse it off."

"Rinse it off? Are you kidding me? First of all, eyeshadow can't be 'rinsed off' because it's a powder and the whole point is not to get it wet. Second, it's all contaminated now!"

"Contaminated? Come on. You, David, Matt and I are the only ones who have been using that toilet."

"It's still contaminated. Just because I have sex with David doesn't mean I want to coat my eyelashes in his poop germs."

"A cell phone has more germs on it than a toilet seat."

"There's no fucking way that's true. You're just like those people who say a dog's asshole is cleaner than a human's mouth because it sounds too crazy to be true, so it must be true."

"I'm serious! And it's not a dog's asshole being cleaner than a human's mouth, it's a dog's mouth being cleaner than a human's mouth. And it is true."

"Dogs lick their own assholes, so that's definitely not true."

"Okay, fine, Emily. Do you want to borrow my makeup for the rehearsal dinner?"

Emily sighed. "No. You only wear bright and dark colors, and I like the neutral look, plus…please don't get offended by this, but it's unsanitary to share makeup."

"With your own sister?"

"What does that have to do with anything? Just because you're my sister, you couldn't ever possibly have a skin infection or be a carrier of MRSA?"

"Oh, for fuck's sake. Fine. I'll drive you to Sephora. You seriously need to learn how to drive, by the way. This is fucking dysfunctional."

They had been driving for a few minutes before Lauren spoke up. "Well, I feel like I have to bring up the gorilla."

"What gorilla?"

"Oh, right. The 'eight hundred pound' gorilla. I try not to involve weight in the idiom because it's yet another micro-aggression against people of size."

"Okay."

"Obviously I don't want you telling Matt about the bartender."

"I wasn't going to. Are you going to?"

"Sure. Because he's my keeper and he needs to hear every detail of what I do sexually."

"Well, yeah, kind of. You cheated on him."

"You really shouldn't judge. What's worse—me having consensual sex, which will never affect Matt if he doesn't find out, or you keeping a pregnancy a secret from David?"

"Those things are not at all comparable. It's not like I sperm-jacked him."

"What the hell is spermjacking?" Lauren was so annoyed she almost ran over a squirrel. She swerved at the last second to avoid it, causing Emily to feel the need to throw up again.

"Jason told me about it. It's basically when a woman wants to score a 'high-value male,' as he puts it, so she pokes a hole in the condom or tells him she's on birth control when she isn't."

"What a crock of shit. Pickup artists think women are so diabolical because they're sociopaths themselves."

"Yeah. They probably do heinous things like cheat on their partners without remorse."

"You know what? That's it. I've had enough. I'm doing you a fucking favor and all you're doing is being a misogynistic hypocrite." Spit shot out of her mouth and sprayed across the windshield.

"Misogynistic? You really think I would have a different opinion about this if you were a man?"

"It's not about your reaction to it. It's about the policing of

women's bodies. There is no historical precedent for policing men's bodies, so when you criticize a male cheater, you
aren't reinforcing centuries of oppression."

"That's insane."

"I don't care what you think is insane."

"Then why the hell did you bring this up in the first place?"

Lauren sighed. "Maybe because I was *hoping* to start a di-
alogue on exactly these issues. I wanted you to understand
all the political and social factors that went into what I did
with Will."

Emily closed her eyes and rubbed her temples. "Let's just
buy some makeup."

When they got to Sephora, two sales associates greeted them:
a pretty woman in her early thirties with dark brown skin, vi-
brant red lipstick and black hair in a sleek ponytail; and a short
South Asian man with spiked hair wearing blue eyeliner.

"Welcome to Sephora!" the man said. "How can we help
you? We have a plethora of age-fighting foundation in our
Clinique section." He directed this pitch to Emily.

"I need new makeup for my rehearsal dinner. I dropped
all my makeup in the toilet by accident."

"Well," he said. "If you're just looking to replace your basics,
I am happy to direct you to some of our highest-rated brands."

"We're on a budget," she said.

"Now we're on a budget?" Lauren said. "After the cost of
your dress?"

"The dress is important to me. Please, just quit it. You keep
nagging me about the dress."

"Well, I'll stop when you stop judging me for every damn
thing I do."

"I get it," the man said. "Weddings are stressful for everyone!"

"Especially us," Lauren said.

His face softened and he smiled. "Wow. You guys are adorable. You make the cutest couple."

"We're *sisters*," Emily said. "Are you kidding me?"

"Why are you so offended by the suggestion?" Lauren asked. "You think there's something *embarrassing* about being a lesbian?" Emily recognized the look on her face. She would have to be careful not to accidentally dangle any more argument bait in front of her for the rest of the day.

"Of course not! I'm just…not." She was particularly afraid of being homophobic in front of the presumably gay male Sephora sales associate, but she knew Lauren would be quick to remind her that "tons" of straight men wore eyeliner and worked at Sephora. It would be a repeat of the "tons of straight men wear thongs" disaster of 2010.

"Sorry about that," said the female sales associate. "Don't listen to Eddie. He has no filter. Let us know if you need anything while you shop."

They ventured farther into the store. Women huddled around the tiny mirrors, applying goopy, used-up samples of sparkling lip gloss to their chapped lips. Emily never understood the people who used the samples on anything other than their wrists. Either they were all trying to inoculate themselves against the flu, or their understanding of germs was that of Medieval peasants.

"The smell in here is sickening," Lauren said. "I'd be careful if I were you. Perfume can be toxic, and you're breathing for two now."

"I thought you were here to *help*. You're just making me anxious."

"Sorry. These places make *me* anxious. Did I tell you about the time I got PTSD when Mom made me wear makeup for cousin Alyssa's bat mitzvah? Speaking of which, was Alyssa invited?"

"No. Nick and Susan probably think our entire family is dead."

"Whatever, Alyssa voted for Obama twice—I don't need her in my life."

Emily turned to look at Lauren and raised an eyebrow, wondering whether she should even bother addressing that comment. Finally, she gave in. "Are you a Republican now?"

"No. I only vote third-party. The lesser of two evils is still evil."

"Okay." She paused for a second, remembering the over-whelming smell of perfume in the store. "Wait, Lauren, is perfume really going to kill my baby?"

"It's not a baby, Emily, it's a fetus. Don't buy into anti-choice propaganda." She fiddled with a Kat Von D black lip-stick for a second before getting bored and moving on to a blue eyebrow pencil.

"Yeah, but I'm keeping it!" Emily watched as a middle-aged woman with her teenage daughter rubbernecked at their conversation. Emily lowered her voice. "Can we put the poli-tics aside for one second? I'm about to get married, I'm preg-nant and nobody knows, and you just told me that perfume could kill the baby!"

"It won't kill it," she angrily whispered back. "I'm just say-ing, it's not healthy. In fact, I'd be suspicious of makeup in general. All the parabens."

"*What?* I've been wearing makeup daily and God knows how long I've been pregnant. Oh fuck, this baby is definitely messed up now."

"Calm down, you're probably fine. But if you're actually concerned about all this, just stop wearing makeup. It's not like you need it."

"I need it more than anyone, Lauren. I'm one of the few people in this cruel world whose acne phase and onset of aging manage to coexist. Fuck, now my own vanity is going to kill my kid!" Emily felt her heart rate increasing, her hairline sweating. At this point, she didn't care who stared at her or laughed at her. This was just like the time she saw a man at the airport using a laptop next to an outlet without charging it. Only a suicide bomber, in her estimation, wouldn't take advantage of a scarce airport outlet. She had frantically called the airport police, completely unconcerned about how crazy she might have seemed. She was saving lives! Who cared that he turned out to be a harmless businessman? On some level she was at least raising awareness.

"Hello, ladies." Emily turned around and saw a young, heavyset makeup artist wearing the all-black Sephora ensemble. Her beige face was matte and completely drawn on. She had dark hair pulled back in a shiny top knot, and highly arched eyebrows that made her look like the love child of Kim Kardashian and Ursula from *The Little Mermaid*.

"Hey," Lauren said. "We're in kind of a hurry, so—"

"I just wanted to let you know we are offering free makeovers today. What are you two looking for?"

"Makeup for my rehearsal dinner tonight," Emily said. "And then for my wedding tomorrow. I accidentally dropped all my makeup in the toilet, and things are just—" She couldn't help it. She started to tear up. She tried to breathe deeply to postpone the tears, but she could feel them rolling down her cheeks. "This whole week has been so messed up. My parents are probably getting divorced, and I'm pregnant and the father doesn't know yet, and the baby is going to die because I've been wearing all these parabens."

The woman looked slightly aghast, then rearranged her face into a smile. "Look, honey," she said. "No shame in drama. We *all* have drama. Just the other day my fourteen-year-old half sister started cyberbullying me on Twitter, and up until then I didn't even know she existed."

Lauren turned to Emily and began rubbing her back. "Calm down about the parabens. Just relax and get the free makeover. It'll save time."

"We can do a free makeover for both of you, by the way," the makeup artist said.

Emily shrugged. "May as well. Lauren, you okay with this?"

"I guess. I could always use the experience for a blog post. Seems like they're looking for more obvious, easy-to-digest feminism over at *Cunt*."

"Excuse me?" the makeup artist asked.

"Nothing."

"Oh, okay," she said. "Let me get Eddie to do her makeup and I'll do yours. What's your name?"

"Lauren."

"I'm Dominique."

Dominique instructed Lauren to sit on a black canvas director's chair while Eddie came over to do Emily's makeup. He smiled and placed his hands on either side of her face. "I am going to make you look *hot*!"

"I just want something that covers up my blemishes. I don't want to look too crazy."

"No worries, girl. I get what you're saying. Mature skin tends to look best with a liquid foundation as opposed to powder, so I hope you don't mind if I stick to that. When I'm done with you, you won't look a day over thirty. Now close your eyes."

With her eyes closed, Emily began to feel her anxiety crawling back into her brain. "Say, you wouldn't know anything about the chemicals in makeup, would you?"

"Uh…maybe, why?"

"I'm pregnant and I'm just not sure what makeup is safe to use...you know, for the baby." That question was innocent enough. Nobody could conclude that she was doing anything but being reasonably cautious.

"Oh, girl, I don't know. How far along are you?"

"That's the thing. I don't know."

"Girl, go to a doctor! You need to know!"

"Why? Why do I need to know?" She was sweating again.

"You want to make sure it doesn't have any birth defects, obvs. If you've been drinking—"

"*I have been drinking! What, are you trying to tell me I've killed the baby?*"

"I think we're done here," Lauren said.

"Girls, you're going to be late!" Marla called upstairs. Emily and Lauren came down the stairs, dressed for the rehearsal dinner. "My God, what happened to your faces?"

"We got makeovers at Sephora," Emily said.

"You wouldn't need all that eyebrow powder if you didn't overpluck so much."

The front door opened. It was Steven.

"Don't mind me," he said sullenly. "I just need to get my suit."

"Oh yes, Steven," Marla said. "Tell us not to 'mind you' when you come in here unannounced looking like a hobo. The least you can do is trim your beard. Photos are forever."

"Hey, Dad," Jason said. "Stay for a beer. We can all head over together."

"That won't be necessary. I'm just going to get my suit."

"This is classic you, Steven," Marla said. "Avoiding criticism even when it's long overdue." Her bracelets jingled against each other as she made a sweeping gesture with her hand.

Steven stopped on his way to the stairs. "Can you elaborate on what criticism is so 'overdue'?"

"Well, obviously, your narcissistic tantrum needs to be addressed. You've completely humiliated Emily on her wedding week."

"No, he hasn't," Emily said. "I mean, Dad, I wish you were staying in the house, but I get why you left."

"Marla, don't involve the children in this," he said, ignoring Emily. "They're too young to process any of this."

"I'm twenty-eight, Dad."

"Yes, Emily, I'm aware, but your brain technically only reached maturity three years ago. And this situation is a lot more complicated than you think."

"Mom cheated on you with Dr. Leibowitz. That's pretty much it, right?"

Marla sighed. "Emily, it's more complicated than that. I have a lot of unresolved anger toward my father and Aunt Lisa, and I can't say I completely dealt with…never mind."

"Never dealt with what?"

"The Cold War."

"What?"

"You of all people should understand. Knowing that Khrushchev was ready to destroy us every second of the day really impacted me in my formative years. It's no wonder that years later I subconsciously sought out a strong, masculine presence who reminded me of my own distant father, while I was married to someone who—no offense, Steven, I'm sure even you would agree with this—is extremely passive."

"I'm done with this," Emily said, throwing her hands up and seconds later realizing she had adopted that tic from Marla. "Nobody in this house takes responsibility for anything."

Lauren pulled Ariel onto her lap. "Emily, you are the last person who should be criticizing anyone right now. We literally just went through this."

"Okay, fine. I take it back. Leave me out of this."

"What is she talking about, Emily?" Marla asked. "Lauren, what are you talking about?"

Lauren shook her head. "I'm not going to say shit. Because I'm a decent person who respects what other women do with their bodies."

"Holy crap!" Jason said, putting his beer down on the counter. "Emily, did you spermjack David?"

"No," Emily said. "Let's just drop it."

"I have no clue what's going on anymore," Steven said. "I'm getting my suit."

"You're not really here to get your clothing," Marla said. "You're here to make a big, passive-aggressive scene. So you know what? You got your scene. Are you happy? Emily is completely humiliated right now."

"You know what? Forget it," he said. "I'll just wear this to the dinner." He motioned to his short-sleeve collared shirt and khakis, then went to the door to leave. "See you at the rehearsal dinner, kids."

He left, slamming the door behind him. Or trying to. The door didn't close properly and swung back open a few inches. Moments later, Steven reached in awkwardly and closed it.

"Okay, I'm calling a therapy session," Marla said. "You kids have barely even been trying. So I have to take this even more into my own hands. It's therapy time."

"You can't do that," Emily said.

"Yes, I can. I'm paying for your wedding and God forbid I also give you free therapy, I really am horrible, aren't I?"

"It's not free therapy, it's just your new way of being able to lecture and guilt us without criticism."

"Without criticism? Ha! I've been getting nothing but criticism this whole week! That's what I get for raising you

kids to be outspoken. Maybe I get what I deserve after all."
She looked at the floor sullenly.

"Okay, fine," Emily said. "You want therapy, Mom? Well,
I resent that you cheated on Dad and had an unethical rela-
tionship with my psychiatrist that confirms my suspicion that
I can never trust anyone."

"That comment carries racial undertones," Lauren said.
"If you use the 'I can't trust anyone' excuse as a way to per-
petuate your inherent biases, then—"

"Oh, shut up, Lauren."

"Mom," Jason said. "I have a slightly different take on you
cucking Dad."

Marla looked perplexed. "Jason, I don't know why that
should bother you, and I think your father would argue I
didn't do that nearly enough. That was a big problem in the
beginning of our marriage. Very mismatched sex drives, and
styles."

"Oh my God, Mom," Jason said, covering his face with
his hands. "I didn't say *fucking*, I said *cucking*."

"Well, I have no clue what that is. I don't have time to
keep up with all your idiotic start-up lingo."

"He's talking about cuckolding," Emily said.

"That's actually a valid kink for a lot of people," Lauren
said. "And queening."

Emily shot daggers at her. "Yes, because that's totally the
subject we're on."

"You know what?" Marla shouted, silencing all three of
her children. "First of all, all of you need to start taking responsibility for how messed up you are. Perhaps it was my
fault to introduce you to the world of psychology so young.
It made you all completely incapable of taking responsibility
for your own hang-ups. You're all officially far too old to be

blaming your mother for your problems, and definitely far too old to be blaming each other."

"But you still blame Aunt Lisa for—" Lauren started.

"I wasn't finished, and Aunt Lisa is hereby a banned topic because you have no insight into how toxic she is. As for Abe, I was wrong to have an affair. Yes, I was wrong. But until you three have been married to your father and dealt with his constant condescension and aggressive boredom, you can't talk. Do you realize how many times I had to listen to him going on and on about Samurai culture while simultaneously giving zero credit to my own academic and professional achievements? Jason, you yourself admitted you cheated on Christina solely because she aged and you were bored. And Lauren, I think we all see how little you respect Matt. I'd be shocked if you made love to him even once a month. I may have cheated on your father but at least I love him, in my own way, and I do respect him both as a husband and as an academic. And Emily—you mean to tell me you have no secrets with David? If you don't yet, you will."

Emily stared into her mother's glassy brown eyes and couldn't bear to imagine how transparent she must have looked in that moment. If Marla didn't know about the pregnancy, she at least knew Emily was the type of person who would hide something that important. Which made her no better than her mother.

"I think I made some good points today," Marla said, with the casual tone of a therapist wrapping up a normal session. "These sessions have been so helpful for all of us, don't you think? Anyway, are we all ready for dinner?"

NIGHT 6
Emily

"WELCOME TO SCALLION," said a bored young woman in a red kimono. She wore a bun with two metal chopsticks through it. "Follow me."

The rehearsal dinner was in the back room. There were two long black-lacquered tables low to the ground, with little red cushions to sit on. The four parents and David's aunt and uncle were seated at one table, while Emily and David's generation sat at the other. Ariel was on Lauren's lap, wearing a shiny blue *Frozen* princess dress and a pair of glow-in-the-dark sneakers.

"Your son is adorable," Jennifer said to Lauren. "And so well behaved."

"He loves restaurants because he has such a sophisticated palate. When he was two, the other kids at his preschool were having Cheerios and he was requesting tempeh, coconut water and heirloom tomatoes."

"I'm starting with a drink," David said to Emily. "What are you going to have?"

"Oh, um…nothing."

"Nothing?"

"Yeah, detox before the wedding."

"Seriously?"

"Yeah. I just gained a little weight and I want to fit into my dress."

"Yeah, Em, but the wedding is *tomorrow*."

"Wouldn't you rather I wasn't hungover on our wedding day? I'll just have water."

The waitress came by. "Have we decided?"

Lauren attempted to order as Ariel struggled on her lap, trying to take off his dress. "I'm a boy. I'm a boy princess," he chanted.

"My child and I will have the tofu stir-*frybulous*," she said, reading the menu.

"I don't want this!" Ariel shouted. "I want grilled cheese!"

"He's testing," Lauren said. "He loves Asian food."

"Hate hate hate hate hate hate," Ariel said, kicking Lauren.

"We've been encouraging him to express himself," she explained to Jennifer. "This is so healthy." She picked him up and carried him, screaming, out of the room.

"I want to be *boy* Elsa!" he cried.

David's drink arrived. It was a girly-looking margarita with a pink fan. He discarded the fan and took a sip. "Oh, fuck," he said. "Nathan."

At the far end of the table, Nathan had gotten out of his seat and was kneeling in front of one of the waitresses. She was in her late teens, thin with a chubby face and braces, wearing a pair of Converses with her ill-fitting knee-length kimono. Nathan, his fedora tipped over one eye, stroked her palm.

"Milady, your palm says you have an old soul. This means you would be better off betrothing thyself to an older gentleman...perhaps one between the ages of twenty-four and thirty."

"Nathan!" David gave his brother a stare. Nathan smiled devilishly at the waitress and released her hand.

"We shall meet again, milady…when you arrive with the edamame."

Lauren

Lauren sat on a bench outside the restaurant with Ariel on her lap. She felt tears in her eyes but couldn't bring herself to cry in public. Looking at Ariel made it worse.

"Mommy, I want grilled cheese!"

"This restaurant doesn't have it. You're going to have to compromise. Besides, vegans aren't supposed to eat cheese. How do you even know what it tastes like?"

"But I *want* it!"

Jason emerged from the restaurant, looking for Lauren. He spotted her and came over.

"Are you okay?"

"I'm fine. Ariel is just throwing a tantrum over grilled cheese."

"They have grilled cheese? Awesome!"

"No. He wants grilled cheese and they don't have it."

"Why are you in such a shitty mood?"

"I don't want to get into it."

"It's the rehearsal dinner, Lauren. David's dad is paying—don't you want to go ape shit and order some Shanghai Shooters on him? Take some body shots off Nathan? Come on, it'll be fun!"

"I said no," she snapped. "When will everyone just leave me the fuck alone?"

Jason threw up his hands and went back inside as Ariel chanted, "Fuck alone! Fuck alone!"

Jason

Jason sat at the bar, drinking something called a Beijing Blue out of a giant plastic goblet haphazardly decorated with twirly straws, fruit slices and paper umbrellas. He sipped on his drink as he watched the women walk by. Many of them were in their thirties and forties, some leading small children whose faces were smeared with teriyaki sauce.

He saw a slender blonde woman in a pair of beige cropped pants. She looked a little like Christina from behind. The woman turned around and smiled at him. She must have sensed he was staring at her. He was officially the creepy guy drinking alone at a family restaurant. He rubbed his forehead and sighed.

Lauren came back into the restaurant with Ariel on her hip. She brought him to the back room and sent him in to sit with Matt, then walked back over to the bar and sat down next to Jason.

"I'm sorry I snapped at you."

"No shit. In front of Ariel? That's unlike you."

She looked around, then turned back to him. "You have to promise not to tell anyone this."

"Okay."

"I cheated on Matt," she said, massaging her temples and closing her eyes. "It wasn't the first time, but for some reason, I just feel horrible. Worse than usual."

Jason couldn't help but smile. "This is amazing!"

"Are you fucking kidding me? I'm trying to confide in you."

"Yeah, I know. But I mean, come *on*. You're so holier-than-thou about relationships, you have to at least appreciate how tasty this is for me to hear. How were you able to cheat on Matt and then yell at me for cheating on Christina?" He tried to keep his voice down, but this was too juicy. He saw a middle-aged couple a few seats away from him staring.

"It's different for men," she said, lowering her voice. "Women haven't been taught to treat men as objects. Men who cheat don't view women as people. But women who cheat—I mean, we always do it for a *reason*."

"There's no good reason for cheating."

"Are you kidding? You cheated on Christina. You're admitting you never had a good reason?"

Jason sighed. "Of course I never had a good reason. I'm not the type of guy that should be married. Too selfish to give myself to another person."

"You're telling me."

"Hey, don't be an ass. You're no better. Where did you even cheat on him? And with who?"

"A bartender at some bar during the bachelorette party. And…it was in the men's bathroom."

"Oh, fuck."

"So what should I do?"

"Leave him. Do him a favor. Don't turn him into Dad."

Emily

"You know, you can get more than just coconut soup," David said to Emily. "You weigh about ninety pounds."

"One hundred and thirty two," said Emily. Her stomach gurgled. She was hungry, but she saw that one of the waitresses had a cold sore and she didn't want to risk it. She hadn't even seen the people working in the kitchen. What if one of them had leprosy? Or that disease that turned a Bangladeshi man into a tree, which she kept seeing every time she watched TLC?

Steven rose and clinked his fork against his glass. "It has

fallen to me to make the first toast of the evening. Emily, I love you very much, and I'm so happy for both you and David. Such an occasion is too momentous for mere words to do it justice, but poetry, I believe, can rise to the occasion." He paused, waiting for a laugh that didn't come. "Anyway, I'll be reading an ancient poem by the Chinggisid prince Tsogtu. I don't want to bore you about Tsogtu, but he was a great poet. I wrote one of my better-known articles about him. There is only one way to properly honor Tsogtu's poetry: to read it as it was meant to be read, in its original language."

He cleared his throat, and then began to recite the poem in Mongolian. He made a mistake after the first few lines, which forced him to start again from the beginning. After what felt like an hour, he nodded, adding, "I love you, Emily," and sat down.

"Thank you, Steven, that was riveting," Marla said, raising her glass. "Nobody here can deny that Emily has struggled more than your average young woman. I still recall the day that an ambulance arrived at our house after ten-year-old Emily was convinced that my husband ate a rotten sausage and needed to have his stomach pumped. And I'll never forget the time that a thirteen-year-old Emily—deeply afflicted with body dysmorphic disorder but profoundly intelligent—wrote a manifesto inspired by Martin Luther, detailing the ninety-five reasons she believed I should buy her a nose job and breast implants. I never thought that any man would be able to handle Emily as David has. David is a man of character—the only man who ever dated Emily and didn't break up with her within six months. If David can see Emily at her worst and love her no matter what he sees her say and do, I'm confident that their marriage is one that will last into Sheol and beyond."

"What's that?" David whispered to Emily.

"The Jewish afterlife," she said. "She doesn't believe in it."

★ ★ ★

Emily woke up at three in the morning with a pain in her right calf. Or was it an ache? After years of Googling symptoms, she had yet to figure out the difference between the two. Muscle aches were painful, and this sensation was like that, but deeper. It was below the muscles. Nerves? What was below the muscles? Veins? *Veins. Deep vein thrombosis.*

She was used to her fears being unfounded, like the time she worried she had MS after her arm fell asleep from carrying a large bag of groceries, or the time she thought she had melanoma when she actually had a pimple, but this was different. This time she was in pain. And as for her risk factors, she had two: she recently took a long flight, and she was pregnant. She had been on birth control *during* her pregnancy too—that would be double estrogen, which would double the risk—right? How could she not have known this? Why hadn't she *done* something? Was there anything she could do? It was the silent killer, after all. Silent killers were never truly that preventable. She breathed in and felt a stabbing pain in her chest, similar to the pain in her leg. It had spread to her lungs. She would be dead within an hour.

"David," she whispered. She nudged his arm and he woke up. His hair was sweaty and messy. He squinted.

"What?"

"My leg is killing me. It's deep vein thrombosis. I've read about it and that's definitely what it is. And now I have chest pain. I need to go to the ER."

"It'll pass, Em. This is another one of your...things."

"No, I really need to go. Come with me, babe. I can't do this alone."

"You want me to drive you to the ER at three in the morning because your leg hurts?"

"It's deep vein thrombosis! And now it's a pulmonary embolism."

"I remember last time you freaked out about this. This only happens to old people. You're fine."

"And women on estrogen! And sometimes for no reason at all!"

"It's so rare. I don't know anyone it's happened to."

"You're about to."

Emily heard footsteps. Lauren peeked in, wearing a big T-shirt and a pair of men's boxers.

"What's going on? I heard yelling."

"I am having a health emergency."

"Are you *sure*?"

"Yes, I'm sure! My leg is throbbing like crazy and I'm having chest pains. I'm having a pulmonary embolism. I could die any second. What is *wrong* with both of you?"

Lauren exchanged glances with David, then looked back at Emily. "This is unhealthy," she said.

"No shit. It's the silent killer!"

"I mean your mental illness."

"So people with mental illness *never* also get pulmonary embolisms? You sound like Mom."

Lauren turned to David. "We should probably take her to the ER just in case. If she doesn't figure out what this is, just imagine what a shit show tomorrow is going to be."

"It'll be a bigger shit show if I'm dead," Emily said.

David lifted himself from his butt doughnut and groggily limped out of bed. Jason appeared at the door. "Why's everybody up?"

"I'm dying," Emily said.

"What the fuck?"

"She thinks she's having a pulmonary embolism," Lauren

said. "It's probably one of her usual delusions, but we're taking her to the hospital just in case."

"Fuck, for real?" Jason looked borderline concerned, which was validating for Emily to see, but also a little worrisome. She almost preferred it when people said she was crazy. At this point, any reaction any person could have would have upset her on some level.

"Yes, for real," Lauren said. "But like I said, she's probably fine. Don't you remember the phantom appendicitis of Christmas '99?"

"Good memory," Jason said. "I'll come with you guys anyway."

On the way to the hospital, Emily firmly pressed her hand into her chest and breathed in and out.

"It's probably just muscle tension," David said.

"How soon would you remarry if I died tonight?" Her eyes were welling up.

"Why would I dignify that question? You're not dying!"

"David, let it go," Lauren said. "Em, how do you feel?"

"Like I'm happy that at least in my final hour, I'm around the people I love." Emily sniffled.

"Hi, I think I may be having a pulmonary embolism," she said to the ER receptionist, a fiftysomething South Asian woman wearing pink scrubs with Care Bears on them. She gave Emily a suspicious look. Emily had a history of arousing the skepticism of medical professionals with her self-diagnoses. Memorably, she had once told a therapist that she was concerned about developing Cotard's Delusion, a mental illness that causes someone to think they're dead despite being alive.

"Are you a nurse?" Emily followed up.

"I just check you in. Can I have your insurance card and ID?"

She handed them over. "This is an emergency, right? So I'm technically covered even though I have a shit HMO that shouldn't even be legal?"

The receptionist ignored her question. "Have you been to West Africa recently?"

"No! I'm not here for Ebola, I'm here for a pulmonary embolism! How long will this take?" She knew she sounded rude, but she didn't care. She was dying!

The woman began typing Emily's information, seemingly in slow motion. Emily looked around the waiting room. A young woman wearing big earmuffs was curled into the fetal position on two chairs arranged to form a makeshift bed.

"Why don't you go sit down?" David rubbed her back. "This is just your anxiety. Take some deep breaths. Lauren will handle the insurance stuff."

Almost as soon as she sat down, a nurse called for her. He was in his early sixties, and looked like a washed-up English rock star, with an earring in his left ear, square black glasses and a fringe of frizzy white hair encircling an otherwise bald head. She would not have thought he was a nurse if it hadn't been for his scrubs. For a moment, she wondered if he was a domestic terrorist posing as a nurse, part of a larger plot to sabotage the nation's health-care system. That *would* happen to her—it was so typical.

Emily and David followed him to an examination room. He took her blood pressure.

"Can you tell if I'm having a pulmonary embolism?"

"What are your symptoms?"

"My chest hurts when I breathe, on my right side, and my leg is throbbing."

He nodded. She wasn't sure if that was good or bad.

"How long do I have?"

"How *long*?"

"Before I die?"

David shook his head and stared at the ground.

The nurse gave her a patronizing look. "Judging by your age, probably fifty, sixty years. Although by the time you get older, who knows what advancements will be made in the medical field?"

"I mean before the pulmonary embolism kills me."

"I don't think you have that. You're able to speak just fine, and you don't seem to be short of breath. Just in case, though, let's get you an EKG." He extended a ruddy hand with tattooed crosses on the knuckles and helped her stand up.

She lay on an examination table with electrodes taped to her skin. As the test began, Emily saw her heartbeat represented on a scrolling piece of paper unfurling from the machine. She saw a lot of harsh, sharp lines. That looked scary. The doctor, a petite redheaded woman with glasses who appeared no older than twenty-five, read the results. This woman terrified Emily for two reasons: if she was really so young, how could she be trusted to do this right? And if she wasn't that young, why the hell wasn't Emily aging as well as she was?

"Your heartbeat is normal," she said. "You clearly don't have a pulmonary embolism."

"Thank goodness," she said. "Can I go home?" She saw David's face light up.

"No, we should do an X-ray," the doctor said, in a monotone voice, her eyes glued to her clipboard. "You said you were experiencing chest pains."

"What else could I have?"

"Oh, I don't want to scare you. But chest pains could be anything. The heart, obviously. But also the lungs. Pneumonia, bronchitis, abscess, lung puncture, lung cancer..." For a second, she reminded Emily of a young female version of her father. Had Steven impregnated some other woman twenty-odd years ago to create this one-note, emotionless woman? Maybe that was what spurred on the affair with Abe. Emily shook the thought out of her head.

"This is insane," David said. "She obviously doesn't have any of that stuff. This whole thing is psychosomatic."

"Let's order an X-ray just to be safe," the doctor said, looking at her chart. "Okay, date of birth?"

"February 15, 1990."

"Can you repeat that for me? Ninety?"

"Yes, I fucking know I look older than my age—I said it right."

"Emily, calm down," David said.

The doctor seemed unfazed. "I'm surprised. I assumed you were in college. When was your last chest X-ray?"

"Gosh. I can't remember. Do I really look like I'm in college?"

"Last February," David offered. He looked at her. "When you thought you had myocarditis, remember?"

"Oh, right." She turned back to the doctor. "Seriously though, did someone tell you to say that?"

"No. Are you on any medication?" She adjusted her glasses.

"Benadryl, when I fly. And I'm not flying now, obviously, so nothing."

"What about your birth control pills?" David asked.

Emily's throat tightened. "Oh, right. Um, birth control pills."

"That takes care of my next question," she said. "But I have to ask anyway: Are you pregnant?"

Emily felt her throat tighten. She looked at David, and then she had to look away.

Emily

WHEN SHE WAS LITTLE, Emily liked to dream about her wedding day. She always imagined her dress as a bright white lacy number with pastel rainbow-colored bows and big puffed sleeves, like those Velcro-fastened gowns her Barbies wore. She would have flower girls and bridesmaids in the double digits, wearing dresses the color of Easter eggs. The groom would be built like one of Jason's G.I. Joes but with neatly coiffed blond hair and blue eyes. He would wear a baby blue tuxedo with a pink flower on it. The cake would have ten tiers, icing roses and a bride and groom on top.

What she hadn't imagined was that she would wake up on the morning of her wedding without her groom in bed next to her, and with no idea where he was.

It had been a long ride home from the emergency room. David had glumly gotten into bed with her and said that he'd talk about it in the morning. Now it was morning and he was gone.

Emily found Marla in the kitchen making coffee, wearing a sheer beige kimono over a pair of linen pants that could have passed for breezy beachwear or pajamas.

"Have you seen David?" Emily asked.

"He went out." She motioned toward the door.

"Did he say when he'd be back?"

"No."

"Oh, great."

Marla opened a container of yogurt. "What are you having a fit about?"

"Mom, it's my wedding day and I don't know where the groom is. I think I'm allowed to be upset."

Marla shook her head. "So I guess today's all about you, isn't it? I'm starting to wonder if you inherited some narcissistic traits from my mother."

"I'm Elsa!" Ariel shouted.

"No, you're not!" Mia shouted. "I'm Elsa!"

The kids started wrestling on the nursery carpet. Jason and Lauren sprung to attention to separate them.

"Mia, stop!" Jason said. "Don't pull your cousin's hair!"

"It's a wig!" Mia said as she tugged on Ariel's hair. "He's a boy."

"Boys have long hair sometimes, Mia," Lauren said calmly. "Ariel, set boundaries. Tell her that contact is not something you consent to."

"I don't consent to this," Ariel said. Mia didn't seem to understand. She kept pulling his hair. Ariel pushed her and she fell backward. Mia paused for a moment, then cried hysterically once she realized everyone was looking at her.

Emily appeared in the doorway. "Guys, I need your help."

Jason picked up Mia. "What's up?"

"I can't find David, and Mom is acting like a complete cunt."

"Are we going to *Cunt* today?" Ariel asked, jumping up and down.

"No. I'm talking to Auntie Emily." Lauren turned back to Emily. "Go on."

She tried not to cry. "David seriously just walked out of the house this morning and nobody has seen him. Mom was no help at all, Dad is still at the Ritz, and I have no idea who else to ask. I've texted Mark and Kevin already, and they both said they haven't heard anything from him."

"I'm sure he'll show up in time for the wedding," Jason said, nonchalantly. "Dude probably just went to get a beer and have one freaking moment to himself. Mia, no! You don't get to kick people. That's not how we do things. Use your words."

"It's not like that," Emily said. "He barely spoke to me last night. And nobody drinks a beer in the morning."

Jason shrugged. "I've already had two today."

"Okay." Lauren pulled Ariel onto her lap. "So maybe David left because he's pissed at you right now. But that doesn't mean he's not coming back."

"I'm not just going to wait around for him!"

Jason paused to think. "Did you text Nathan?"

"Why would David choose to hang out with him at a time like this? Nathan drives him crazy."

Her phone buzzed. She eagerly checked it. "It's a fucking calendar alert. I have my hair appointment with Eva in fifteen minutes."

"Wait, you're going back to her?" Lauren said. "I thought you hated her for wrecking your hair."

"I have a two-for-one coupon, and I don't want to waste money. Also, my hair is kind of the least of my concerns right now."

Lauren shrugged. "Okay, so skip the appointment."

"Are you kidding me? I don't want to look ugly."

"Ah, yes," Eva said as Emily settled into the chair. "You the lady who get very angry about the hair."

"Yeah. That's me. I'm over it. I have bigger issues to deal with."

"Bigger issue is when your town mayor steal your only pair of Levi jeans to pay off his mob debt. Bigger issue is when pet rabbit thrown out window to ward off evil spirit that make your dog make sex with grandfather clock."

"Does that happen in Russia?"

"Who say I from Russia? So what is your bigger issue? It couldn't be bigger than when my last husband was stolen by twin sister saying she was me. He still believe it." She stared sadly into the mirror from behind Emily.

"I'm pregnant."

"Pfffft. That not big issue. Come back when baby born with head of goat."

"That happened in your village?"

"No, it just a saying. You don't say that here?" She shrugged. "It mean bad luck with money." She tied the plastic cape in the back of Emily's neck and brandished a curling iron.

Emily nodded. "Well, the father isn't very happy about the baby. Or maybe he's just mad at me for not telling him about it. I don't know."

Gabrielle, who had been flipping through her thick binder of hairstyles, rushed over at the sound of the word *baby*.

"You're *pregnant*, oh my gosh!" she said, hugging Emily's neck. "This is *amazing*! How could David be angry? Oh, he'll adjust. He's just freaked out! Who could blame him? I'm sure he'll be fine by the time of the wedding. Even though our baby was planned, when Mark found out about it, he scheduled a boys' trip to Vegas and lost a thousand dollars on blackjack. Men are so weird."

"You tell husband *night* before wedding?" Eva gave Emily an incredulous look in the salon mirror. She lowered her voice to a secretive whisper. "That not smart. What you do—you wait until after honeymoon, then you tell. Then he cannot leave even if paternity test is false and it belong to mayor."

"It's *his* baby. He just freaked out that I didn't tell him right after I found out."

"He the real baby. In my village, when woman get pregnant, all men in town bring their guns out to town square for dancing and shooting ox."

"Well, in America, men are usually pretty freaked out when their girlfriends get pregnant accidentally."

"Nonsense. He forget everything at wedding. Like we say in my village, men are like shallow pond—they catch fire easily."

"What?"

"They have quick temper. Then they get over it. He just need vodka. Also in my village we have problem with ponds catching fire because of pollution. So what kind of hair you want for the wedding?"

"Loose curls!" Gabrielle squealed. "Sorry, you get to choose—but my vote is for loose curls!"

"What about Jennifer's vote?" Emily asked. "I don't know how much longer we should wait for her."

"She hasn't been responding to my texts," said Gabrielle. "I hope she's okay."

"Fuck. This is so typical. Loose curls it is."

Emily sat in her bedroom in her white strapless wedding gown, which, though it had been let out a little, was still dangerously tight around the expanding waist and bust. Gabrielle had done her makeup using her new products from Sephora—matte and soft, as she put it. Emily couldn't look at herself in the mirror. She felt like Miss Havisham haunting a spooky Victorian manor in her old wedding dress. Lauren and Maddyson, both wearing their bridesmaids dresses, looked at their phones, avoiding what Lauren no doubt would have called "the gorilla."

"Where the fuck is Jennifer?" Emily finally asked.

"Oh, that reminds me," Gabrielle said. "I should check my phone. I turned it off to save battery." She opened her gold clutch bag to retrieve her phone.

"*You're* low on battery? How is that possible? You're the most organized person ever."

"Oh, I'm not low. I just wanted to conserve it in case there was some emergency and I needed a fully charged phone. Like, what if there's a blackout?"

"Don't say that," Emily said. "That's the last thing I need. Maddyson, have you heard from Nathan?"

"Nope," she said, swiping through her phone and lounging back on Emily's bed. "I have no idea where he is."

"When was the last time you saw him?"

"This morning. He just took my mom's car and drove off somewhere."

"Seriously?" Emily's heart raced as she sprung up. "Nathan took off for no apparent reason? Fuck, Lauren, that's a clue! Nathan never leaves the house, ever. That's what David is doing. He's with Nathan!"

"Maybe," Maddyson said. "What's the big deal?"

"Emily told David she's pregnant and he freaked out," Lauren said, as if recounting the plot of a boring Kate Hudson movie.

"You're *pregnant*?" Maddyson said. "Shit."

"Don't," Gabrielle snapped. "Don't freak her out."

"No, I mean, she looks good for being knocked up," Maddyson said. "No offense, Gabrielle."

"Thanks," Emily said. "Weirdly, that does make me feel better."

"Now I see why your boobs are so huge," Maddyson said. "Hashtag, jealous."

"Oh wait, I missed a call from Jennifer!" Gabrielle smiled and swiped her phone.

"Call her back!" Emily said. "Ask her where the fuck she is!"

Gabrielle rang Jennifer. Her brow raised in relief when Jennifer picked up, but her facial expression quickly changed to one of disappointment and confusion. "Oh, hey, Jennifer? Yep, thanks for picking up. We're all sitting here wondering where you are. The wedding starts in—oh, really? Are you serious? Do you want me to tell Emily? Yeah, well, she *is* going to be mad. Jen, wow. Are you serious?"

"What? What is it?" Emily asked.

"Okay, Jen, I'll call you back later." Gabrielle hung up and turned to Emily. She exhaled deeply. "Jennifer can't make it."

"Can't make what?"

"The wedding."

"The wedding? She flew out here for my wedding! She's a fucking bridesmaid. What could possibly have come up?" Emily hated the fact that she was screaming while wearing a bridal gown, which probably made her look crazy, but this was just too infuriating for her to worry about how she looked.

"Apparently Kevin thought she hooked up with Jason and lost interest in her. She was really upset about it. So last night she splurged for a ticket to Los Angeles to see her ex-boyfriend. Apparently he's still in love with her and she felt like everything with Kevin was a sign that she should go back to him. You remember her talking about Carl, right?"

"Los fucking *Angeles*? Carl? She couldn't have done this after the wedding?"

"I'm just the messenger," Gabrielle said weakly, her hands in her lap.

"Well, this is just great. I'm one bridesmaid short."

"I say we make the best of this," Maddyson said. "Let's pop some champagne."

"Sorry to be a downer," Emily said. "But fifty percent of the people in this room are pregnant."

Maddyson shrugged. "I'll have some then." She took a bottle of cheap strawberry champagne out of her oversize tote bag and untwisted the cap, drinking directly from the bottle. She took a quick selfie before screwing the cap back on.

Emily looked aghast. "Where did you get that? You're eighteen."

"Nathan gets me alcohol sometimes. In return, I let him touch my hair."

Emily was not going there. "Speaking of Nathan, we need to find him," she said.

"Jason knows Nathan better than either of us do. He'll find him."

"How about some tunes?" Jason asked. Lauren was driving and he was riding shotgun. "We need some finding-the-groom music!" He pumped his neck forward and back like a clucking chicken.

"No," Emily said from the back seat. "I don't want to listen to anything right now. What's Nathan saying?"

"Seriously, Jason, do your job," Lauren said.

Jason looked at his phone "He says...and I quote... 'Good sir, my brother has entrusted me with his privacy. I have no honor if I give this information to anyone who asks.'"

Emily lunged forward, reaching for the phone. "Let me have your phone. I'm going to kill him."

"No, we can't be mean to him," Jason said firmly. "We

need to speak his language. We need to get him to agree to give up the info. Otherwise he's just going to get off on this whole 'honor' thing."

"Jason's right," Lauren said. "Nathan gets bullied all the time. Telling him off won't intimidate him. If anything it will encourage him. He loves the 'me against the world' narrative."

"Okay, fine," Emily said, sitting back. "Jason, is there anything you could offer him? Anything he really wants?"

Jason paused to think. "There is one thing."

"What?"

"I could take him out on the town in New York City. I offered it to him after the bachelor party, mostly because I was drunk, but I think he really wants to do it. He wants me to show him how to talk to girls."

Lauren rolled her eyes. "Right, because you're such an authority."

"Whatever," Jason said, texting Nathan. "I'm a hell of a lot more of an authority than he is. I'm pretty sure the only girls he talks to are cartoon characters."

Jason's phone buzzed.

"What, what?" Emily asked.

"He went for it. He's telling me where David is."

"I love you," Emily said.

The patrons of Jojo's Ice Cream Shoppe in Fairfield turned and stared as Emily rushed in, pushing the door open so fast that the little bell around the doorknob rang and smashed against the door as it slammed shut. The vibrations from the slamming door caused the pink-and-white-striped awning outside to shake. Emily looked around and saw a couple with a young child looking up from their banana splits to gawp at her. The pudgy teenage cashier stopped chewing her gum and stared. It was only then that Emily remembered she was wearing a wedding dress.

Nathan and David were seated by a window. They were in their tuxes, which Emily took as a good sign. David's face, however, told another story. He looked sullenly into a barely eaten ice cream sundae that was made to look like the face of a teddy bear.

"Seriously?" she asked.

"I just wanted a moment."

"You had your moment. What were you going to do, not show up to our wedding?" Emily was too upset to care that the teenage checkout girl was taking a video of her. She could imagine the viral clip on YouTube now: "Epic Ice Cream Bride Fail."

"He had no intention of jilting you," Nathan said. "I would never permit him such an indecorous gesture."

"Thanks, Nathan, but he's being pretty fucking indecorous already."

"Let's talk outside," David said. He got up, and noticed Lauren and Jason outside the front window, staring into the shop. He sat back down. "Fine, let's talk here. Nathan?"

Nathan made a deep ceremonious bow and peeled off. Emily sat down. David resumed morosely eating his ice cream sundae.

"Why would you do this?" she asked.

"I just needed some time alone to think."

"You're being such a child!"

"I'm not being a child!" he said, stabbing his spoon into the teddy bear ice cream sundae. He lowered his voice. "I just…"

"Yeah?"

"Why didn't you tell me? Did you think I couldn't handle it?"

The words started tumbling out of her. "I don't know, I

just… I've had so much pressure on me this week with my family and the wedding, not to mention your job and… I screwed up, I know I did, but…"

"It's not about stress. I'm going to be your husband and you can't even tell me you're pregnant? What the hell was your plan?"

"You can do better than me!" Emily blurted out, fully aware that everyone was staring, but no longer caring. She was holding back tears. David looked taken aback.

"Why…why would you think that?"

"Just look at us! You were popular in high school, I wasn't—"

"Oh, come on, we're adults, who cares about—"

"Let me finish." Emily inhaled deeply. "You're handsome, you're smart, you're successful—"

"Not really anymore." David smiled self-effacingly. "I'll allow 'handsome' and 'smart,' though."

"You will be successful, though. If not with Zoogli, somewhere else. You have everything going for you. I don't know why you're even marrying me! Am I like…some kind of reliable starter wife? Or are you subscribing to the idea that ugly girls are more grateful and give better blow jobs, which I know I'm very good at?" She heard some fourteen-year-old boys laughing from behind giant sundaes. At the very least, she had given them a funny story. She shuddered to think that all the funny things she witnessed in public were the ends of other people's lives.

Although she feared her comment would insult David, he started to laugh. "You're not ugly by anyone's standards, Emily. You know how when you walk into a room, you think everyone is staring at you because you're ugly? They're staring at you for the opposite reason. I'm flattered that you think I would marry someone I find unattractive for the sake of a good personality, but come on. You think I'm that deep? Of course I think you're beautiful. It's one of the many reasons I'm with you. You're caring, you're smart, you're funny in a way that so few people are, you don't judge me, you like all the weird food shit I like, you and I can stay up till two in the morning making each other laugh…and, actually, your blow jobs could use some improvement. Not enough hand use. But it's okay, we have sixty years to work on that." Emily was too busy holding back tears to worry about the teenage boys knowing her blow jobs were subpar. Sixty years with this wonderful man. She wished it could be two hundred.

She couldn't help staring at the ice cream bear. "Are you going to finish that?"

He slid the bear over to her.

The wedding party was mustering in the lobby of the Ritz. Gabrielle checked her phone. "Well, now we're missing the bride *and* the groom. I don't know if that counts as progress."

"Wait, here they come," Mark said, spotting Emily and David, followed by Lauren, Jason and Nathan.

Gabrielle embraced Emily. Her black binder cut into Emily's back. "Ow."

"Sorry." She spoke in a hushed tone. "Is everything cool?"

"I think so. I don't know. I hope so."

"What's up, motherfuckaaaaas?" Emily wheeled around. It was Stephanie Morris, the old high school friend she had seen at the airport. "You have got to be *kiiiiidding* me!" Stephanie shouted, running over. "You look am*aaaaaz*ing!"

"Stephanie!" Emily said. "What are you doing here? I thought you had a bonfire…"

"Oh, that fell through. The dude who was supposed to provide the peyote couldn't make it. Plus, I figured your wedding would be *way* more awesome. I know I don't technically have an invite, but that's so lame, you know? I can't believe your mom wouldn't let you invite your best friend!"

"Best—"

"You look so hot. Your boobs are so big, Emily! When did that happen?"

"Since I got pregnant."

"Whoa," she said, covering her mouth. "That is like, a normal person's life on molly. But not during the high. After the comedown, when you're depressed."

"Thanks."

"Can I be a bridesmaid? Can I please? I've never been one. No one's ever asked me, not even my sister, that bee-otch! I know I'm not wearing the *exact* same dress, but I'm wearing peach!" She motioned to her casual long sundress. To her credit, it was peach, but it was strapless and patterned.

"I say, let her," Gabrielle whispered. "She's far more dedicated than Jennifer would be. And besides, didn't you want the number of bridesmaids to equal the number of groomsmen?"

Christina arrived, holding Mia in her arms. She came over and joined the rest. "Emily!" she gasped. "You look beautiful!" Mia's hair was curled. She was wearing a mint-green flower girl dress with white patent leather Mary Janes. "Jason, where's your tux?" she asked.

Jason was wearing a faded tee with a picture of a big-eyed kitten under the words Pussy Monster.

"I'll change," he said sheepishly.

"Just turn it inside out," Emily said. "You don't have time. I'd rather you look like an idiot at my wedding than not be there. Although to be clear, that T-shirt is a disaster nonetheless."

"I heard about Jennifer," Christina said, ignoring Jason.

She gave Emily a deep, perfumed hug. "It is what it is. But what a bitch."

"Yeah, we're kind of one bridesmaid short," Emily said. "I feel like such a loser."

"Oh, I'll step in!" Christina said. "I knew I'd be escorting the little ones down the aisle for the procession, so I wore the right colors!" She motioned to her dress—a knee-length peach chiffon cocktail dress with beige pointed-toe pumps. Her hair was done up in an effortlessly pretty chignon, and her earrings were ivory pearls. She looked like a J.Crew model.

"The thing is, Stephanie also wants to do it." Emily motioned to Stephanie.

"Who are you?" Christina asked, only just then noticing Stephanie.

"I'm only Emily's best friend from high school."

"I'm sorry, sweetheart," Christina said. "I'm Emily's former sister-in-law. I think if anyone should take the missing bridesmaid spot, it should be me. Your dress is also extremely inappropriate. This isn't Coachella."

"Seriously?" Stephanie said. "Her *former* sister-in-law? I'm her *current* best friend!"

"I…don't want to be mean," Emily stammered. "But Stephanie, I haven't even seen you in years."

"You saw me at the airport, dude."

"I meant, you know—on purpose."

"Whatever," said Stephanie, not showing a hint of being insulted. She turned to Christina. "I say we both do it. Girl power." They both turned to look expectantly at Emily.

"Fine," Emily said. Then she laughed. "Fine."

"We are gathered here today to witness the union of David Porter and Emily Glass," the officiant, Katherine, who had come highly recommended on Yelp, said, "who have come all the way from San Francisco to wed in the presence of their families."

"Woohoo! San Francisco!" shouted Stephanie, standing with the other bridesmaids. All eyes turned to her. "I've never been, but I've heard it's cool. So awesome that you guys live there. Represent!"

"Emily and David met a few years ago at a start-up expo event, as they said in their email to me," Katherine said. "One might say this is an unexpected place to meet your future spouse, but their love has only grown through the years. Today, they will join together in a union of loyalty and devotion. They have written their own vows. Emily?"

"Oh, um…" Emily stammered. "I never got around to writing mine. So I guess I'll be winging it." She heard murmurs from the wedding guests. Who *were* these people? Her parents invited way more friends than she had expected. She looked out at a sea of Judy Steins. At least Dr. Leibowitz didn't seem to be there. Maybe Marla got the message after all. Emily cleared her throat.

"Some of you already know this, but this has been an insane week. First of all, I'm pregnant." There were gasps and giggles. "Yeah, I know. And I was so busy with that, and freaking out about it, that I didn't tell David or write my vows. This is basically the shittiest thing I've ever done. So I'm just going to say—I don't know, I guess, just…" She turned to him. "David, I'm sorry. I was wrong to hide this from you. I know you'll be a great father. I've never doubted that. I'm sorry that I didn't tell you and I'm really kicking myself for it."

She turned to the guests.

"This wedding is kind of a mess," she said, feeling as if she might laugh or cry or both. "My parents aren't staying in the same house—"

"Emily!" Marla snapped.

"Well, it's true, Mom, and everyone knows. Not to mention, one of my bridesmaids is missing because she decided it would be reasonable to go to Los Angeles today instead of coming to my wedding. And, of course, none of that compares to the fact that David and I had the biggest fight today that we've ever had. But I guess that's life. Life is just…it's just one long shit show. And David, there's no one I'd rather go through it with than you, because there's no one in the world who can make me feel as calm as you do. Whatever happens, whatever scary shit life throws at us, I know I can handle it as long as I have you."

He took her hand and started to speak. She didn't hear a thing he said. She just looked at him and thought, *he is perfect.*

Jason

"Good sir!" Nathan said joyously, waddling over to Jason as he sat at his table, next to his father's empty chair, drinking Scotch on the rocks. He wasn't completely sloshed yet, although he intended to be by the end of the hour. "You won't believe what just happened!"

"What? If this is about video games, you need to reevaluate everything."

"It isn't. I finally had a successful interaction with a female. Nay, a woman. A beautiful woman."

"Oh really?"

"Yes! I joined a dating site for LARPers and found someone named Daenerys95. She lives in Greenwich with her parents and she's looking for like-minded *atheist* males. She specifically said 'non-WoW players need not apply.'"

"You realize that just because you found a woman's profile doesn't mean you have a girlfriend, right?"

Nathan pursed his lips in frustration. "You underestimate me so. I never said she was my girlfriend. But we have a date next Saturday."

"No way, man! What was your strategy—did you neg her, maybe say something about her weight? She sounds fat."

Nathan looked perplexed. "No. I just sent her a message asking what her favorite book was."

"And that worked?"

"Yes, good sir. I mean, I question some of her taste, she still has a fairly rudimentary understanding of atheist litera-ture and she glorifies the frankly overrated George R. R. Martin, but I can enlighten her further."

"You need to make sure she sees you as the top dog." Jason took another sip of his drink. "When you go on the date, make some joke about how she looked hotter online and then say, 'just kidding.'"

Nathan scrunched up his face. "You may be my best friend, Jason, but you are, for lack of a better term, a douche."

"I take more of an issue with 'best friend,' but point taken. See you around, buddy."

Nathan returned his attention to his phone, where he pre-sumably messaged his fair maiden as he walked off toward the buffet.

"Your turn," Christina said, walking over and plopping Mia on the floor next to Jason.

"I'll take her," he said. Mia was clutching her mother's iPhone firmly in her hands.

"Can I seriously trust you with this task?" Christina asked. "Just play *Frozen* clips for her if she gets unruly."

"Sit down for a sec," said Jason. He pulled his father's chair out and patted the seat, hoping that didn't make him look too pervy.

"I'm supposed to be getting Susan a drink. We were in the middle of a conversation about the Rockettes."

"I only need a second," said Jason.

Christina rolled her eyes and sat down with a huff, crossing her freckled arms and legs. "What is it?"

"I just wanted to say," said Jason, "I'll try harder. I'll be a better dad. I'm sorry I'm not always there."

Christina opened her mouth as if to say something, but stammered. Finally she said, "You're telling me you *haven't* been a good dad."

"Yes," said Jason. "I admit it. The whole marriage and fatherhood thing... I screwed it up. But I love Mia, and I want to be there for her. I want to be in her life. I think I can be there for her, be what she needs. I think I can learn to be a good dad. I don't want to be the...the douche anymore."

Christina nodded as if she was waiting for Jason to shout, "Psych!"

"Also, I'm sorry about you...about everything I did to you," he added. "I don't expect you to like me, or be friends with me but...for Mia's sake, let's at least be polite to each other."

Christina nodded. "I want you to read some articles first," she said softly. "I have a very particular way that I'm raising her, and if you're going to get involved, I want us to be on the same page."

Jason shrugged. "Sure, what are they?"

"I'll email them to you, but just to give you an idea, I am raising her to believe that all women are goddesses. I am raising her to believe that if she wants something, she should go for it. And I am raising her to believe that she should never, *ever*, compromise anything she wants for a man or back down for anybody."

"She's three."

"Yeah, but this kind of thinking starts early, especially with girls. I'm never going to let her make the mistakes I did."

Jason paused for a moment. "Christina, those are *all* the mistakes you made. You never compromised. I'm not saying I was a good husband at all, but if you want her to have healthy relationships, she needs to learn give-and-take."

"And *you* know give-and-take?" Christina snapped.

"No, that's what I'm saying. I sucked at being a husband but at least I know it. I'm not going to tell her to do what I did either."

"So I sucked as a wife?"

"Not nearly enough." He smirked to himself. He couldn't help it—she had put it in his lap. Well, not literally. *Zing again,* he thought.

"I should have known better than to talk to you for even *five* seconds," she said. "A-s-s-h-o-l-e." She stood up, but Jason grabbed her hand.

"Don't touch me," she snapped.

"I'm sorry. I didn't mean to upset you. I just feel like if we're going to do this together, we need to agree on some things, and I didn't agree with what you said. You know me, I like to joke around. I just don't want her growing up to be entitled. I don't want her growing up to be a princess. I want her growing up to be a healthy adult with self-respect, and respect for other people. Not that I'm a healthy adult, but the least I can do is try to help Mia become one."

Christina sat back down and cocked her head. "I suppose we can compromise on that," she said. "Will you still read the articles?"

"I'll read them," Jason said. "Can we compromise here? Can we coparent? Can we spend a few minutes around each other without fighting?"

Christina looked at Mia, then back at Jason. She nodded.

"I guess," she said. "But I have some rules too. No smoking or drinking in front of her. No McDonald's in the house, even if she's not eating it and *no women whatsoever*, unless I've met them first. I don't need her meeting all your bimbo girlfriends."

Jason laughed. "You obviously think I do way better with women than I actually do. I mean, I banged this girl from Celebz but she seemed kinda unhinged and it was only oral."

"Shh! Not in front of Mia!"

"She doesn't understand," he said dismissively. "Anyway, what I'm trying to say is—you don't need to worry about me with women. And if, by some random turn of events, I actually want to get serious with someone who wants to get serious with me, I'll have her meet you before she meets Mia. Fair?"

"Fair," said Christina.

"And that goes for you too," said Jason, smiling at her. "Any dude you're getting serious with, have him meet me first."

"Why?"

"So I can provide suicide counseling to him ahead of time," Jason murmured.

"What?"

"I'm joking. I just think everything should go both ways. I don't want some creep hanging around my daughter."

"Can we at least not joke around in front of Mia?"

"Deal," said Jason. "Now go have fun. I'll watch her for the night." He dislodged the iPhone from his daughter's tiny hand and led her to the dance floor.

Emily

"Care to dance?" Steven asked Emily. Emily nodded. She hadn't seen him interact with Marla since the ceremony. On the bright side, worrying about her own marriage all week made her a bit numb to any fears about her parents' marriage.

"Sure, Dad." There hadn't been an official father-daughter dance, mostly because Emily knew it was accompanied by a mother-son dance, and as much as David would be happy to dance with Susan, she didn't want to run the risk of bringing up unwanted feelings about his mother. When Lauren noticed that Emily had declined to incorporate this tradition, she congratulated her for "not pandering to that patriarchal father-as-husband bullshit." Emily just said thanks.

Steven took Emily's hand. In heels, she was almost taller than him. Neither of them knew how to dance, so they merely stepped in rhythm, going in a slow circle.

"You're going to be a great mother, Emily," he said.

"Wow, Dad, really? You mean that?"

Steven shrugged, keeping his hand on Emily's. "Well, being a parent isn't particularly difficult. You don't exactly need to be a genius."

"Thanks, Dad."

Emily looked to her right and saw Lauren waddling around on the dance floor alone. Matt was nowhere to be seen. Nathan approached her, bowed with his fedora in his hand, and asked, "May I have this dance, milady?"

Lauren shrugged and sighed. "Oh, what the hell. But I'm taking the lead." Emily smiled as she saw Lauren and Nathan waltz off together. Nathan's hand grazed Lauren's lower back and she quickly swatted it away.

Earlier, Emily had seen Jason bending over to dance with Mia, but that was five drinks ago. Christina was entertaining Mia and Ariel with *Peppa Pig* clips on her iPad while Jason danced with Stephanie Morris, who was twerking upside down on the wall. Her maxi dress draped down over her head, and she was wearing a faded white thong that was so old that it looked dirty. What Jason was doing couldn't really be called "dancing" as it would have been impossible to truly dance with her without getting a face full of ass. He was bopping in place, staring directly at her butt. At least he was showing a mild amount of restraint. At the end of the song, Stephanie got back on her feet, wrapped her arms around him and began making out with him furiously.

"Hello, Steven." Emily turned around to see Marla. "I hope you're having a nice time."

Steven stopped in his tracks. "I am."

Marla lowered her voice. "You know, it may be a bit embarrassing for Emily to be dancing with you for this many songs. It's her wedding, after all, and she probably wants to spend time with her peers. Perhaps you should let her find her husband."

"Yes, I'll dance with you, Marla." Steven let Emily's hand go, and placed his hand around Marla's waist. Emily watched as they held hands together through the crowd.

Emily ran into Lauren again at the buffet toward the end of the reception. She was sullenly gazing at the array of desserts but neglecting to put anything on her plate.

"Matt knows," Lauren said, looking at Emily with dead eyes.

"I'm… I'm sorry. I didn't tell him, if that's what you're getting at."

"He doesn't know the literal truth, and there's no reason for him to know something that will only hurt him. But we were sitting at our table, and he just turned to me and said, 'You don't love me, do you?'"

"And?"

"I told him I didn't. It isn't fair to waste his life like this. He stormed out. Of course he's angry, but he'll be better off without me. And frankly, I'll be better off without him. He's quirky and all, but can a white cishet man ever really relate to my struggles? If anything, his hipsterism is an appropriation of my otherness. He's queering himself because he lacks any markers of real oppression, and frankly, that's emotionally abusive."

Emily sighed. "You're allowed to just be sad about losing him, you know. You don't have to come up with all these… reasons."

"I know." Lauren popped a mint-green chocolate almond in her mouth. "I think I just need a hug." They hugged and Emily found herself silently whispering to her baby, *That's Aunt Lauren you're hugging.*

NIGHT 7

Emily

"AVON," DAVID SAID, lying on the hotel bed and staring at the ceiling.

"What, like the makeup company?" Emily was wearing a white bra and underwear with matching thigh-highs, an ensemble she had originally bought with the intention of seducing him on their wedding night. However, after four pieces of wedding cake, they were both bloated. Before they could even think about consummating their union, they needed to digest.

"No, like Avon Barksdale from *The Wire*. It's an awesome name."

"No. Our kid is going to have to deal with having me as a mother and having my mother as a grandmother. His life will be hard enough, let's not also give him a name from an HBO show." She paused. "Although, if it's a girl, I wouldn't mind Arya."

"So Avon is stupid, and Arya isn't?"

"Boys can't get away with these weird names. Girls can. Like, you can name your daughter Meadow and her life would basically be normal, but if you name your son Branch, he gets his ass kicked."

"What about Bamboo?"

"He gets his ass kicked more. As his ass is being kicked, he's wishing we named him Branch."

"I meant if it's a girl."

"You're joking, right?"

"No, I think it sounds nice."

She noticed that the tiny bottle of hotel shampoo on the nightstand was from a brand called Bamboo. "This isn't *The Usual Suspects*," she said.

He shrugged and adjusted his butt doughnut underneath him. "It's just a cool name."

"What about one of our dads' names? Nick and Steven. Those are normal names."

"Those names suck! They're so boring. Everyone in his class will be named Nick and Steven."

"Hardly. Go to a baby-name blog. Everyone in his class will be named Brayden, Aiden, Caiden and Braydynn."

"What's wrong with Brayden?" He sat up suddenly as if he had had an epiphany. "Actually, I really like that. It's so different."

"No, it's not. It's the name that pretty much every twenty-two-year-old Southern Pinterest mom gives their kid. I mean, sure, a three-year-old named Brayden is adorable, but can you imagine a fifty-year-old Brayden? Dr. Brayden Porter? Would you trust a lawyer named Brayden?"

"You're overthinking it."

"Look, if you like Brayden so much, how about Brandon? That's a normal name."

"Brandon sucks."

"Why does Brandon suck?"

"Braaandon," he said, in an annoying high-pitched voice.

"What was that supposed to mean?"

"I don't know, I just feel like anyone named Brandon would suck. And besides, if Brandon is so similar to Brayden, why can't we just do Brayden?"

"Because they're not that similar, and Brayden is by far the stupider name."

"I don't know, I think you want our kid to be boring."

"Well, we have seven or eight months to figure this out," she said. "Hopefully we'll agree on something before then."

David lay back down on the bed and smiled. "That's so crazy. Seven or eight months! I can't believe I'm going to be a dad that soon. Oh, shit, maybe you're one of those women who's actually secretly six months along and just has no idea."

"Don't freak me out. I already considered that possibility. We'll get an ultrasound when we get home."

"Is it safe to…you know?" He trailed off, and then to make things more obvious, made the international sign for sex with his index finger going in and out of a ring he formed with his other hand.

"Real mature," she said. "Yeah, it's safe. Why wouldn't it be?"

"The baby can see it, right?"

"What are you talking about? The baby can't see anything. It probably doesn't even have eyes yet."

"Yeah, but what if it gets, like…dislodged?"

She started laughing. "You can't possibly be this misinformed. You really think pregnant women can't have sex?"

"I mean, I know they can, but isn't it one of those 'you probably shouldn't' things, like eating oysters?"

"Was your plan to go the next eight months without any sex? You really planned on doing that?"

He shrugged. "I mean, we didn't plan on anything."

"We can have sex. I'm sure I won't be up for it when I'm

nine months along and the baby is the size of a giant watermelon, but for now it's really fine."

"Good to know. Actually, can we give it a go in the morning? Right now my stomach feels like it's going to explode."

"Me too. I feel like a pressurized can of farts."

"Very sexy." He rolled over and spooned her, running his
hands through her hair, which was sticky from twelve-hour-
old hair spray and gel. "How about we run a warm bath and
I'll set up some *Game of Thrones* episodes on my laptop?"

"Sweet," she said. "You're the best."

He got up to run the bath. Emily stared up at the ceiling,
feeling so heavy that she wasn't sure it would be possible for
her to get up even if she tried.

Surely this child would need a relationship with his grandparents, and both sets would live a six-hour plane ride away.
Maybe that was for the best. Emily couldn't hide from Marla
forever. She had largely ignored her at the reception but someday she would have to attempt at least a cordial relationship
again. Perhaps she and David would eventually live somewhere closer to their parents. Not New York, of course, since
it was a hotspot for terrorism, disease and Brazilian models
lying in wait to steal her husband. Maybe somewhere on the
East Coast, a short plane ride away.

Maybe they'd be better off in Boston, if David could get
over his irrational hatred of Red Sox fans. Or Virginia. David
once said you could buy a house in Virginia for what it cost
to buy a steak in San Francisco. Virginia, of course, posed its
own problems. For one, she always assumed that any place
south of New Jersey was loaded with anti-Semites and neo-
Nazis. This was the reason Marla never let them go to Dis-
ney World. Plus, some Southern women actually put effort
into their appearance, and if she felt as ugly as she did in San
Francisco, the Birkenstock Empire of the World, she could

only imagine how she would feel in Virginia where women wore heels to the supermarket. Fuck. There was nowhere they could move. Everything was a disaster.

"Hey, babe, the bath is ready and I downloaded the episode where that little bitch Joffrey gets slapped."

"I think I just want to cuddle with you for the rest of my life."

"As you wish." David laid the laptop on the dresser by the window and hopped into bed with her. His body still fit hers perfectly. She knew it always would.

★ ★ ★ ★ ★

ACKNOWLEDGMENTS

To my father, thank you for your tireless work, reading and critiquing this book, helping me to become a better writer, and always encouraging me to be funny, a worldview that solidified itself for me during a certain recorder concert in 1998. To my husband, Jeff, thank you for reading this book more times over than anyone should ever have to, for keeping my confidence intact throughout the whole process, and for your love, support and cups of morning tea. To my mother, thank you not only for reading and critiquing this book, but also for your amazing sense of humor, your willingness to make fun of yourself and all the work you put into planning the wedding that gave me so much inspiration—the Fire Department's visit due to Tentgate will never be forgotten. The artistry and devotion with which you sewed my Halloween costumes as a kid stayed consistent throughout the wedding planning. And to Max—euyl. To my sister, Madeline, I have no doubt that one day you will have a book in stores too—I will be one of the first people to buy it. Thank you to my stepmother, Olivia, for your support and advice during the publishing process—you helped me to stay positive. Thank you to everyone who attended and helped plan my wedding in 2014—you provided more inspiration than you know. I would also like to thank Elisa, Christine, Tory and Samantha for always being available on Google Chat when I'm bored—I couldn't make it through a day without you guys.

Thank you to Allison, Luke, Emily and Heather for all your support and work throughout this process!